beautiful garbage

Published 2013
Printed in the United States of America
ISBN: 978-1-938314-01-8
Library of Congress Control Number: 2012951918

For information, address:
She Writes Press
1563 Solano Ave #546
Berkeley, CA 94707

beautiful garbage

Jill Di Donato

She Writes Press

Chapter One

The cafes and bars around the Met were all bland. Tourist traps where the wait staff scoffed at a punk like me with my leather mini, ripped hose, and spiked hair. At the wine bar on 80th Street, they sat me in the back and kept looking over to make sure I wouldn't run out on the tab—rightly so. I barely had enough to cover the glass of Malbec. It was with a bit of spite that I lingered out front smoking a cigarette well after I'd paid my check. Which is when I saw her. At first, I thought I was mistaken. The way she was walking, arm-in-arm with a dark-skinned older man wearing a porkpie hat, pointy wingtips, and shiny slacks beneath his overcoat. This Monika was completely foreign to me. And the way she was done up—pastel makeup, soft blond curls pushed away from her face with a headband—she looked unrecognizable. What caught my eye was the silver, floor-length ball gown that I'd seen buried in the back of her closet one day when I was going through her things. She was always insisting that I borrow something from her fabulous collection of clothes.

I stubbed out my cigarette and looked down at the gnarled pavement. Earlier, I'd asked her if she wanted to come to the museum so I could peruse the Ancients, but she'd said she was taking her book to a photographer who was doing Nan Goldin. On the way over here, I'd witnessed a homeless man drying his socks over a trashcan bonfire.

They were across the street, walking east on 5th. In the

months I'd been living with her, Monika had often said she'd never be caught dead above 14th Street. But here she was, without a doubt the girl who'd taken me in, helping me do what I'd come to the city to do: make art. The man stopped for a minute to light a clove cigarette for her, which she held between her perfect, plump lips. Monika hated clove cigarettes; she said their stench made her sick to her stomach. After she exhaled, her companion grabbed her arm, almost too aggressively. Something about the way he touched her was off.

I had no choice but to follow them. Digging my hands in my pockets, I managed to cock my head so that my chin nestled into my ratty scarf while my eyes fixed on the target. The click of her stilettos echoed, my curiosity keeping pace. As she tilted her head, laughed, and turned around, I ducked into a storefront before she could notice me. A swarthy merchant tried to sell me a gold chain and an *I Love New York* tote bag, but I shoved him off, picking up speed as they hit Madison and started downtown. It was a short walk before they reached their destination, the Mark Hotel. The man in the porkpie hat nodded towards the concierge and led Monika by the arm into the elevator. I stood in the arched entrance, questioning everything I'd just witnessed and wanting to ignore the sickness brewing in my stomach.

The concierge emerged from the revolving door and gave me a once-over. "Excuse me, Miss," he said. "Are you lost? I'm most certain you don't belong here."

Chapter Two

The night I met Monika at the New York opening for *L'Architecture Gonflable*, I could tell she was the type of girl who took you places. She shimmied through the exhibit, not once stopping to examine the odd, inflatable models of French housing. She had a fierce brow, long chin, and high cheekbones that suggested a life that had been lived hard and fast. Her hair, bleached so blond it looked white, was sprayed into a cone-shaped bun with shiny lacquer. Yellow eyes, hard as marbles, penetrated the crowd of art critics and downtown intelligentsia who always turned up at these things, where booze was served in plastic cups and avant-garde rifts filled the room.

This was exactly where I was supposed to be.

It was the winter of '84. I would come into the city on Amtrak, spend the night at an after-hours club if I had to. Not that I knew anyone by name: *he* could always be found on Christopher Street with an aluminum tray of poppers; *she* was the fag hag who danced on the piers with the drag queens, blasting Afrika Bambaataa from boom boxes; *he* was the guy in the Pierre Cardin suit who still believed in disco.

Perched in Monika's hand was a champagne flute; how she came by that, I didn't know. She studied it for a moment, almost as if she didn't know herself, and then raised it to her lips, which were plump and pink and freckled like the rest of her.

"What's your take on ephemeral architecture?" I managed

shyly, begrudgingly trusting my instincts to approach her. I swallowed. "Any good?"

She finished her sip and smiled. "You're not supposed to ask that. This is an art show." Then with a wink, "Love your boots."

"Thanks."

I swept my dark hair from my face and the studded bangle bracelets cascaded down my forearm.

She said, "You look like somebody."

"Who?"

"No one in particular, but like someone I should know."

I bit my lip, a bit nervous, but keyed up, flattered. "I'm Jodi," I said.

"Monika."

Truth was, I'd seen her around but didn't want to admit it right away. It was much more fashionable to play our meeting off as a chance encounter.

I was learning the subtleties of social interaction that seemed so important to these people. Most of it was pretentious as hell, and I didn't know why their silly rules and shenanigans bothered me so much, but what I did know was that I'd made the right choice to get back on the Amtrak tonight and walk through Lower East Side tenements to the show, where fabulous parties were held in burnt-out buildings.

"It was my birthday earlier," she continued. This sounded like a lie, like something a child says when she wants attention. This deception made me feel good about myself. I reached into my pocket for some lip gloss.

"I turned 27," Monika continued. "Nearly a hag. You can't be more than what, 20? 21?"

"23."

She drew a pack of Kool 100's from her purse. "Fag? Though we probably shouldn't smoke around the art. Want to get out of here?"

"Absolutely." I couldn't believe my luck.

"Just let me get my coat," she said. As she walked towards the coat check, I took one last look at the city of little domed cubes. Blow-up houses, an engorged cathedral, so much might, so much mystery. I wondered if this girl, decked out in PVC pants, chain-link jewelry, and plastic high heels, was for real or just full of hot air.

She came back wearing a floor-length leather trench, carrying a bottle of Chardonnay.

"They always keep a couple extra in the coat check," she said. "Come on, before someone sees."

Stepping outside, I could tell my luck was changing, a good thing considering that creep Vincent Frand. I couldn't believe that had only been *last night*. It felt a lifetime away. Just this afternoon, back at my mother's house, I'd wanted to crawl out of my skin; I'd started panicking that my art career would be over before it began. But just before sunset, I'd decided to come back to the city, because, I don't know, I was feeling restless.

The February chill was overwhelming, but as Monika and I walked west on Delancey, crowds were lined up for a Fellini revival festival. We passed a row of tenements with people flowing in and out. The entire street hummed. Everyone seemed oblivious to the cold. By then, Monika had wrestled open the bottle of Chardonnay. We were just about to make a toast when a squad car pulled up, the cops inside sipping something from Styrofoam cups. They gave us a once-over, and for a minute I thought we were done for, then the light turned green and the squad car sped away.

"What should we drink to?" I asked. "Your birthday?"

"Oh God no."

"You never answered my question," I said, pointing my finger at her, my purple glitter nail polish sparkling under the street lamp. "What did you think of the show?"

"What did *you* think of it?" she replied.

"Interesting… kind of smaller-scale than what I'd been picturing," I began. "But incredible, really, what it says about structure."

"You're smart," she said. "I can tell. That's a good thing, too, because this town is filled with idiots."

"That picture of Lynda Benglis all oiled up," I said. "You know, the one where she's wearing nothing but rhinestone-studded sunglasses?"

"Umm," she said. "Posing with a gigantic dildo."

"It's pretty cool. Let's drink to Lynda."

We each had a long slug. Suddenly, she took off running down the block, stopping at the side of a building where narrow steps led to an abandoned alcove. She climbed up, hoisted herself onto the ledge, then dipped into her purse, taking out a can of spray paint. As I caught up to her, she was spraying something indecipherable on the blank wall in front of her. I could hear police sirens off in the distance. She laughed and tossed the can of Krylon into a pile of garbage.

There was no one around to catch her; still, I was afraid she'd get in trouble. I began to have reservations about following this girl. Who knew what kinds of things she was into? But I was doing it again; walking that line between excitement and danger. "Sure you're okay up there in those heels?"

"Used to it!"

"Here, let me give you a hand," I said.

"It's easier going up than coming down; that's for sure."

Taking another gulp of wine, I had a feeling she was talking about something else.

"Hey, you gonna help a girl or what?"

"Sorry."

She just kind of dangled there for a minute. "What's the matter? You don't dig on graffiti?"

I couldn't tell her that her tag was impossible to make out; I wouldn't even call it graffiti. "It's cool," I said, helping her down. "I'm a sculptor. How about you? What do you do?"

"Take pictures," she said. "Look for pictures that haven't been taken yet. Tagging is just a hobby. You know, one of my boyfriends ripped a tenement door off its hinges because it had a SAMO tag. I hear it's worth thousands."

"Yeah it is."

She smiled, "Come on, I know a speakeasy around the corner. This place is exclusive as hell. Want to go?"

So I went. Owner of a Basquiat and woman about town, the girl had to know what was what. Yet there was something self-effacing about her—her quiet desperation. It made me wonder, what would make a girl like this be vulnerable?

✶

The silver doorway looked like any other tenement on the block, but inside the walls were laced with fancy paper, and a mahogany bar dominated a parlor packed full of rockers boozing and smoking it up. One of the hosts led Monika and me to a private table. We had cocktails immediately.

"I can't believe we've never met before. Who do you know?" she asked.

"Alex Czh—Czekinsky, from the Laundromat."

Everyone called her the Alchemist. Six feet tall with a red buzz cut, Alex Czekinsky had this habit of taking young unknowns and turning them into solid gold hits in the galleries. She knew all kinds of people: Peggy Guggenheim and Mary Boone, Susanne Bartsch and the painter Alice Neel. She ate dinners followed by cheese plates and million-dollar acquisitions.

"Mmm," cooed Monika, "You're one of Alex's."

"Not exactly. I don't *really* know her. I've been trying to get a meeting." I wanted to tell Monika about what happened with Vincent Frand. How many girls before me had he done this to? Something about the throatiness of her voice, the way her breasts fell suggestively into her knit top, told me she'd understand. But we'd only just met.

"I'm beginning to think I'll never get anywhere," I said.

"Not with that attitude. Attitude is everything. I was out the other night, and this fantastic Spanish woman was dining with a bunch of suits. She wasn't beautiful by any means, but she had this energy, this charisma, that kept all the men doting on her, vying for her attention. They were on their third bottle of champagne when she decided to take her shoes off. Can you imagine? Barefoot in Beretta. If it had been anyone else, the hostess would've come over and made a fool of her, but no one said a word, not even when she started pouring champagne into her shoes and passing them around the table. Everyone just acted like it was the most normal thing in the world to drink Veuve from alligator pumps."

"Motherfucker! I totally forgot about my train," I said. "The last one's at 1:30."

Monika smirked and sipped her cherry-colored cocktail. "You'll never make that."

Chapter Three

I'm nine years old the first time I encounter pornography. I've seen and experienced inklings of desire before, but never as blatantly as this, as *Playboy Magazine*. The little girl in me likes the image of a rabbit wearing a tuxedo bowtie. I know there's more waiting, and I wander to the inside pages. I can feel that what I see will leave an imprint.

I open to the center picture and close the magazine right away. I re-open it and unfold the center page, and up pops a glossy spread of a brunette taking a bath. My mom is the only other woman I've seen naked; she's a china doll, perfect and fragile. The woman in the magazine is sun-kissed and freckled, doe-eyed with pigtails, taking a bath. Her bare breasts, accented with the sheen and sparkle of soap bubbles, mesmerize me. Beyond kissing and childlike strokes, her glistening, hard nipples signal possibilities. A tingling sensation courses through my thighs and finds a center between my legs. I don't understand this feeling, but I like it.

I'm falling into this woman. One of her legs is cocked on the outer rim of the tub. She's smiling, lips poised to blow a kiss at the person taking her picture. I imagine the photographer as a man, a handsome one. She's having such a good time in the bath. I want so much to know what that feels like, what *she's* feeling in the soapy, warm water. There's so much she could teach me. I stick a thumb in my mouth. I haven't done this in years. My father hates thumb sucking and used to punish me for it.

I stare at the picture. I want what she has. Her buoyant breasts and smooth calves are where it all begins. Her beauty seems unreachable, like the perfect, pretty girls who have everything, like Isla. But maybe, if I work hard enough at it, I can be like the picture. The pulse between my legs intensifies. It's building to something—a hiccup, a release, I don't know what, exactly, but I like it. And just when I feel myself expanding, the door opens.

"Jodi!" The feeling is like having my heart broken and being lifted up at the same time. My father is standing there with a mean look on his face. "What are you doing in here?"

A warm gush, then the flow down my leg. The pungent smell of piss gives me away. The magazine still flapping in hand, I slink down to the puddle settling into the carpet.

"What's wrong with you?" he says, snatching the *Playboy*. He roughly folds the picture of the nude woman back into the magazine. "Little girls don't look at those things. You better stay out of my stuff and out of trouble. I don't want to have to worry about you yet."

My shorts are wet in the crotch area. I don't dare speak.

He shakes his head. "What would your mother say?"

I know she hates it when I wet the bed. But this is different; both Dad and I know it. I want to cry. "Are you going to tell?"

"Go get yourself cleaned up," he says. "I'll take care of the closet."

"Are you going to tell Mom?"

He takes a long, deep breath like he's really thinking about it. Then he says, "We're going to forget all this. It will be like it never happened."

He smiles awkwardly, like he wants to hug me but has decided against it. We've entered into some kind of pact, and for the moment I'm relieved. But then comes the creeping sensation that he can expose me at any time.

When I was five, Dad gave me a porcelain brush and mirror

set. The gift made me feel special, adored. Later, I found out that Mom had bought it for him to give to me.

All I wanted to know: "Daddy, am I pretty?"

"You, baby girl, are so smart."

Chapter Four

Vincent Frand was more wheeler than dealer, which is why so many artists wanted him to represent them. He was a man who dyed his hair, eyebrows, and mustache deep black and had thick, wet lips that never stopped moving.

When he grabbed my hand on a random street in lower Manhattan, he pumped it violently and introduced himself. I should've known right then, but instead, I searched my purse for a pack of matches. "We're going to Mudd Club," he announced.

Until tonight, I'd only seen pictures of Mudd Club in the paper. The vinyl booths were just like they'd looked in the photos. The party was packed, even though it was still early. I figured this was some private get-together for the brand of liquor the sequined-dressed cocktail waitresses were pouring into an ice sculpture at one of the bars.

"Stay close, baby," he said. "Can't hear a word you're saying."

People were pressed up against the velvet rope that blocked off the seating area, and there wasn't an inch of space on either side of the crowd.

The next minutes were a swirl of introductions and the rub of unfamiliar bodies mashed up against your skin. Champagne bottles were popped; glasses clinked. There was a constant influx of people, and they all seemed to know Vincent Frand. I held onto him for dear life, not daring to correct him when he introduced me as Jamie. I was the girl who nothing happened to. But I wasn't going to be stuck in the suburbs with no imagination, like my mother.

"I've only just met her," he shouted to someone called Steg, a tall, tattoo-covered guy with a silver ponytail down his back. "Found her right across the street. You know how I'm always losing lighters?"

"I lit his cigarette." I said it like I'd accomplished nuclear fission.

Vincent Frand laughed. "Isn't she adorable? Adorable is the word of the day."

When I smiled, two little-girl dimples popped out on either cheek. I was surprised "adorable" even fit into Vincent Frand's vocabulary. But they poked through, without my consent, my dimples—and my face took a wrinkled, chubby, clownish (though also, so it seemed, *adorable)* shape. I held my jacket close to my body. It was vintage, something from my mother's closet: a cropped ski-coat made of purple rabbit fur.

A sudden waft of smoke caught my attention and I turned my head. A man and woman, both so beautiful they had to be models, were passing a joint between them. They were staring at a poster someone had ripped down and propped up in one of the club's corners. It was an advertisement for men's dress shirts.

"He was the hottest in the business," the angular woman said, pointing to the man in the ad, a statuesque Adonis flanked by a model and a Great Dane. "Everyone wanted him. His face was his trademark!"

"And now..." began the man. He and the woman looked at each other. "I can't get his face out of my head."

"It haunts me too."

"He looks so old," said the man. "Enough to make me go straight again."

Suddenly, the woman had a thought. She turned to the man and said, "Do you think the makeup artists soak the brushes in alcohol? I mean, every time?"

The smoke made me cough and then the man and woman

noticed me, turned their backs, and began talking again. But by then, I'd realized that I'd lost Vincent Frand.

"Jamie!" It was Steg, the tattooed guy with the silver ponytail. "Over here."

When I smiled, at least I could feel good about a set of even, white teeth. But were fine teeth enough to get me —"Jamie"— whoever this made-up girl from Connecticut was—to Vincent Frand? He'd had me by the arm, and then I'd lost him. But a jolt of adrenaline hit when I played the fantasy out: Vincent Frand would make me a star. Music was pumping; I felt very sexy.

"Over here!" I called to Steg.

All of a sudden, Steg was in front of me. He handed me a long shot glass filled with blue liquor.

"Here, baby doll. Drink this."

"What is it?"

"Curaçao. You'll love it."

I downed it and then said, "Where's Vincent?"

"I'll take you to him. Don't worry."

"Did he tell you I'm a sculptor?"

Steg didn't seem to hear me. If he did, he pretended like he didn't.

"Wait!" I yelled, and stopped us short. "Are my teeth all blue from the drink?"

This seemed to crack Steg up. He bellied over in laughter and started singing, *Feeling blue over you, my one and true...*"

"Where's Vincent?"

"Don't worry, Jamie," he said. "Vincent's got a table for you and a nice bottle on ice that's being cracked this second."

"It's Jodi."

"What?"

"Never mind."

Steg led me around a corner, and there he was, Vincent Frand with his dark hair, dark suit, and thick lips pursed in the biggest smile, all for me.

"Safe and sound," said Steg, who disappeared as quickly as he dropped me off. And then it was just Vincent Frand and me.

I reached into my purse and, next to the matches, felt for what had really brought me here. When my fingers reached it—the leather box containing twenty-five slides of my best pieces—my entire body tingled.

"Are you enjoying yourself?" Vincent Frand said to me. He generously tipped the waiter. Then, "Leave it; I'll pour the glasses myself."

I slid into the booth. Immediately, his arm fell around my waist.

"Did you say you work in plaster?"

"I do." Breathing a sigh of relief that he remembered something about me, I settled into his arm.

"Nobody's using plaster," he said matter-of-factly. "These days, shape is abstraction, not formula."

I loved this part. This was when I got to defend my whole artistic sensibility and sound original. I felt for the slide box in my purse. It was a real professional job, and I was proud of it. Cost a fortune to make: I had to pay a photographer $500 to shoot each piece individually and another $130 to have the slides made. Then there was the slide box itself, which a Swiss antique dealer at a flea market had let me have for $85. I was about to pull it out when a girl walked right up to Vincent Frand and kissed him on the mouth. The girl looked like expensive blow, wearing the type of dress that only the thinnest girls can wear: a powder-blue, flimsy number trimmed with curly white feathers that made her look like an ostrich. Pinched between her index and middle fingers was the longest cigarette I'd ever seen. She sipped a tall glass of champagne.

"Here you are," she said to him. "I've been looking for you all night."

"Not now," he said to the girl, annoyed. "Can't you see I'm in a meeting?"

"But baby..." she went on. Vincent Frand shook his head at me and shrugged. I looked at him and then the girl and didn't know what to feel.

"Here's fifty for a cab, and another two-hundred to spend on drinks with the girls before you take the cab. I'll catch you later."

The girl took the money and extinguished her cigarette in the ashtray on our table. My presence didn't seem to faze her in the least. "Okay," she agreed. "I'll be seeing you." She waved a finger in his face and kissed him again, this time missing his mouth and hitting his chin.

"Take your jacket off." Vincent Frand's attention was back on me. He unzipped my rabbit fur, revealing a plain black spaghetti-strapped dress. "I'm sorry for the interruption. What were we talking about?"

I took a sip of champagne and tried to hold my chin like the Ostrich Girl. She was the type of girl who could look fabulous while getting blown off, so I figured I should learn something from her. "We were talking about how I work in plaster." Then someone bumped me and I spilled champagne down the front of my dress.

"Beasts in here," said Vincent Frand, dabbing my chest with a napkin. "That's putting it mildly. The whole downtown art scene is a miraculous disaster. But you." He paused to take a drink. "You," he began again emphatically, "*you* just have to be a part of it. Don't you?"

"The whole star bit—I'm not playing into that."

"Oh no?"

I was a little nervous, knowing how important this moment could be. I pursed my lips, then spat out, "It's about making—objects—that make people feel."

"And you're unsigned? Looking for a dealer?"

"Yes."

"You know all about me, I assume."

"I do."

"Well," he said. "Always on the lookout for new talent. That's what I'm all about. Maybe why I met you tonight. You think we'd be a good fit, you working in plaster and all? Everyone I'm seeing, fuck, everyone I'm selling these days is very modern."

"But that's what sets me apart," I began. "Besides, figurative isn't dead."

He laughed. "No, it just won't die."

His hand was starting to move beneath my skirt. I couldn't tell if what I was experiencing was fear or excitement.

"My slides," I said. "I've got slides I could show you."

"I'm just thinking how I would position you."

When I looked at the ceiling, I could see the lights that lit up the dance floor below. They were connected through a complex series of rigs. On the floor, people writhed, arms and legs wrapping around each other. It was like everyone was in on this pact to explore an infinite exchange of desires, and so was I.

"Let's go somewhere; I know a private room," said Vincent Frand, rising and taking me by the hand. In his other hand, he grabbed the ice bucket with our bottle. "And baby, give me those slides. When I say I'm in a meeting, it means I'm gonna make something of it."

I was beginning to see how things happened. I passed the box from my hand to his, and watched his face for an expression. Of course he didn't open the slides right away, but I thought the box would impress him, which it did because he smirked, "Lovely box."

The "private room" turned out to be a john with a toilet, sink and mirror, a small divan, and a folding table that must've been some kind of spare used in club emergencies. Covered with a thick white tablecloth, it gave the impression of a doctor's examination table. But then I remembered this photo of Bettie Page, heeled legs up on a folding table covered with a white tablecloth. In the photo, a crowd of men in suits with cameras are jockeying to take her picture. With her head flung back, she looks like she's having the best time on earth.

Vincent Frand had put the ice bucket on the floor, and after swigging from the bottle he hoisted me up onto the table and started kissing my neck.

It felt wonderful to be kissed like that by a charming, powerful, attractive, and important man. As he kissed me deeper, the feeling grew more intoxicating. When it came to men, I had limited experience. No man had ever made me climax or ever filled me with any great passion. I hoped to God I wasn't one of those girls who couldn't come from the touch of a man.

Before I knew it, Vincent Frand's pants were around his ankles and he was going at me pretty hard, but sometimes, all of a sudden, he'd slow down to touch my face and say, "Baby, you all right?"

This was going to be my chance to feel something, I could tell. I let myself fall all the way back on the table and pulled the neck of my dress down, exposing my small breasts. I hoped Vincent Frand would mouth them, which he did, one by one, slowly then ferociously. I began to concentrate very hard on my slide box inside the pocket of Vincent Frand's dress shirt. I could feel it pressing up against me when he brought his body down on top of mine. I fantasized about him opening the box and examining my slides, one by one. I knew he would love them; what my work would say about form. Form requires solidity... and then I let out a groan and the throbbing inside me released.

This was an unexpected twist: a hot dealer in the palm of my hands—*and* my very first orgasm from sex with a man.

"Oh yeah, baby, come on my dick."

The lewdness of his response snapped me back to reality. After coming, I immediately wanted him out. I couldn't stand him inside me a second longer. I wasn't stupid; I knew Vincent Frand was crude and a sleaze for paying off his girlfriend to screw some other girl in his private room. But he could be all those things as long as he was my dealer, too. That may have been calculated of me, but that's how bad I wanted to make it, and this right here was my ticket. I could've just lit his cigarette and that would've been it, but something had made Vincent Frand take me for a ride this evening, and I had to go along. I wondered who that girl was with the strange man on top of her. Was that really me, or was it that naughty little girl? *She* could be very suggestive.

"That was fucking amazing," he said. "I'll call you."

"My number," I was particularly proud of this, "is in the slide box." I'd made two miniature business cards with my name and contact info. The paper was a thick, hand-cut stock, and I'd used a calligraphy pen to make each letter precise yet artistic.

I lay on the table, trying to act nonchalant about the fact that we'd just had sex and that I'd had an actual orgasm from intercourse. I didn't want my inexperience to show as he preened himself one last time in the mirror before blowing me a kiss goodbye.

Only after he exited the room did I get up from the table and attempt to make myself feel respectable. The whole thing was so exciting I couldn't believe it. Then I glanced down and saw my slide box floating in the ice bucket. The leather case had opened and some of the slides were drifting in a pool of melted ice, spilt booze and several cigarette butts.

There was no salvaging the box; most of the slides were damaged. I collected them anyway. All of a sudden, I vomited in a small puddle next to my feet. I wiped my mouth and held my face in a napkin until I could catch my breath.

Then came the frightening thought that I couldn't stay in the john forever. Eventually, I'd have to brave the labyrinth of Mudd Club without seeing that creep Vincent Frand, Steg with the gross ponytail, and Ostrich Girl, who thought she was so much better than me. Screw them all. And screw the universe for giving me five lousy seconds of sexual ecstasy—for which I'd been waiting years—to be followed by a grotesque insult to my entire body of work, my entire existence.

I wrapped my arms across my chest. I was a stupid, stupid slut. If he wasn't interested in seeing my slides, he could've just said so. I could take it, even if I did fuck him to make him like me. I figured if I were going to be that type of girl, I'd have to get better at doing that kind of thing. Much better, in fact. I wasn't sure I wanted to make it like *that*. Something like *that* could follow a girl, and not in a good way. I punched the wall.

"Okay in there?"

So much for a stealthy escape. I wrapped what was left of my slides in a cheap towel and shoved them into my purse.

It wasn't midnight yet. I could still catch a train back to Danbury. I had to get my rabbit fur; it was freezing, but I couldn't risk running into Frand and his cohorts. I was so pissed that I'd probably kick him between the legs.

That was bull, I was humiliated and just wanted to get out of there without being noticed.

On the ride back home, *sans* my mother's coat, I tried to tell myself there would be other chances. Suddenly, I remembered that they all thought my name was Jamie. That was something positive. Another good thing: I'd had anonymous, orgasmic sex with a stranger. But I couldn't think about sex. Things I didn't know I was capable of doing had occurred. I couldn't believe that was me fucking Vincent Frand on a table in a private john in Mudd Club. I'd been using him just as much as he'd been using me, or trying to.

The train paused between stations and the conductor announced the stop. I shivered a bit when the doors opened.

A final thought came to me: Tonight I learned what I was willing to do to get what I wanted. This was terrifying and exhilarating and I didn't know what to make of it. It wasn't the first time I'd felt this kind of power and submission at the same time. I just wasn't sure I was ready to get into all that again. Bad little girl: so desperate to be seen, she did horrible things. When she surfaced, there was nothing I could do to stop her. I didn't want to deal with her right now. In fact, that was the last thing I wanted to do.

I was unnerved and a little off-balance. This was the night before I met Monika.

Chapter Five

"Sleep well?"

Monika was standing over me, fresh-from-shower hair dripping all over my face.

"Hey," I said, not quite bothering to sit up.

She was naked. In contrast to her angular face, her figure was generous, not chubby, with soft, feminine flesh around the hips and thighs. I could tell she was muscular from the way she skimmed the water from her body.

"Phone's over there if you want to call your mom. You kept calling out for her in your sleep."

I groaned. "How embarrassing."

I rose from a platform bed in the middle of a gigantic loft. I wasn't used to such high ceilings. As I yawned, I noted how the absence of furniture added to her presence in the place.

"Is all of this yours?"

"Impressed?"

"It's amazing." I looked towards the window, waiting for the river to empty out, but like Monika's view, it seemed to go on forever. "Beats the hell out of living with your mom in the sticks."

"I'll say."

"I'm assuming you want a shower after last night," she said, tying the sash to a satin kimono. "I left you a towel."

"I feel like I'm in a hotel."

"We *are* next door to the Olympic," she said. "Ten bucks a

night. Sometimes I pop in just for a change of pace. Of course, if I don't find a roommate soon, I'll be forced to check in for good. Solitude is not good for my soul."

The shower had washed away the lacquered stiffness of her hair, and her cropped, tussled cut made her look a little like Deborah Kerr in *From Here to Eternity*—except for the sides, which were shaved. Illuminated in the kitchen alcove, she appeared to me like one of Giacometti's miniatures, a halo of light crowning her head. Later, I learned that she'd had the alcove specially built so she might appear like that to morning guests. She believed people had their own exposures in which they appeared their best. She called herself a student of light.

But we'd only just met, and I didn't know that about her yet.

On the surface, she came off hard, but I sensed something fragile in her despite the bravado. Even if she knew she needed mending, she didn't let on—and if she did, she wasn't going to make it easy for you to fix her. It was obvious what needed fixing in my life. I needed to get out of my mother's house, but I also wanted a friend again.

"Is that your darkroom?"

Her work was all around us. Blow-ups and miniatures, double exposures and negative strips, all of the same image: a little black girl spinning a pinwheel.

She showed me some portraits in her look book—mainly close, cropped, head-on shots that were designed to confront the viewer. I noticed that all of Monika's photographs read like prayers for girls with longings.

"I don't juggle plates; my trick is, I reduce life to film. Like this, click!"

As my image materialized onto the Polaroid, I felt embarrassed to have been shot fresh out of bed. "I look like hell," I said, rubbing black from the rings under my eyes; picking fuchsia crumbs of lipstick from the creases of my lips.

"Check out those dimples!" she said.

I got the feeling that I was being swept out to sea by a powerful tide and immediately, I liked it.

*

An hour turned into a day, another night, another morning. I worried about my mother alone in her condo; then that feeling of worry turned to nausea. Another shower in Monika's gorgeous stainless-steel shower, where the water pressure was heavy enough to wash away the feelings of disgust, fear, and guilt I felt for Mom. These days were precious gifts; time meant nothing. I had no past and didn't look further than the next hour. Another meal at a fabulous restaurant. Another night of vodka and opium-laced reefer. You could tell Monika was one of those people who couldn't stand to be alone. As soon as we exited the loft, she would clutch my arm so tightly I couldn't even consider letting go. And when we arrived at our destination, she made a big show of introducing me to everyone as her best friend. She paid for everything like money was nothing. I felt elated, like I was existing in some kind of primitive painting, early Matisse with a looseness of brush stroke. A place where people relied on simple, reciprocal signs for the basic, boiled-down expression. I noted the following: whereas some may be referred to as flakes, Monika was a dreamer.

I told her what had happened with Vincent Frand. She seemed to think it wasn't all that big of a deal. "You need to work with Alex Czekinsky. She won't fuck you over." Monika paused to wink at me. "At least not literally."

"Guess I had that coming."

"No, seriously," she said. "You *must* work with her. Your dealer should be a woman. I know some people who know her. I could get you a meeting."

"Wow! That would be fantastic. Could you really do that?"

"Of course. But first can we get breakfast? I'm starving and I know this place that has amazing Eggs Florentine."

The Lower East Side, as always, looked like it had been hit by a bomb. But among the tenements and dilapidated buildings, every block or two there'd be a boutique that sold outrageously expensive Danish boots.

I didn't know what to do with the fact that Monika reminded me so deeply of Isla. The little girl in me sensed that right away. But *I* saw Monika as a way out of that life with my mother, where I was inescapably tied to my past with Isla—what we'd done together, and what I'd done to her.

Isla had been the one in charge. Though it was true, I'd gotten sadistic glee out of watching that little boy beg. Isla and I both had, and this had bonded us in a way people shouldn't be bonded.

I had to wonder if we were flesh and bone girls, or simply afterimages: two teenagers alone in a suburban bedroom one hazy afternoon. It was the last time I saw her alive.

*

"When I first moved in here, all I had was a fish tank," Monika said. Something about the careless tilt of her head told me that this was true. And dear lord, I wanted so badly to believe in that kind of spontaneity.

It was her apartment, her bed, which she'd get out of in the middle of the night to wash her face to "contemplate my place in the world. Besides," she said, opening one of her bottles filled with creamy, pastel-colored cleanser. "You know what they say about cleanliness…" When she was done washing up, she perched on the bathroom vanity, fingering a cascading tower of miniature soaps wrapped in parchment that appeared too precious for use.

"Where'd you get all this stuff?"

"Sweden, Geneva, Capri—this is the way Mum says she cares. Today I got a caviar facial and a bottle of beluga ass cream from somewhere in the Greek islands. You know," she continued, "I went home about a year ago. The rapid growth of ivy had covered the entire façade. The house looked ancient, and I couldn't remember if it had always been like that or it was me. I nearly had a breakdown."

"Where's home?"

"Gone now," she replied wistfully. "When I first moved in here, I started growing ferns in old pickle jars. I spread cheese-cloth on the floors, cut it into strips and hung them as curtains. You should move in with me."

"Really?"

"Why not?"

Outside on the street, a parade of worshippers chanting "Hare Krishna" shook tambourines and sang about love and devotion.

"Do you believe in idols?" I asked her.

"Always."

Chapter Six

In the den, not a single light was on and I could smell peppermint schnapps. Peggy Lee was crooning from the Hi-Fi. An afghan covered my mother's slight frame and I realized, all of a sudden, that Mom was older now. I turned on the desk lamp, waking the cat in the nook of her arm.

The cat mewed. I hated the fact that my mother had become a cat person.

My mother sat straight up with a jolt and shrieked.

"It's me."

"Who's there?"

"It's okay, Mom."

"Oh, Jodi. You startled me. I didn't think you were ever coming home. How long have you been gone?"

"Couple days."

"And already you forget about your mother."

"Mom, please. I called and left two messages."

Her cat was obese. It tried to jump from her arms, but was too slow and my mother was quick to grab its neck and force it down into her lap where she could stroke it.

"You want to be *That Girl*," she said, referring to the Marlo Thomas show we watched together. "It's not all it's cracked up to be, you know, that kind of life."

"Mom, please. I'm not in the mood."

"How'd you get home from the station? The roads are terrible. Let me fix you something to eat."

"I'm fine. What are you doing sitting in the dark like this? It's not even five."

She waved me off. "Never mind. What's the difference?"

That nausea returned, traveling up my stomach into the bulb of my throat. I worried for her. I was terribly angry that she *made* me worry for her, and even more afraid of becoming her. "What's with you?"

"Oh, I'm just being dramatic."

We laughed about it and my stomach settled. She began humming along to "Mr. Wonderful" and I joined in. There was something soothing about the way she hummed, something that made me forget my disgust, and anger, and fear for her.

I untied my boots and joined her on the couch under the afghan. The night was extra bitter, and even though she was annoying and could be stifling as hell, I was still a daughter trying to get warm.

"Why are you home, anyway?"

Mom was the director of the Danbury Historical Society. The notion that Danbury had anything historical to contribute was laughable. Still, the town had money for that kind of thing, and the money made it important. Her executive position was impressive. She was the only woman in the condo who worked, though it was out of necessity.

"I'm not driving on these roads with black ice. It's hazardous out there. I hope you called Charlie from the station. Don't take those other cabs. They're gypsies who drive them. You want a drink? I want one. We should have some vodka."

As she got up from the couch, her oversize glasses slid to the tip of her nose. Her mahogany hair fell in spirals to her shoulders. I could tell from her scalp that she'd missed a couple touch-up appointments.

"I was thinking we'd escape to Los Angeles for a little sun. What do you say? My treat."

"Calm down. I can't just go run off to L.A. on a whim."

"It's not a whim. We've never been to L.A. together."

I rolled my eyes. "Come on."

"When you're a forty-something *divorcée*, I'll take advice from you. I know I'm not crazy; women still give me looks at the market. They talk."

"No one's talking about you." I hoped she hadn't noticed that I'd lost her ski-coat. It was a good sign that she hadn't said anything about it yet. "L.A. is so tacky," I began. "I don't know how you don't see it."

"Golden sunsets, bellinis, and bungalows; that's the life I'm talking about."

"You mean beaches crowded with women who wear pearl necklaces devoid of irony."

Mom chipped away at a block of ice for the drinks. "This coming from you, Ms. Vassar College."

"I'm a scholarship girl, remember?"

"Of course I remember. You act like I don't want you to make it, but I do. As long as you don't forget about your mother, that is."

"There's something I need to talk to you about…" I wasn't exactly looking forward to telling her I was going to move in with Monika.

"I," she went on, wagging her finger at me, "I support my daughter. Whatever it takes. I'm your biggest fan."

"Sorry," I said. "I didn't mean to upset you." I felt lousy about losing her ski-coat. She still looked great in it and it had been really nice of her to lend it to me. I couldn't risk disappointing her. She'd never understand about Vincent Frand, and besides, I didn't want her to.

Leave it to her to say something nice right then. "You just don't see it, do you? What's wrong that you can't see how beautiful you are? Even with that black hair and crazy cut."

"Mom, stop."

"And your makeup. You want to use colors that *enhance* your natural features, not cover them up."

Mom could've been a beauty queen if she hadn't been a hippie. She'd always been tall and thin with lustrous Rita Hayworth hair, and as a teen she had modeled at our local department store. I was too plain to be one of the beautiful people. Not that there was anything wrong with me; my nose was straight and my ears small, eyes brown and medium sized, though I did have naturally long lashes. My hair was thin, which made it easy to dye and cut in layers with a razor. This created the illusion of a fuller style and allowed me to have an edge, which is what girls who aren't beautiful strive for. She would never admit it, but Mom was disappointed that my face was so ordinary. You could tell by the little things: the way she left her jar of cold cream on my pillow or how she would hand off her tube of lipstick to me before we entered the grocery store. "You never know," she'd say, "you could meet Mr. Right."

"*You're* beautiful," I said, sipping my drink. "I'm average."

"I was and you are. But can't you do something about your hair color? It's not natural with your pale skin tone. And if you're going to wear nail polish, you shouldn't let it chip; that just looks sloppy. No matter what, a young girl has to take care of herself. Now's the time. You don't realize it until one day you look into the mirror and say, 'I used to have a neck. What the hell happened?'" She sighed, draining her cocktail. I had a long way to go on mine. "I should've been a dancer. Your father and I used to go dancing. He couldn't keep the beat. But I would get up there and…"

"Dance in the cages."

"That's right. Of course I was hopped up on amphetamines and your father had quite the affair with Benzedrine. Not that I'm endorsing drug use. It was a whole different time. Drugs these days aren't like they used to be."

As irritating as she could be, I knew that on some level I would miss this. Smiling, I passed her a bowl of peanuts off the coffee table. "That's why I just say no."

"Oh yeah, I bet."

As she worked on the bottle of vodka, I went to the kitchen to fix us something to eat. There wasn't much, mostly pre-packaged stuff that my mother used to pass off as corporate poison. "Hungry-Man Dinner" is what the label said. I could hear her calling from the other room, "What happened to my neck? Have you seen where it went? Look at all this loose skin. That's what I'm left with. Jodi, do you hear me? Doesn't anybody ever listen anymore?" She was drunk.

I put my head in my hands. When I was little, Mom would tell me to put my head between my legs and take deep breaths whenever I felt panicked. She'd bathe me in a tub with bubbles and read to me from a book of Greek mythology. When I got too old for the bath, she'd sit in the bathroom while I showered and tell me about her day. It was the most calming feeling in the world to know that she was there. After Dad left, she didn't do it anymore.

I hurled the plates into the sink and began pounding on the frozen dinners with my fists until my knuckles were white and numb. I had no choice. I'd tell Mom that I'd lost her ski-coat and that I was moving in with Monika. And whatever she had to say about it would be too bad.

Chapter Seven

When I got to my studio, also known as Mom's garage, I found my damaged slide box, still wrapped in a cheap hand towel on my drafting table. I tossed it in the garbage. There was no reason for me to hang on to it. In fact, I wanted to erase all evidence of that night, like when Dad caught me with the *Playboy* in the closet. Besides, new things were happening; I was going to have a meeting with Alex Czekinsky. Monika would pull through for sure.

But before undertaking the meeting, I'd have to have some spectacular stuff ready. I surveyed the room. Working in plaster was a process. I used it for both molds and casts. Aside from being cheap, plaster easily took the shape I wanted it to. I had a mold waiting for me, and like all my molds, this one was two-layered. I dyed the inner layer with laundry-bluing solution and kept the outer layer white. When I chipped through the white and hit the colored layer, I'd know I was getting close. When I hit white again, the cast would emerge.

I dipped into my dope stash and rolled a joint to settle my stomach while a bust I was working on softened in a sink of warm water. The martini and Chinese take-away I'd ended up ordering for us wasn't sitting right. I'd chickened out and decided not to tell her about moving out. But I wouldn't let tonight be a total waste; I'd finish something. There was a precision and neatness to casting molds that kept the messiness of life out of my reach.

Plaster wasn't marble—and it wasn't plastic. The materiality of it struck me as traditional yet ephemeral. It combined the spontaneity of plastic with the austerity of marble—and for a fraction of the cost. Artists working either figuratively or abstractly would not invariably desire to have their finished product in plaster. But this was something I embraced. Reaching—stretching towards something.

I always loved the tin flowers Andy Warhol made from flattened cans. Warhol knew what made garbage valuable. I wanted so badly to have the eye he had, but more than that, to have that kind of spontaneity. But something was standing in the way. I looked at the plaster. So much precision. So many rituals. In ancient times, rituals existed to ward off dark spirits. What was I doing? I wasn't being spontaneous. Something unsettling enslaved me and kept me from really being able to attack the clay. I wasn't talking about Vincent Frand. I was talking about that little girl who had done gross things. Like a cancerous thought, she always ruined my fun. But there was nothing I could do. What had happened *did* happen, and the little girl was to blame. She and Isla, the two of them, really, they were at fault. The two of them, yes, but now only one.

Isla was gone and I was left. Which is why the little girl couldn't let go; why she felt entitled to her interruptions.

Chapter Eight

After she had me, Mom grew a tumor on one of her ovaries, so the doctor removed it. To be safe, he took the other ovary out also, and now she can't make eggs. I pray daily for a sister but know it will never happen. Unsure of whether to curse God or science, I curse them both.

The fact that I'm an only child makes this all the worse. Dad's leaving for sure. He's not coming back. Not this time. Don't ask me how I know this; I'm thirteen, which means I know a lot more than people give me credit for. But nobody sees that I get shit; all they see is a little girl with dimples. But I'm a little girl who understands suburban architecture: all façade, no substance. I can hear everything: glass shatters and then the sound of skin being slapped. Mom yells, "Go back to your whore!"

This is the moment I lose everything. I begin to dissociate. This is the day I say fuck suburban architecture.

I open my door and chase after my father. He's down the stairs by the time I get to the top landing and Mom has come out of her room. I call out, "Daddy!" but Mom has one hand over my mouth so I can't say anything else. Her other hand pins me to the wall so I can't rush down the stairs. Dad looks up at us once before he turns and leaves. It's like he sees us, and then he doesn't. I thrash to get away from Mom but she won't let go. Then I notice her red face. I don't know if it's from crying or from being hit.

"Daddy!" I keep calling after him in muddled screams despite my mother's hand. Then she moves it down to my throat. I try to scream but can't.

"Let him go," she tells me with a frightening calm in her eyes. I want to answer but the force of her arm on my throat scares me quiet. Dizziness takes over and I feel myself disappearing into a whirlpool of blackness. Who is my father? I don't really know. I know he has an office job that he hates, but I don't know what he does. I know sometimes he can be bossy and mean, and that Mom hates it when he gets like that. One time he made her change her outfit when we were going out to dinner, and my mother refused to speak for the whole meal. Another time Mom says he was flirting with a woman at a party. After that we never went to any more parties. He can be weird about people touching his stuff, especially this old-fashioned model train set that his dad gave him. I broke the chimney off a train and he spanked me. Mom gave him hell for it. She says it's amazing how much people can change right before your eyes until you can't recognize them anymore. But what she didn't know was that after he spanked me, Dad took me to the ice cream parlor and let me order whatever I wanted, even though it was before dinner. Mom wouldn't allow sweets during the day.

Mom and I are crying. I'm lying down on the hallway floor, my head in her hands. It feels like I'm waking up from a bad dream. My head hurts and I wish it would just fall off. Mom keeps asking if I can breathe. I tell her I'm fine. She grabs hold of me and starts rocking me like a baby.

Then, suddenly, she turns her head like she doesn't want me to see her tears. Mom's profile is striking, like that of an exotic bird. She's had many hairdos, but still comes back to the original, long and simple. Everyone else's mother has stiff, feathered hair. Mom's is soft because she brushes it fifty strokes every night before bed.

I'm afraid she's going to get up and then I'll be lying on the hallway floor all alone. I don't want to be left alone right now; I can't be.

"Don't feel that sweet love, Jodi. Don't feel it or else you'll lose it." She turns to me and purses her pink lips. Then her smile goes wildly wrong, and she begins to scream with no regard for the neighbors. She keeps repeating the same question over and over: "What have I done?" and I can't do anything to shut her up.

Chapter Nine

Nineteen in all: bottles of Schlitz that Monika had managed to bring home from an open bar. I imagined her at the gallery, digging in the icy garbage can for the coldest ones.

"We're artists!" we'd say, all the time, not only when making art. Everything was an exercise in expanding boundaries.

I opened another Schlitz and drank it lying down on the cool loft floor, stretching out my back vertebra by vertebra.

Monika was at a party and I had the night to myself. Bliss. I could work in silence, feeling indulgent and raw all at once.

Outside, I heard a car screech to a stop. I got up and ran to the window. A cab was pulling away and Monika, one hand holding her face, stumbled to the door. I opened the window and called down to her.

"Are you all right? I'll let you up."

I couldn't tell what, but something was definitely wrong. I flew down the stairs and opened the front door.

"Oh my God!"

Her face was a swollen, bloody mess; she tried to cover it with her hands as soon as she saw me.

"Looks worse than it is," she mumbled. I held her close and locked the door behind us. The only sensible thing to do was carry her upstairs, but my frame couldn't support hers, so I carefully rested her chin on my shoulder and slung an arm around her waist, and we took the stairs gingerly, one by one.

We were silent the whole way up. She stank heavily of bourbon.

I lowered her onto the couch and took her purse and coat. Her nose was bleeding, so I gave her a rag and told her to keep her head up. By now, she was kind of giggling, and kept saying, "Jodi, you're so nice." She was obviously high.

"Keep still," I said, and left her momentarily for a towel, which I wet under the warm tap in the bathroom. I moved quickly, searching her toiletries for balm and antiseptic. "Be right there, Monika. Keep your head up."

I took the rag from her hand and gently swathed her face in the towel. That's when I noticed something was off. Her jaw was protruding from the left side, and when she bared her teeth they formed a Z.

We locked eyes and she gripped my leg, her nails digging deep into my thigh.

"You're going to have to pop it in," she stammered.

"Shouldn't we go to a hospital?"

"No!" Her nails furrowed themselves in my flesh.

"You can do it, Jodi. You're a sculptor; I trust you."

"I can't!"

"You have to," she pleaded. "You're the only one who can help me."

The insanity of the situation took hold. I broke free from her grip, found my beer and chugged it. "Okay," I said, rubbing my hands together, the friction feeling powerful. I cupped my hands on either side of her face, right beneath the ears, and then drew my fingers away. *Just clap.* But at the last second, I couldn't do it.

"Sorry!"

"Please," she snarled.

"Okay." I bit down on my own lip and steadied my hands. Pressing them against her face, I felt the awkward displacement of her jaw and nearly threw up. But Monika was counting on me, and this was a chance to help her, despite my own personal fear and repulsion. She groaned in agony. I couldn't let her bear the pain alone. Holding her head in my hands, I snapped her jaw back into place. At the moment of impact there was a popping sound, and then Monika drew a long breath of relief.

"Thank God!" she said, her face relaxing. "Feels so much better."

"What the hell happened?"

She didn't answer. She didn't speak for a long time, and then she asked me to fill a silk napkin with ice and make a compress for her face. After that was done, I took off her shoes and made her comfortable. For a while, I brushed her moist, matted hair and we sat in an anxious silence.

Before she drifted off, she said, "You should see the other bitch."

"What do you mean?"

"Bar fights," she mumbled, "will be the death of me."

The entire night I sat up on the arm of the couch, uneasy and awkward. I didn't believe her. This wasn't the handiwork of a woman. A madman had done this to her; there was no doubt in my mind about that. I didn't sleep a wink, but instead wondered where Monika disappeared to at night while I was working in my corner studio.

"That compress worked wonders," she said the next morning. "Didn't it?"

It had; her face looked as good as ever, her sharp, sweeping features no worse for wear. For a minute I thought it'd all been a dream, but then I flashbacked to the sensation in the palm of my hand when her jawbone had realigned.

"What really happened last night?"

"What do you think?" she asked, sitting up and lighting a cigarette.

I looked sideways, swallowed. This was familiar territory. To really pay attention in life meant seeing things you don't want to see. I was beginning to figure out more and more what connected us. It's strange how that bond can form without a word spoken.

"So I went out with a louse? I'm not embarrassed. This town is filled with jerks. I just happen to attract them."

"It's not okay, Monika. A man should never touch you like that. Should I be worried?"

"Yes," she said, drawing on her cigarette. "You should be very worried about the state of chivalry in New York City."

"I don't get it. You could have any guy you want. Men call off the hook for you."

She looked at me funny. "Really, Jodi?"

I crossed and re-crossed my legs, then cast a glance at my corner studio. "Have you ever been in love?"

"Once," she said. "I was seventeen. He was older, of course: the groundskeeper at my boarding school. He'd steal books, and eventually he asked me to steal him books, like, you know, the sexy ones. God, he was hot. He had long hair that would fall in his face when he'd make love to me. I could never fully see him, but I'd feel a throbbing from every crevice of his body. It was that intensity that made me love him, even though it was just sex." She took a deep breath.

"He made me feel like I was the most special woman in the world. What did I know?" she asked. "Maybe that's not love, but it's the closest I got. But why are you asking all these questions about love? Of the two of us, you're the talented one. Put your focus on that, and let me worry about men. There's no shortage of them, and trust me, they're not going anywhere."

She stubbed out her smoke and fell on her back, kicking her legs up in the air and screeching at the top of her lungs. *"Mama may have, Papa may have, but God bless the child that's got her own."*

Her parents had set her up with some sort of trust fund. She didn't tell me this outright but it was the only explanation for her lifestyle, how she lived with complete abandon. She didn't work and acted like it was the most normal thing in the world. I knew some rich kids in Danbury, but Monika was on a different level. She didn't really talk about her parents, but every now and again a package would arrive from some exotic locale, and Monika would say something like, "On and on, goes the hag, about scarlet sunrises and purple sunsets."

"Tell me about your mother."

"What's there to tell? She comes from a long line of cold Swedish twat."

Only when I pressed her did she recount some elusive anecdote. But the details of her childhood changed every time.

"I don't believe in God! Jodi, we need a cappuccino maker. That's the only thing we're missing."

"I should get my own bed," I said.

"Why? I never bring dates home. Besides, I like sleeping with you. Sorry about the farts, by the way. I've always passed gas like that," she said. "I mean, I keep it under control when I'm with a man, and I know this sounds rude and all, but it's tiring keeping up appearances all the time. Sometimes you just want to let things go. You know?"

I wanted to tell her I did know—that I had suspicions she was lying to me. I tried to reason that the way she behaved with men was none of my business and something you just don't bring up to a person. Besides, this was my opportunity to make art, and I couldn't let that go to waste, especially since I was right here, in the thick of everything.

✶

For money, I found a job in a hat shop visited infrequently by trophy wives. I was the only salesgirl. The milliner, a flat-footed curmudgeon with long, silver whiskers, liked to think of himself as a scholar of nineteenth-century literature. For some reason, I was quite good at making sales when the infrequent customer meandered in. Hats are very personal accessories, meant to be tried on, cocked, and preened just so.

"I'd settle for nothing less than the red fox fedora this time of year… oh, do you prefer something more demure? The velour cloche, yes, *that* is your hat. I knew it the moment you walked in. Not just anyone can pull off a veil these days."

Such nonsense appealed to the clientele. I'd spend a whole hour with customers talking to them this way. When it was quiet, which was often, the milliner would insist I model hats for him. Then he would go on about how the sloop brim reminded him of Shelley.

To fuck with him, I'd insist, "*Mais non.* It's reminiscent of Dickinson."

My real work was scoping galleries. Monika should've been going with me, but she was too busy going out on dates. I had to remind her to call her friend about Alex like she'd promised. She assured me, "Of course, you know I haven't forgotten. You can't rush these things, Jodi. Your problem is that you think too much. It's what you don't plan that can revolutionize your life. Trust me, it will happen."

Rene Ricard had written in *Artforum* that you're "at the mercy of the recognition factor." In moments of supreme doubt, I wanted to believe that this wasn't totally true, that talent and brilliance were more potent than fame. I also knew Monika was right. I thought too much. So I put on a brave face and did the gallery crawl. While I was waiting for my meeting with Alex, I attempted to be seen as much as possible. It was hard to silence that nagging little voice that whined and told me I was no good. But I did it, struck up conversation with airhead gallerinas who'd always look fabulous and the so-and-sos who'd curate group shows. Even though it was work you had to trick yourself and pretend that you were just out having a good time, otherwise you came off too stiff, like an outsider. It was my dream to strike up the kind of conversation that was remembered.

People would start to think of you as part of the scenery. That was my plan. But I was intrigued by what Monika had said about what *you don't plan*. That was living automatically, being plugged in, just like she was.

★

Life at the loft was very ordered. We kept the place clean, never acquiring anything without first establishing its purpose. Wheatgrass juicer to provide daily juice ridding the body of toxins. String of lost keys to remind us that when one door closed, another opened. Everything had a distinct place. Cooking utensils went in the ceramic vase next to stove. Exercise mats were rolled taut, and stowed atop the cupboards.

The only things we had in random abundance were starfish. Some, Monika had saved from family vacations. Others I'd collected at seaport gift shops and maritime museums. We'd hide them around the loft—inside a Pabst bucket, behind a soapbox—only to come across them each time with a sense of discovery, like *objets trouvés*. When we did, we'd watch them change texture by candlelight, drinking, of course, Kentucky moonshine. In these moments, I felt like I was getting to know the real her, not the good-time gal who was known by half the city. If only people could see this side of her—smart and irreverent—maybe she wouldn't feel the need to go out all the time. Still, her nocturnal abandons were incentive for me to work—time when I had the entire loft to myself to make objects out of myths.

Next door to us, just east of Canal Street, the Olympic Hotel provided shelter to squatters and thrill-seekers. With its saltwater swimming pool and half-dozen ballrooms, the Olympic had been all the rage in the 1930s. These days, it was rumored to be a men's hospice, a place they went to die.

"That's what they're doing," she told me one day when we were on the fire escape watching squatters go in and out of the hotel. Her expression took on a sudden and quiet desperation, so I took a moment to brush the hair from her face in my best attempt at a maternal gesture. "The people who stay at the Olympic, like starfish, they wash ashore."

Then Monika became friends with one of them. He couldn't have been more than twenty-five, but he was bald, as if all his hair had suddenly fallen out. His bulbous head, spotted with brown flecks, immediately offended the sense of order we'd established. I'd never known anyone with it—the bug—and didn't particularly want to think about it. But Monika had been watching him for weeks from the fire escape as if he were a circus act. All she could talk about was how she wanted to take his picture.

"Why?" I asked. "Why would you want to document something like that?"

And then I came home to, "Jodi, this is Walter. He's staying for dinner."

Chapter Ten

A woman without a man is like a fish without a bicycle. It's 1976, the message is everywhere: men are expendable. My friend Isla's always telling me this, and she should know. She knows all kinds of things about men. We used to be a lot closer, but we're in high school now, and suddenly she's got boobs and hips and wears blue-tinted mascara and shiny pink lip gloss that makes you want to stare at her perfect, plump lips all day long. What goes into becoming like someone else is never simple. I don't quite get it, I just wish she would teach me about makeup so I wouldn't have to rely on Mom. But now Isla's popular, and because of how I look, the whole school sees me as a little girl. Therefore, I'm not important. I'm the expendable one, not like the popular girls who travel in a swarm, tight and impenetrable. To be part of the swarm, you must possess the power to read the minds of other girls. All girls seem to know how to do this, but only a select few, those who can do it the best, make it into the swarm. Isla makes it in.

The boys seem to know about the swarm. They make it their goal to break it, us. But they're sneaky about it. So when Joe Smite passes you in the hall and says, "Hey baby," you stop and say hello.

"I'm talking to you!" Joe knows to pick one girl, to single her out. When he says it, he's not just saying it to the girl he's chosen; he's saying it to all of us. But today he picks me. He takes my hand and places it firmly on his crotch. He squeezes.

Trembling, my hand wilts beneath the weight of his sweaty fingers and endures the humiliation. But this is not enough. He must make the other girls laugh at my expense. Melissa, Sally, Jen, and Clarice, they all find this exceedingly funny. He's testing us: if you laugh, you get to leave, make it to Algebra with your dignity intact. If you don't laugh, you're next.

As it swells, he squeezes my hand harder. Maybe I come off as moody—or rude, even—but I don't mean to. No one understands the horror that comes with being ordinary, invisible. But this is *too* visible.

Isla breaks from the circle and pushes her way towards us. She flips her hair, which is long and curled at the bottom and, I notice, recently tinted with golden highlights.

"Why pick her?" she says. "Jodi's a carpenter's dream, flat as a board."

A roar of laughter.

"You think *she'd* know what to do with *that*?"

My stomach turns and I'm afraid I'm going to puke all over Joe's white sneakers.

Isla's relentless. What's she doing? I wish she'd stop.

"Everyone knows it's *me* you like." She smiles with her huge eyes and sticks out her chest, where ample buds pop out of her blouse. All of a sudden, Joe releases my hand and I'm left dangling, no longer the focus of attention.

"Oh yeah, baby," he says.

Everybody's looking at Isla, beautiful and weightless.

∗

Mom says men are expendable too. It's been more than a year since Dad left, but I hear her crying at night. The sound kills me. I go downstairs to the kitchen, where she sits with her head in her hands. I don't really know how to comfort her. I try reason instead.

"You told him to leave. I heard you."

"Jodi, go watch TV."

I go back upstairs. For months now I've been avoiding her room. But I'm curious to see what she's done. I still can't understand how he'd just leave. The perfect triangle has become something else. A line, uniquely determined by two points: Me ———————————————— Mom. Thanks, Euclid and Mr. Finer, my stupid geometry teacher who can't stop staring at Isla's tits.

The room is dark and I keep it that way. I head for the closet. All his clothes are gone, and so is the train set he loved so much. I search the top shelf for something. The *Playboy*. It's been years since he caught me with it, but somehow I know it's still up there, and it is. It's like he left it there for me.

I take my shoes off so I can feel the bare carpet on my feet. I hold the magazine close to my body. I try for that old feeling, that pulsing, the best feeling in the world. If I could feel that again, things would be okay. I'd be connected to something.

I open the magazine to the centerfold and there she is. She's not like I remember. In the picture, she looks like a cartoon with that vapid smile and those orange nipples. She appears oblivious to the world seeing her with no shirt on. I don't get what makes her so special, and who she thinks she is to show herself off like that. I hate that there's such a thing as a centerfold. Even the word makes me cringe. It annoys me that she has to be the center of everything. It annoys me that this is where the world puts women—folded between ads for aftershave and sports cars.

Mom tries to fool me into thinking she didn't see Dad. She never gives me enough credit. She thinks I don't know that divorce involves paperwork.

Let her think what she wants. It's easier on everyone if I pretend I don't know he doesn't want to see me. If he had wanted to see me, he'd have made it happen. It's not like he ever listened to anything *she* said anyway.

I'm just a little girl, and he doesn't know what to do with little girls.

"Jodi." Mom stands in the doorway. I hide the magazine

beneath my flannel nightgown. I don't know what I'm going to do with it, but it's mine and I must keep it, protect it at all costs.

"If your father were here, you wouldn't get away with so much."

"But I don't *do* anything."

"So go do something. You've got your permit and it's Saturday night. Get dressed; you can take the car."

Being a teenager in the suburbs is kind of like riding a carousel. You're riding your pastel-painted horse, holding on to a gilt-covered pole, round and round. Saturday nights, the place to be is the 7-Eleven parking lot. It's a real free-for-all. Leaning back onto other people's vehicles, the boys have a swagger that eludes them in any other place on earth. In the fluorescent glow of the neon awning, no one's going to ask them to get out of the way; people walk around them.

The swarm spends the entire night entering and exiting the store. In to sip on cherry-flavored fountain soda, out to watch the boys do tricks on their dirt bikes. In to flip through the glossies and read about the latest starlet, out to sneak drags of the boys' cigarettes.

I pull up in Mom's car with no real plan. I never know what to say or how to act when there's a crowd. I wonder if everyone sees the world like I do.

You feel it when the carousel is about to stop. Your painted horse slows down; his prance becomes lumbered, as if he were trying to get through quicksand. One final lap, and then the ride is over. I get out of the car and walk towards the 7-Eleven. I bite my nails. Then I see Isla getting soda. I walk over and say hi, but Isla grabs some other girl's arm and the two of them run out of the store giggling.

The clerk comes over and tells me I have to pay for their sodas.

"I saw you," he insists.

"But I didn't do anything."

It's no use. He says if I don't pay for my friends right now he'll hold me in the back until the cops come. I hand him the five Mom gave me and wait for change. The clerk takes a long time counting out singles like he has all the time in the world. I pick up an issue of *Cosmopolitan* with a beauty on the cover and a blurb that reads, "Positions You've Never Tried." It's simple; I know that now. The world wants beautiful people. The rest of us are just here to serve them and pretend to be happy with ourselves. I flip through and read something about how aging men seek out younger women as evidence of their vitality and prowess. I wonder if my mother's replacement is a younger woman.

"Are you going to buy that?" the clerk wants to know.

I take my change, slam the magazine on the counter, and turn to exit.

Outside, I hope for the power of invisibility so I can make it to the car. But Isla stops me, and, sucking on a straw full of cherry soda, flashes me a pair of wide, sorry eyes. "Thanks," she says. I start to say something, but she's already across the parking lot letting some boy show her his bike.

When I get home, I really let Mom have it.

"Back already?"

"Where's Dad? I know you've seen him. I saw the papers."

She turns down the volume of the TV. "I don't know where he is. I told you before that he's not in Danbury."

"He's just gone?"

"This happens to women all the time."

"That's what you have to say to me? I'll never see my father again?"

"He can't face you," she says. "He's too ashamed."

"He was here, wasn't he?" Stomping my foot like a real brat, "You did this! You told him to go back to his..." I can't say the word, but I remember what she said. *Whore.*

She starts to cry. I lunge at the TV and turn the volume all the way up.

Chapter Eleven

Walter, I could already tell, was going to be a problem.

Leading him out to the fire escape, Monika said, "Come, Walter. You must see our view of your room. Jodi, would you open a bottle of red? Do you like red, Walter? I've got a nice Malbec."

As I pulled the cork out of the bottle, I listened to their chatter on the fire escape, and quickly made my way outside. I offered our guest the first glass, and he raised a pinky as he drank, with prim, polite lips that just barely touched the glass.

"Thank you," he said in an affected tone. "I don't usually imbibe."

It was one of those early summer nights when it's just beginning to get warm. He said something about how pleasant the breeze was. "Oh, yes," Monika gushed.

"I see what you mean about the change in perspective," he whispered.

Swilling my wine, I rolled my eyes, predicting Monika's train of thought. She'd been talking about parallax lately and, of course, everything she encountered was somewhat relevant to her philosophy *du jour*.

When it came time to eat, he pulled a fork and spoon from his shirt pocket that had been rolled in a cloth napkin. None of us said anything. We all acted like it was the most normal thing in the world for him to carry around his own utensils.

"Are these water chestnuts in the salad? I love water chestnuts."

After a couple bites and too many thank-you's he dabbed his lips, wiped his fork and spoon, and then asked us if he could shoot up in our bathroom.

"It'll only take a minute. Then we can play Gin; I haven't played a good hand in years."

Monika laughed gutterally. "Love those odds!"

I'd hung out with junkies before, but only at parties. When he emerged from the bathroom, he seemed to float above us like he was riding a hot air balloon. The contours of his face had become more boyish. His cheeks seemed to have more plump to them.

Then the three of us played Gin Rummy. I used to play with Mom and her friend, and put them both to shame.

"This is so much fun, Walter," said Monika. "You absolutely must come over tomorrow and the next day after that."

Walter looked at me, smiled, and swallowed. "Good night, Jodi."

Cleaning up the kitchen afterwards, Monika got on my case.

"What's with you?" she said, filling the sink with soap bubbles.

"Nothing. Why?"

She dried her hands on a dishtowel in an exaggeratedly theatrical way. "Will you please bring in the glasses from the fire escape?"

When I returned with the glasses, I opened the trash bin and gently, shamefully, dumped the glass Walter had so politely sipped from.

"What are you doing?" said Monika. "You can't catch it that way."

"We don't have a dishwasher," I said.

"Jodi, sometimes you're such a child."

I was filled with things I wanted to tell her about herself. Like how pretentious her thrill-seeking lifestyle was; how easily she slipped into a vortex of men and champagne; how she cared only when it was cool, or, as she'd say in a phony French accent, "super-cool." Maybe she became friends with Walter out of guilt, or maybe because of the bug he represented. I wonder if she thought being friends with a sick person made her deep. Still, there were times I suspected it was because she knew it made me uncomfortable. Suddenly, he was always around. But I couldn't say anything about it; she'd been so generous to me. And though she might've been disillusioned and glamorously damaged, she didn't have a cruel bone in her body.

The way Monika would shoot off at a party and leave me while she worked the room was how she befriended Walter. You couldn't be mad at her—it was her spontaneity that had attracted me in the first place, and that was, maybe, her true artistic calling.

She loved taking Walter's picture. She'd take rolls and rolls. Close-ups of his face, so close you could see every pore. She took close-ups of his hands, neck, toes, and other parts and strung them out with clothespins on a clothesline. It was a little grotesque, but I never said so. It wasn't up to me to critique her vision.

He would come over, marvel at his string of portraits, call Monika a genius. I didn't like the way he looked at me—apologetically. People like that made me nervous, because it's always people who look at you apologetically that think the worst, most sordid things about a person.

✶

Saturday morning, nothing excited me more than the flea market in Alphabet City. I'd made espresso so Monika would get out of bed at a decent hour.

"We have to get there before noon if we want to find anything worthwhile."

Reluctantly, she lit her morning fag and had two cups of espresso, which I delivered to her while she smoked in bed. She stubbed out her cigarette and rolled over.

"I'm not feeling up to it," she said.

"What? Why? We haven't gone forever, and you promised."

"Don't be such a child," she said.

I got in bed with her and softly rubbed her temples. She flinched.

"What's wrong?"

"Nothing, Jodi. I just don't feel like being touched right now. Is that too much to ask?"

I stiffened and bit my lip. "Sorry."

"It's fine."

"Monika, are you okay?"

"Fabulous," she answered, almost convincingly. "I'd just like to get some sleep if that's all right with you. Damn it, this coffee you made is going to make that impossible."

Her mood was startling, a bit frightening. I'd never seen her this cranky, even in the morning.

"I didn't mean…"

"I know you didn't, sweetie. Just hand me my purse, the patent one by my pumps over there."

"We don't have to go," I said. "I'm sorry."

She didn't respond, only pointed to the purse on the floor. I got up from the bed and brought her the bag. I knew she wanted her "dolls," and had reservations before handing it over to her, but she'd been taking care of herself long before I came around, and seemed to be doing just fine. Still, I figured I should stay and keep her company.

"You'll do nothing of the sort. Besides, I'm in too much of a mood to be around anyone. It's better for both of us if you just go." She rummaged through her purse until she found what she was looking for.

"Monika, sometimes you worry me."

"Please. I can't deal with a headache right now," she said, and swallowed the pills. "What? Don't look at me like that. It's Aspirin."

"I hope you know what you're doing."

"Always," she said. "Now go to the flea market, and get your picture in the paper!"

Forcing a smile, I closed the curtains, ensuring that not even a sliver of light could enter the room. "Are you sure you don't want me to stay? I won't bother you."

"Before you leave, can you bring me my spoons?"

"Okay," I said. I opened the freezer and took out the tiny demitasse spoons she used on her eyelids.

✶

I had a love affair with the flea market, the open-air museum of Americana. Here, I could covet the ritual search for archaic, broken, and delinquent objects.

A breeze passed and the morning light cast cross-shadows on the juxtaposed objects: prosthetic legs, rolling pins, throwing dice, pin-ups, milk bottles, miniature bonsai trees, pipe cleaners, a coo-coo clock, bell jars, used car parts, butterflies, mounted and framed.

Still, I couldn't fully enjoy myself without Monika by my side. The Saturday flea market was *our* ritual. The two of us sifting through junk was quite a sight. Part of the fun was dressing for the day: giant sunglasses, chiffon scarves hiding our hair—hers, white-blond, mine, jet-black. She'd wear things like a string of pearls, a camisole and a leather vest, a pair of skimpy jean cut-offs, and combat boots. I'd put on a backless cocktail dress, ratty zip-front sweatshirt, and heels. On more than one occasion, our photos had turned up in the paper, via a well-known fashion photographer who would stake out the corner of Avenue B and 12th.

Something was off. I couldn't ignore the way she'd flinched when I touched her. I didn't really know all that much about her. Perhaps I didn't want to know all that much about her. The image of her laid up in the dark loft stirred something deep within. I wasn't completely sure I could handle it.

The other night, I'd come home, and she was sitting cross-legged on the floor in the loft just staring at the wall. She was pale white, even by her standards.

"Monika? Monika?" Three times I called her name until she answered. And when she did she told me that she'd spent the afternoon at the dog park.

"I can relate to those animals," she said, without looking at me. "But not people."

I didn't know what to say. But I knew enough not to say some cheesy sentimental crap that everything would be okay.

She was in desperate need of repair. This I understood, but didn't really want to acknowledge. I started feeling sick to my stomach. I eyed a Kineflex twin lens camera and thought of all that parallax stuff she'd been going on about recently. I had to buy it for her no matter what it cost. Suddenly, the things we had in common seemed to be dwindling.

✶

After the flea market, I figured it was a good morning to gallery crawl, or at least stop in to this coffee shop Whispers where, I'd read, Ultra Violet and Jackie Curtis would sometimes meet up for fruit cocktail.

That must've been a while ago, because there was no one at Whispers except for an old lady eating an ice-cream sundae in a corner booth. The way she lifted her spoon was depressing because it made me think of my mother, who I hadn't seen in ages. I pulled a stool up to the counter, lit up a cigarette, and ordered black coffee. I liked the picaresque walls—chintz murals recounting the adventures of roughish heroes, beasts slain, treasure recovered.

The waiter brought me my coffee. "Want a piece of pie? Last slice. On the house."

"Why?" I asked.

"Can't have coffee without pie."

"What kind of pie?"

"Key lime." The waiter was young, nineteen or thereabouts, and very cute. His facial features were feminine, but his body was broad and cabled like a man's. He had dark hair pulled back in a hairnet and a five o'clock shadow you could tell he was proud of. He began to hit on me.

After two coffees spiked with Irish whiskey, the waiter's shift was over and he asked me over to his place.

"I'm staying with my uncle on Loisaida. He's not home right now." Outside Whispers, two men sat at a folding table playing dominoes.

"Okay," I said. "Let's go."

We didn't talk at all on the way to his uncle's. I could tell he was nervous from the way he opened the door to the apartment: a little boy, sneaking a girl home.

Immediately I began to make out with him, grabbing him by the back of the head and sliding my tongue in and out of his mouth, across his neck and into the recesses of his ear. He groaned a little, and I whispered, "Too much?" In moments, I had his pants around his ankles.

I started to go down on him. I wanted to feel him expand and then explode in my mouth. He was happy to oblige. While I was going at it, I kept thinking about Monika. She must do this kind of thing all the time. It was a strange but intoxicatingly powerful feeling being this intimate with someone I didn't know at all. But then I started to wonder how well we knew anyone; how well I even knew myself.

After he finished, he wanted to go down on me. I toyed with the idea for a minute, imagining how good it would feel to have this stranger's lips kissing and caressing me in that hidden place. But I told him I had to be somewhere. After all, this encounter wasn't about my pleasure, but something else entirely.

✳

Walter was over again. "I was stoned out of my mind," he was saying, "And the delivery guy tried to kiss me." He and Monika had made a fort of sheets and pillows and a cheap drugstore fan oscillated between them.

"It's hot in here," I said, opening a beer. "How can you stand it?"

"Oh, honey," said Walter. "Can I have one of those?"

"For someone who doesn't usually imbibe, you sure drink a lot."

"Come join us," said Monika. "Get under here; we've made a fort."

"What's that over there? A pile of toenail clippings?"

Monika giggled. "Oops." Then in her baby voice, "I forgot to clean them up."

"That's gross," I said. "I hate it when you leave that shit around the house and then disappear with some guy."

"Jodi never goes out on dates. She's too busy being an artist."

"Perhaps," I sneered, and tossed my hair, thinking about the waiter I'd just blown in Alphabet City. "I see you're feeling better. I got you something from the flea market."

"A camera!"

"It's a Kineflex. You know… parallax and all that shit."

She stared at it a moment, then tossed it on the bed.

"Monika, I paid a lot for that."

"I know, darling. You can consider it a thank-you gift."

"And what am I thanking you for?" I asked, handing Walter a beer.

"People are primal," Walter interrupted. "As in primates." What was he even talking about? But I had to hand it to him, the way he beamed up at you, his pale, blank face like a fetus. It made me want to puke.

"Walter! You didn't let me finish." Monika started giggling again, the way she did when she took her red "dolls" and drank too much beer. Then she turned her eyes on me. "You better get busy being an artist, because I've done my duty and arranged your sit-down with Alex Czekinsky!"

Chapter Twelve

Here comes that sad little girl again. She's always getting in the way, spoiling things for me. I'm leaving my body, just like the day Dad left. The further from myself I go, the clearer the flashback becomes. Wouldn't it be worse if I were one of those types who got depressed but couldn't be bothered to figure out why?

Someone at Danbury Community High gets the stupid idea of starting an art club. This puts Isla and I together again for the first time in years. The faculty advisor is an old man with a high-pitched, sniveling voice named Mr. Winters. Why he volunteers for the job, I don't know; he doesn't even teach art. He teaches history, intense stuff like the birth of civilization. Anyway, Mr. Winters saunters in and challenges us to observe and create. We all have tricks up our sleeves, so we need to start with what we know.

"Do that," he explains, "until the subject exhausts itself."

"Isn't that, by definition, death?"

It's Isla. Her long, feathered hair frames her tanned, oval face and she's wearing gigantic gold hoop earrings that vibrate every time she tilts her head, which she does obsessively when she speaks aloud in class. On other people, this tic seems nervous or tackily flirtatious, but on Isla it's inspired.

Mr. Winters offers a satisfied, "Precisely."

She's won all the top prizes in art and everyone thinks she's a creative genius. I'm sure I downplay her talent because I'm so grossly jealous. I'm aware that I'm jealous, that I envy Isla and want everything she has: beauty, friends, talent, popularity, the admiration of others. Despite all this, and how she left me behind, I still want her to be my friend in art club. The wish to love is very basic.

She takes a seat next to me and flashes a conspiring smile.

The wish to be loved is more complicated.

I return the grin and wait for the opportunity to whisper a crack about Mr. Winters under my breath.

Next week I come prepared to complain to Isla about how stupid Winters's assignment was. To my surprise, she's going on about how brilliant he is.

"I really learnt something," she says. "I *was* drawing stuff that I thought other people thought was important, and that kind of made me feel like an imposter. But with this assignment, I felt myself really let loose. How 'bout you, Jodi?"

She asks me this like we're old friends. And we are, except we haven't spoken since sophomore year, when Isla got popular. It's funny how stuff like that happens. I know it happens all the time, but you never think it will happen to you. Then it's Saturday night, you're sixteen, and you have nothing to do but listen to Peggy Lee with your mom. But in art club, none of that matters.

"To be honest, I didn't really spend much time thinking about what he said."

"Oh," she says. "Would you like to see my sketchbook?"

She places a black, leather-bound book on my lap and nods for me to open it.

Her sketches are done lightly in pencil, and gone over with ballpoint. The shading effect adds to the dimension of her drawings, like they're sculptures on the page. I open to an Eden of wild grasses, which I recognize immediately as her overgrown front yard. The next page is a close-up rendering of a heart-shaped leaf, and on the next page, the same leaf cut diagonal. Her dissection gives the impression that a palm leaf has entrails, and that plants feel things like love and pain.

Next comes a diagram labeled "the sex-cycle of a fern." She's drawn each spore, as if seen through a microscope. The spores, they intermingle, form courtships and pair up for a grand orgy, which explodes on the final page of her assignment, in a finale of flora and phantasm. These simple drawings of leaves and grasses floor me. They evoke stories of passion and possession, suggest that plant life is sordid and complicated and fraught with sexual tension. I look at Isla and am mesmerized because all of this came out of her.

There are seven of us including Mr. Winters. Sometimes he brings in a cassette player and lets us play tapes. Isla, in side-buttoned pants worn so tight they look painted on, and I sing along to songs about pot, even though neither of us has smoked. At least, I haven't. Even if she has, she sings along like she doesn't know what it's fully about. I'm still nymphish, a carpenter's dream, flat as a board. My mother suggested I cut my hair short and wear it like Twiggy, but the look is off by a decade, and I've ended up looking irrelevant. To compensate, I wear tons of bangles and hoop earrings and the type of makeup my mother tells me is good for girls with plain, pale complexions.

There are other people there, people who smile and nod my way in the cafeteria, but I don't really care about being friends with them. I'm trying out papier-mâché, layering sheets of paper pulp, newspaper, and stinky glue. Mr. Winters is overly enthusiastic, but not so you lose respect for the man, just enough so you like him for going that extra mile. I make masks and boxes, simple objects. I am relaxed and hopeful. I focus on the dampness of the newspaper, the texture of the glue. This is the closest I've come to true happiness. As my hands caress the soft, fleshy pulp of the paper, a soggy mass emerges. This will soon dry, harden, and take form. Form will rise to function. The object in my hands becomes something with meaning.

Next to me, Isla works in her sketchbook on piths and various flora innards. She pauses to contemplate the anatomy of a flower. Where, exactly, is the part where the stigma and style meet? I don't mind one bit that our friendship is confined to the art room on Tuesday afternoons. I think about her drawings and the questions they pose long after class is over, like they are teaching me something sincere, something made real by the curve of Isla's neck, regal and knowing.

At the same time, her talent makes me hate her a bit, and just like that, the happiness I felt making something that was mine is interrupted. It doesn't seem fair that she can be so talented and so beautiful. I can't decide which I feel more, the desire to be like her or the frightening urge to stop her.

Then, one day after art club, she invites me home.

Chapter Thirteen

I couldn't believe this was finally happening. Nervous as hell, I wrapped and packed my best pieces and set off for the Laundromat, Alex Czekinsky's gallery. It had been a laundry in Alex's husband's family for years. When her husband ran off with their neighbor's daughter, he felt guilty and left Alex the Laundromat as collateral. With vision, she managed to turn a dingy Polish laundromat into one of the hottest galleries in Manhattan.

When I arrived, two of her boys were painting the walls. After about five minutes, one of the boys put down his roller and came to the door. "She's in the back office," he said in a German accent.

Without an exhibition up, the gallery could've passed for one of Jeff Koons' factory-esque studios, its staff of minions occupied with odd jobs. The enormous, obsolete washer and dryer combos functioned as sculpture when there was no art in the gallery to define space.

"Vestige of my ex-husband," Alex said from the doorway of her office. "I'm so glad it's you. I was frightened you were Suzie Gibbons. I never should've signed her. She's here all the time, always asking for something. Painters can be so needy, you know? Especially the tragically insecure, neurotic, and damaged ones. Fuck, sweetie, I shouldn't be telling you this. Come in. I see you brought work." She gestured for me to leave my crate on the table, which I was glad to do, since my arms were nearly ready to snap off. It was exhausting carrying that crate and all the while making it come off like no big effort.

I took a seat in a white swivel chair across from her desk.

"Oh, no, dear," she said. "That's a piece by a Danish artist I've just signed."

I scrambled to my feet. Alex pulled up a low stool for me to sit on. On the brick wall behind her hung a tapestry of flyers from shows she'd put together.

She straightened her thick, red spectacles and said, "You've got quite a press agent." Monika, I thought. What had she told her?

"Tell me, Jodi, what interests you?"

I'd imagined this question many times and had rehearsed the list of important artists and sculptural works, works that inspired me. Works like *Guitar* and *The Palace at 4 a.m.*—hardly considered figurative—the opposite of figurative—but nonetheless those that had taught me about the conception of space and the body and its wants. But just as I was about to open my mouth, I realized what a pretentious fool that would make me sound.

"You're not from New York, are you?"

"Connecticut." I cracked a witty smile. "It's morning everywhere in America, though."

"Borrowing phrases from Ronald Reagan." She looked at me curiously. "That's one this studio hasn't heard."

Hitting my stride, "He's an acting vanguard."

"Indeed," she said, tucking her lips into her mouth and laughing with me.

"But really, he's a wonderful metaphor for our time," I said quickly. "And what I'm trying to get at. Beneath his sunshine grin lies this terrible and profound fear of chaos, calamity."

"You talk about the grin, what's he laughing at?"

"He's in on the joke, that's for sure."

"And what do you think the joke is?"

"I'm not so sure there's an actual joke; I mean, something with a punch line."

"Well," she began, pausing to straighten her glasses, "the joke's always there. Self-consciousness will inhibit it, but you're young. Young people always try to be so serious. On the other hand, Pop is beginning to bore me. That's why that plaster stuff you do interests me. Working in plaster is, I imagine, a directly representational, almost academic idiom. But for what?"

"I guess I like the idea of reclaiming the tradition of antiquity."

"You guess?"

"I do like the idea; that's what I'm going for."

Alex paused and thought about it for a minute. "The Greeks, they were all about tragedy, and tragedy is all about loss. What have you lost, Jodi?"

The question shook me. I wasn't expecting it. "When you lose someone, part of the trauma is losing the future with that person, the stuff that you imagine but will never happen."

"Go on," she said.

"I don't know what to say." I could feel my head swelling and a burning urge to urinate. "The desire to have my father back was, for many years, just so overwhelming. It made me do horrible things."

Chapter Fourteen

Isla breezes through her porch door with two glasses of lemonade. Clearly, she's in charge. It's her house and I'm her guest, grateful for the invitation, and we both know it. She's changed out of her tight pants and is wearing a see-through nightshirt that stops mid-thigh. What's she doing? Teasing me? Testing me? She's doing what Isla always does: push things—people, I think they're one and the same to her—to the limit.

We drink lemonade and don't really talk about anything, just stare off into the white sunlight. We comment on the latticework of the trees in the sky. Behind us, the dark woods gape. I ask her where her folks are, and she corrects me. "He's not my dad."

Isla's father died from a brain tumor when she was two. Her mother remarried a couple years ago, so now, according to my mother, it's perfectly acceptable to look at her in the supermarket.

"I know," I say, trying to conjure that conspiring smile she flashed me that first day in the art room. She's still Isla, and despite her faults, there's something perfect about her.

"Do you ever hear from your dad?"

My face stiffens and I fold my arms across my chest. "Nope."

"I wouldn't have expected that from your dad. I mean, not like I really knew him. But he always struck me as a family man. I guess you never can tell."

"He's got a new family now," I said. "A new woman, anyway. I wish I knew what she looked like."

"I know what you mean. Hate is so much stronger when it's abstract." God, Isla was smart. The way she put things. Everything seemed to suddenly make sense. "Hey," she went on, "It's like I've been telling you for years, men stink."

I shrugged. "It's not like I expected a custody battle. It's like he doesn't even care if I'm okay. That's what kills me, you know, wondering if he ever thinks about me."

"You'd like to think he does. That people try to do the right thing."

I'm now thinking about the boy. She must be thinking about him too, but with her, you never know.

I look at her and she looks at me.

"Well," she goes on. "They usually don't."

Something's different about her face. Then I notice; it's her eyebrows, thinned out to a pencil-thin arch. Suddenly, I feel unspeakably self-conscious of my eyebrows and their un-manicured state.

We spend the rest of the afternoon picking the neighbor's dandelion stalks. By then, I've forgotten about her eyebrows, her seductive beauty, her prowess. We stand at the top of a little hill and blow dandelion seeds into the wind. The sunlight is strong and Isla lets herself be goofy.

"Want to see what I look like naked? Now that you're into sculpture, I'm just curious to get your reaction to my body."

I don't know what to say. "Okay."

She strips down to cotton panties and then giggles before thumbing them down, tripping on one leg as she manages them off. It's exciting having her strip for me—not because I want her sexually, but because her naked body is so beautiful.

She's just Isla: my friend. The sun is strong as I look at her.

"So, what do you think? What is your artistic opinion of this bod?"

"Pop your hip forward. Yes, like that. That's your best pose, I think. You have the body of a goddess."

"Do you really think so, Jodi? You don't think I have a big stomach?"

"Are you crazy?" I say. "It's flat and cut. One of your best features."

"You're not just saying that, are you?"

"You should get dressed," I tell her. "Someone will see."

She's playing with me. Remember… what we did to that boy. And just like before, I'm her willing accomplice. But I don't want to think about what we did to him. The sun's about to set and I realize we've been outside for hours.

"You know what I like about you, Jodi? You're such a pure person. Pure as driven snow."

"I used to be Snow White until I faded." It's a lyric from a popular song.

Isla looks at me and I look at her, and we burst out laughing.

Maybe she wasn't thinking about the boy. We've never ever talked about it, so it's possible that the whole thing didn't even affect her. I would never bring it up. What's there to say? I'm always over-thinking things, and here I am doing it again. Maybe Isla just wanted me to see her naked because I'm studying all this sculpture stuff. And it would be impossible to be as beautiful as Isla and not be vain. Besides, she's such a show-off.

When Isla is dressed she lights a cigarette and I tell her I have to get dinner with my mom. Next Tuesday, I wait for Isla in the art room, but she never shows. She's not in school on Wednesday.

Chapter Fifteen

"Jodi?" Alex was looking at me, perplexed. "Where'd you go? You were telling me about your father."

It took a minute to register that I was sitting in the Laundromat with actual pieces—not slides this time—waiting for Alex's appraisal. I had to pull it together. I noticed a note hanging above her desk. It was scrawled in messy ink and framed in a tile mosaic. It read:

Dear Alex,

Poppy and Vesna built this place with their sweat and blood so we could have a better life. I can't give you that. Sorry, for what that's worth. I'm leaving you this laundromat and hope you can make a decent life for yourself washing other people's clothes. That came out wrong, but you know what I mean. I'm a coward for leaving like this, and for not leaving alone, but I hope this makes up for it in some way.

X

Alex had balls to post that note up there for all the world to see. A rejection notice from a former lover—but she made it be about something else, and that's what good art does. She made it the punch line of her gallery, and the beauty of it was she got people to laugh with her. No wonder she was called the Alchemist. I had to stay intact and keep a muzzle on the little girl. No room for her here. I couldn't stomach hearing her voice whining to me, being the burden she always was, *not now*.

If Alex could lay it all out there, so could I. If I could be honest with her about my father, she could tell I was for real. She'd relate to that, and when she looked at my work, she'd understand me.

"I didn't understand what I'd done wrong for him to leave like that without saying goodbye or anything. After the emptiness comes the anger, which is a weird feeling. And that's the worst part," I said, telling her with a heavy sigh. "Hate is so much stronger when it's abstract."

"Ah," she said, nodding. "That's why you gravitate to form. But why not marble?"

"Too expensive."

"Right," she said, nodding, playing it out. "And why not plastic? That's the preferred medium of the fetish minimalists…"

"…of the '60s. I'm right now. Morning in America, remember?"

She was interested. "What was it you called it? Reagan's sunshine grin?"

She was getting me. I started to feel a little lighter. Relieved.

"Yes," I said. "And beneath it lies a horrific, gaping mouth…"

"Go on," she encouraged.

"Ready to swallow you." I felt alive. "Can you imagine what it feels like to be swallowed without consent?"

"You are very intriguing," she said.

I paused, giggled a little on the inside.

"Reagan is a gargoyle of a man, and simultaneously the Leader of the Free World. Still, the art market has always been the emblematic stronghold of *laissez-faire* economics," she conjectured, straightening her buggy glasses. "But enough about Ronbo, tell me about your father."

"I just have no need to ever see him or deal with him again. Really, I've lived my whole life without a father; I don't need him now."

"Father issues are very hot these days," she said. "Trust me. Especially for women artists who can pull off vulnerability in a controlled, representational, almost academic way. I get a sense you can do that."

It was more than getting me; I'd fooled her. She saw me as an intact, competent and integrated woman.

"You're smart," she went on. "And that counts for a lot. It's tricky operating from a place of loss, but if you could pull it off, well, the results would be unparalleled."

"This is about something bigger," I said.

"Of course it is," said Alex. "Loss is always about something bigger. I got news from South Africa today. My friend was murdered. Government spies shot her in the street in broad daylight. We all told her, warned her that it didn't matter she's American, a woman. Her face is black. She thought she had to go. She said she knew it unlike she'd known anything in her life." The features of Alex's face were crisp as she spoke. "We were in this very studio when she described this feeling that had overtaken her, that everything in her life had been moving towards this moment. Everybody sees the horror on TV. They watch it and are horrified. Then they go about the rest of their lives. You know, that doesn't make them bad people; she'd always say that."

"That's terrible," I said.

"She was over there trying to do something. I suppose you're trying to make a statement. That's why you're here; that's why you do art."

Neither of us said a word. Together, we listened to the faint patter of paint hitting the walls outside her office. Finally, as the silence started to become a drag, an assistant knocked on the door and called, "Your car's waiting."

"Thank you, darling. *J'arrive*, as the French say. *I'm coming.*" Then to me, "I've got to go. But leave your pieces with me and do excuse me for hurrying off like this."

My heart dropped. That's it? "Oh," I said, feeling the bite of disappointment. She wasn't even going to look at my pieces tonight. What a total waste of time.

"I assume you're free to join me at Beretta on Saturday. Reservations are for eight."

"Beretta?"

"You know it?"

"Of course," I said.

Reaching in her pocket for lipstick, she got up and applied the bright shade to her lips blindly. She looked hard and cocky, even with the red lips.

"Good," she said. "I'll see you there. Wonderful of you to stop by."

Like that, things started happening.

Chapter Sixteen

"Where is she, anyway?" Walter asked. "I thought she'd be home by now."

"Tai chi. She tried to get me to go; no thank you."

We laughed. Laughed about Monika. It was the type of laughter between two people who don't really know each other, but share a close friend. I began to think maybe Walter wasn't that annoying. He was just filled with this awkward neediness that took some getting used to.

Then he started twiddling his fingers, tapping his foot. He was always fidgeting.

"What's up with you? I hear you're Aleksandra Czekinsky's next find, her newest protégée."

"Thanks to Monika. It's kind of mortifying." I paused. "I mean, in a good way. I've got this dinner thing at Beretta tonight."

"Monika told me. You know, Alex would have never invited you out if she wasn't into you."

I couldn't tell if he was for real or just flattering me to get on my good side. Then, "Look at this bitch."

It was Monika on the street below us. Carrying a bag of take-out from Su Su Yum Yum, our favorite Szechuan restaurant. She waved up with a big smile.

"We're not going to eat from containers like savages," she said, coming in the door. "We're going to eat like a family."

"I've got my dinner with Alex tonight," I said. "Remember?"

She looked disappointed. "Oh, that's right. I'm such a ditz."

"And I'm not staying either," said Walter, looking at his watch. "It just creeps up on you, doesn't it?"

Code for: time for my next fix.

"What? Why? I just got home. That's not fair. I never get the both of you together. So you just go to the bathroom, Walter, do what you got to do; Jodi, you don't have to eat, just sit with me while I eat, and then after I'll find you an outfit and do your makeup."

Walter and I looked at each other. "Do we have a choice?" I said.

"No. No," he repeated, puckering his face into a tight knot. "I've really got to go."

"No way!" Monika insisted.

"It's been lovely." He made for the door.

Heaving herself into a statuesque pose, her arms crossed in front of her chest, Monika blocked his way. "Oh no you don't."

"Look, chica, I've got no time for your reindeer games. I'm not holding."

"You?"

"Shocking, right? I've got to make some phone calls. One phone call, really, and I've been waiting exactly three and a half hours to make it, so if you'll excuse me…"

"We've got a phone," I said. "Make your call here. There's no reason to go off and be alone."

"He usually comes to the Olympic."

"Walter, we're right next door. Just make the call."

"You don't understand," Walter explained. "These guys are resistant to change. Any kind of change, even the slightest thing."

"Don't you think our place is more discreet than the Olympic?"

He shifted his weight and looked at his watch. "I guess I'm wasting precious time just standing here arguing about it."

When Walter got on the line, I tugged at Monika's waist. "I miss you," I said.

"I'm right here!" She looked at me kind of funny and made me feel desperate for wanting her whole, undivided attention. But I did, especially considering my big dinner with Alex.

Walter hung up the phone and announced, "Ten minutes."

"Oh, good," began Monika, opening a carton of moo shu. "Who'd you call?"

"Dirty Lonnie. He's very reliable. No thanks," he said, pushing away his plate. "Later."

"Dirty Lonnie?" I'd heard the name. A real fucked up guy. Violent as hell; into crazy schemes like home invasions and kidnappings. "That guy's a Molotov cocktail. How do you know *him*?"

A sly smile crept across Walter's face. Pinky raised, he sipped some of the plum wine Monika had poured for us. "I know him from Tennessee. And don't believe everything you hear."

"Do tell." Monika lit a smoke and leaned in.

"We were in grade school together, Lonnie and I. Met each other quite by chance here in the city one night when I was cruisin'. He's done well for himself! Everybody knows he's the only cat below 14th Street who's got pink rocks."

"I certainly hope you're talking about heroin," I joked.

"That whole Dirty Lonnie rep is just hot air, for business— street cred. So fools won't mess with him. I'm swearing you to secrecy, ladies. What are you waiting for? Swear!"

Monika shrugged, stubbed the cherry out, and stuck her Winston behind her ear. "Cross my heart."

On the table lay a British rag featuring a tribute story on the Sex Pistols. Monika would always come home with foreign tabloids from a newsstand by the Trade Center. I picked it up and said, "I swear by Sid Vicious—can't really do any better than that."

"No, you can't," Walter agreed. "He's actually part of the pocket protector posse, but does more business on the east side than the Estevez brothers. He pays a dozen or so Cuban kids to run deliveries but makes his real money with prep school kids and television actors. He meets up with me only because we go way back *and* because he knows I can handle my gear. He's very low profile, which guarantees he ends up with the *hush-hush* users."

"Like you," Monika teased.

"The types with loads of money for clean hammer."

"The Cubans don't rip him off?" I asked, skeptical.

"The kids? Oh, he's playing them. He knows they're not expecting a guy like him to run such a good business. So he keeps them busy, overpays for the shit deals. And these are kids from Miami I'm talking about. Thirteen, fourteen years old. They get lazy, think they're scamming some nobody under-boss, not even worth it. Meanwhile, Lonnie's handling top-notch clients and no one even knows where the money goes. The guy is a masterful illusionist. He's got an elaborate imagination and the skills and resources to use it."

"Sounds like a lunatic," Monika said. I was intrigued.

"It's just smoke and mirrors. Trust me, when you meet him you'll see. He wouldn't hurt a fly."

✳

A slight man, about five-foot-five, Dirty Lonnie inched his way through the door like a worm. He was dressed inconspicuously in K-Mart slacks and white tennis shoes, and he wore thick, black-framed glasses. He and Walter shared some kind of awkward embrace, and then it was straight to business.

"This is my homegirls' place; these are my homegirls."

"You know I don't do introductions."

Monika and I looked up nonchalantly, without too much interest.

Outside, two Chinese merchants screamed at each other. We couldn't understand them. I thought perhaps it was a fight over the garbage now that the garbagemen were on strike, but it could've been over anything.

"Only for you, Walter. This Sri Lankan gear is pretty good.

Brown, alkaline. You could fix it up with a little lemon if you got some. That'll run you longer than the pink."

Whatever distinction, it seemed to excite Walter, who nodded, "Oh yes, I'll take that."

Dirty Lonnie opened a brown paper sack and searched through it for the Sri Lankan. Walter palmed him a wad of cash, which he'd counted out several times before handing it over, but Dirty Lonnie counted it himself all the same.

"You're a real champ, pal," Walter said. Dirty Lonnie grunted and looked over at Monika and me. I wanted to do something funny like salute him, but didn't want to piss Walter off after he'd been so fussy. So I just said, "Bye, nice to meet you," and Monika giggled. Walter shut the door and gave us each a look. Then he set about unloading.

"Wait," Monika began, "I want to film you shooting."

"Oh, come on," I said. "Ever since she got that thing she's been wanting to use it. I mean, isn't that in bad taste?"

"Stills, then. What do you say, Walter?"

"I don't care what you do, all I know is it's about to be a beautiful thing."

Monika jumped up and ran into her darkroom for her camera. I was getting nervous about my dinner with Alex, and I slumped headfirst onto the couch. I wanted to be able to talk to Monika about what I should say, how to get people to talk to me, and what to order. I really didn't want to watch Walter stick a needle into his vein. But it was too late. He'd emptied the contents of his knapsack onto the table. A leather shaving kit held his spoon, lighter, and syringe, which looked like a clear plastic rocket with a ring of dried crimson where the needle began. I didn't want to watch but couldn't look away. He was already dead; he might as well stick a needle in his arm.

Opening the tin foil of drugs, he asked for a slice of lemon, and since Monika was looking for her camera I assumed it was my task to get it for him.

"Jodi, just get me a slice of lemon, would you?"

"What if I don't want to play accomplice?" I said, annoyed.

"No one's asking you to tie a tourniquet, just hook up a slice of lemon, will you?"

My head felt so heavy, I couldn't pick it up from the couch.

Chapter Seventeen

Thursday afternoon, I come home from school to find Isla at my door.

"I tried to pick your lock," she tells me. "Just kidding. Can I come in?"

"Sure," I say. "My mom's not home."

"So, this is your new place."

"Not really new. We moved in two years ago." I try not to sound bitter, but part of me wants her to know that she's been a lousy friend and should feel guilty.

"It's nice," she says, eyeing the den.

"Yeah, it's not so bad."

I wait a beat, then ask if she wants a soda. She follows me into my room.

"I have to tell you something," she says, closing my door with lithe fingertips.

I plunk down on my bed and feel a sense of relief that I cleaned my room two days ago. It's strange and exciting having Isla over again.

"I'm late."

I must have given her a blank look because she cocks her eyebrows and repeats, "*Late.*"

"You mean?"

Her nail polish is chipping and her nails bitten down. "I'm pregnant, Jodi."

"How do you know?"

"I took a home test. Actually, I took five. All the same results."

We're sixteen. Isla can't be having a baby.

"Are you sure? Can you trust those things?"

I don't know what to say. Isla's a girl who uses words like "nihilism" and "trope" in Junior English. The model student: assertive, strong-willed, yet a team player who brings out the best in her peers. Remarkably talented, guaranteed an art scholarship at a top school next year. Yet here, she's reduced to a quivering mess on my floor.

"I won't do it; I won't have an abortion."

Everything is happening too quickly.

I reach for her hand and clasp it in mine. She continues to tremble. "What are you going to do?" I don't know what else to say. We're silent. It's not the normal type of silence between two people, even between two friends estranged and recently reconnected. It's a dark, dead silence that frightens me.

All of a sudden, her mood changes. Suddenly, she becomes very calm, phantom-like, as she begins to ramble. "It was my stepdad. When my mom was at her book club. It'd be us two in the house and we'd watch TV together on the couch. We started sitting real close to each other. I remember him inching closer. The closer he got, the more he'd look at me, like he was trying to sense if I noticed what was going on. It was nice to be held like that, so I let him kiss me. I have to say, I was flattered, he smells like a man, you know, and when he kisses, he kisses like a man with a strong jaw and scratchy face." She begins to talk faster and faster. "We were just watching TV, that's how it all started. But it got me excited. And I kind of liked having something over my mom; she thinks she knows everything. I'd look forward to her book club night, wash my hair and paint my nails. I even bragged to my friends about the Hi-Fi my stepdad got me special for my room. And I swear to you, Jodi, I didn't think I was doing anything wrong. I felt like I was steering the ship but I wasn't steering anything. One night he tells me he knows what I really want, and there's nothing wrong with it because he's not my real dad, that I was practically a woman already when he married my mom. And I'm so fucked up, Jodi, I am, because *I did want it* and so I let him reach in my pants. Before I knew it, all of him was inside me."

I swallow. Long, hard, deliberately. Part of me is jealous that this has happened to her. Isla's stepdad is cool and handsome with strong, defined muscles, an earring, and a sports car. He could have any woman he wants, even married to Isla's mom, who's gorgeous and sexy and rich enough she doesn't need to hold down a job. I don't blame Isla for one minute for desiring him, even though it is wrong. I wonder what it must feel like to *be* desired. What is it like to be adored in that savage way? A desire so strong you risk everything for it... take something you shouldn't... Didn't Isla and I experience something like that with the boy?

"And after, he tells me to take a shower, that I'll be okay if I take a hot shower. A shower, not a bath. I remember he said that specifically because he knows I like to take baths. So, I did what he said. How could I have been so stupid?"

This, from an artistic prodigy. What did she think would happen?

As she keeps talking, I wonder why she hasn't once asked me not to tell. Suddenly, I realize why I've been chosen as her confidante: I'm nobody. I have nobody to tell.

"I was in that shower for like, a half-hour. But, Jodi... What am I going to do?"

Here's my chance to be important. She's scared. I can tell she's trying to gauge my reaction. Am I shocked? Horrified? Impressed? Repulsed? This isn't some leather-bound drawing of ferns fucking; this is the real deal.

I lower my voice and try to steady her gaze. "You can't tell anyone. What if they don't believe you, and even if they do believe you..."

"I know," she interrupts. "I know what people will think. With boys, it's all, they've got raging hormones. It's normal. But with girls..."

I nod. The girl who feels desire, who asserts her desire is a slut. A whore.

She begins to cry.

"You can't tell your mom," I tell her.

"I know. She'd kill me. But I can't just get rid of it. I don't even know what's real any more."

I want to tell her that I'm real. That this right here between us is real. That she's confided in me, and the secret we share is real. Only, my mind's spinning. I can't get my arms around what's happened to Isla. It's too frightening to think that her desire somehow caused all this, so I think about it very distinctly as something that's happened to her. But that's not entirely true. I know how Isla can be, what a temptress she is. I know what she's capable of. It was her idea to do what we did to the boy.

What would people say if they knew? Beautiful, talented Isla who draws tear-stained entrails of palm leaves with assertive, brilliant strokes. Chatty, popular Isla, with long, feathered hair that hits her midriff, a midriff that is always tanned and flat and gets displayed days when she knots her T-shirt just above her belly button. This same Isla is filled with horrible secrets. But I know them. First the boy, and now this.

I feel a very sudden and intense urge to destroy her. It's a crazy anger that sickens me to my stomach. I begin to question whether I ever really liked Isla. I couldn't for sure say she's a good person. As usual with her, she has me all turned around, inside out.

Chapter Eighteen

Walter fixed the spoon and heated the stuff with a little water.

"Here," I said, handing the lemon wedge to him. "What's it like? Does it make you forget?"

Walter rolled up his sleeve, held out his arm.

"I'm not indulging Jodi the naïf right now. You're charming and all, girl, but reel in the Pollyanna bit a little. At least when I'm about to fix myself up."

You could tell he knew the drill and could whack up on autopilot, tapping the smooth skin on the inside of his elbow. The needle slid in easy. As he pulled the plunger back, a mushroom of red liquid erupted in the barrel of his plastic rocket. He rammed the plunger forward.

Ecstasy.

The needle hung there limp for a minute. All the while Monika snapped away: click click click.

After a couple minutes he was tidying paraphernalia, putting everything back inside his knapsack.

"Fuck," he began. "Fuck, fuck, fuck. I've never done that before. Geared up in front of people who don't use."

"Really?" asked Monika, capping her camera. "I feel honored."

I was beginning to feel sick again. I remembered footage of Edie Sedgwick at one of Warhol's dinner parties. How she cut her meat with her fork, raised the bite to her lips, but nodded off before it got there. The whole thing was happening in slow motion, how I assumed everything happened when you were drugged out.

But I didn't have time for this. I had to get ready for dinner at Beretta with Alex, and Monika had promised to help.

*

The maitre d' clasped his hands at the swell of his chest, the rosaries around his neck swinging with the softest of undulations. He bowed and led me towards Alex's table. Suddenly, I realized that Alex and I were not dining alone. There was a party of people, art people, waiting. I couldn't have felt worse. Then I remembered I was wearing Monika's blouse, a paneled, translucent, azure number that looked terrific with my skinny black trousers and black pumps. I always looked good in Monika's things.

I was relieved that sitting catty-corner to me was a willowy girl with black, wavy hair, milk-white skin, and a pierced septum, who I recognized as Kade. Or Kate, Katie, something like that. She owned a silk-screening warehouse and was a well-known kleptomaniac. The other guests included two Euro-fag dealers on the downtown circuit I'd never met but recognized, a green-eyed stunner with a cherubic face hidden beneath a ratty beard, and his date. The stunner was wearing a bowler hat with such panache that he had to be somebody. Seated next to him was his lady friend, the type of wispy girl whose job it is to look dazed and beautiful and occasionally rummage through her purse while paying un-devoted attention to her date.

I nodded to willowy woman, whose name turned out to be K.T. She was polite, not friendly, and I had to rethink my original impressions. It was obvious that Alex was taken aback by the stunner, and the Euro-fag dealers were taken with each other. A round of introductions quickly ensued, which was made for my benefit.

Frederick Nunch sat to my left. I liked him immediately. He

wore a live orchid in his lapel. He was thin-moustached and slack-jawed, and it was clear that his partner, Vlad Kelisky, was the dom. An eyesore of a man, not meek, but not a brute. At least not physically. For no apparent reason, every couple of minutes he'd take a pair of dice from his pocket and roll them on the table.

The stunner was none other than Jan—not pronounced, "Yan," though the Euro-fags continued to mispronounce it all night. No last name, just Jan, the guy was a grafter-cum-conceptual artist who claimed to be personal friends with Mapplethorpe and de Kooning.

"I thought de Kooning was spending all his time in Long Island," said K.T. with a cocked eyebrow. "How have you two been crossing paths?"

Jan glared at her. "Wouldn't you like to know?"

He was always changing his look, which was why I didn't recognize him. The last time I'd seen him—in an issue of *Artforum*—his hair had fallen in Hasidic-like curls to his shoulders. Sierra Walker, Upper East Side coffee heiress, played his debutante of the night.

Our waiter came by to replenish the table's carafes with red wine, and we all had a toast.

"Amen!"

"Must you be so crass, darling," Sierra whispered loud enough for me to hear. "Claire and Mummy have reservations later this week. I told you."

As Frederick passed me the basket of flatbreads, I snickered to think what Mummy had to say about her daughter's latest conquest.

"You women want me to apologize for my phallus. Well, I'm not gonna."

"Oh, Jan," cooed Alex, "I know you don't mean *all* women."

"Look, there are females and males. It's biology."

"Oh, brother," began K.T. "That argument is so tired."

I nodded. I knew I had to join in the conversation right away, otherwise I'd be branded with silence all night. So I tried to think of a sassy remark. "Next you're going to say that us women were made from your rib."

"That's just a signifier. What you call a rib is really…"

"Your cock," interrupted K.T. "Yeah, we know."

"What I mean is, my phallus is bigger than me, bigger than my life or your life or anyone's at this table."

"Do tell," said Vlad.

"I'm working on a collage of penises. All types: erect and throbbing, flaccid, freckled, black cocks, white cocks, Chinese cocks, those that swerve right…"

"I think we get the point," said K.T.

"Oh no," said Vlad, "Don't stop him now."

"And then I'll jizz all over it. The glue that holds the whole goddamned thing together is my come."

"Arresting," gushed Alex.

Sierra looked bored. Frederick asked her to join him at the bar so he could "stretch his fingers." The heiress nodded and tossed her strawberry-blonde hair onto her bony shoulders.

Jan didn't seem to notice she'd left the table. "The other night I did a line of coke off an erect cock, and I thought, yeah…"

Vlad wanted to know, "Was it the high of your life?"

I wished I'd joined the other two at the bar. This wine made me want a cigarette.

When the smokers returned, our waiter recited the specials and Alex told me that I must order the shoulder of veal.

"I'm telling you, Jodi, it's butter in the mouth."

It so happened that this particular cut of meat had been getting a lot of bad press lately from the animal rights people. We were making small talk about the menu when Jan interrupted. "Jodi Plum. You haven't said anything about my penis project."

The table fell silent.

"Why," I began, "I just love cock. Can't get enough!"

The entire table roared with laughter. Jan shifted uncomfortably in his seat as the gaze was no longer on him, but on my successful quip. I felt like a million bucks.

In the midst of all the laughter, wispy Sierra leaned into me and said, "He wants me to wear a strap-on and fuck him in the ass. Only if the camera's rolling, of course."

We looked at each other and smiled, and I thought maybe she wasn't so bad.

After ordering the eleventh-century Crusader mutton for herself, Alex ordered for me and K.T., who ended up with grilled quail with a yoghurt mousse.

"Guess you're getting the veal," Sierra said in one of her whispers. She unfolded her napkin and placed it on my knee. "Don't worry," she assured me. "Why do you think I carry such a big purse?"

"Did you know," Alex began, "Jodi makes the most incredible frescoes and plaster busts?"

"Really?" inquired Vlad. "Plaster? How retro. Everyone is using neon this and plastic that; plaster castings are so out-of-fashion, you'll be avant-garde."

"Precisely," answered Alex, turning to me. "Which is why I've decided to use you in my next show."

I could hardly believe it. "Really?"

"Yes!"

"When?"

"Don't worry about that. There's a sixty percent chance I've got a buyer for that one piece, what's the name? Oh yes, *Persephone Weeps*. Those odds, my finesse and your honest-to-God earnestness will get you into one my shows."

I was in shock. "Wait, who is he? Who wants to buy it?"

Alex swirled a mouthful of wine. "What difference does it make?"

"Shouldn't I care who collects my work? I mean, for the long haul. If he's the type of collector to buy on a whim and then sell at auction, isn't it doing me a disservice?"

To this, Frederick laughed as if I'd made the biggest gaffe. "Do you believe this? An unknown questioning her first sale. Now I've truly heard it all."

I took a gulp of wine.

Alex said dismissively to me, "I think not. In the meantime, stop reading all those art rags. Rene Ricard is a sour grape."

Once again the table surged with laughter.

"She might have a point," said the other Dutchman. Just as I thought I might have an ally at the table, he quipped, "I remember when *Artforum* was my bible."

"This is all… so exciting, a dream come true."

"Now, Jodi, is it? Enthusiasm is nice," Frederick began. "But if you want the art world to take notice, you better be a little more, how do you say? Cynical. Nihilism sells art, my dear."

"Amen, bitches!" Jan took a drink and smacked his glass on the table. "Worked for me."

K.T. grimaced from across the table. "Who are you calling bitch?"

"Girls," began Alex. "I worry about your generation. You take yourselves so seriously."

"You can't be for real, Alex," said K.T. She wore her hair wild and unkempt. "Everything Jan does is a pathetic attempt to objectify women."

Jan blew K.T. a kiss. "You know you love me, baby."

Alex said, "Are you forgetting that it was women like me who fought for and won, might I add, the freedoms you enjoy today? I don't regret it for a second, darling, but I, more than anyone, have a right to enjoy whatever type of art I see fit."

"Ejaculate art," I said. "Seminal work."

I thought K.T. or someone might snicker at my joke—if not joke, entendre at least—and that we'd emerge from the evening great friends. But K.T. was fingering one of Vlad's dice that she'd somehow managed to steal away. She popped it in her mouth like a cube of gum. It was like she didn't see me watching her, but we both knew she did. The die had disappeared, but she couldn't have swallowed it just like that. She turned to me and said, "A magician never gives away her tricks."

Sierra nuzzled in the crook of Jan's arm like a china doll. Craning her wealthy, nimble neck, she whispered in his ear and made him smile.

"Of course we will," he told her. "We'll go by Nan's after dinner."

Like that, they'd all turned on me. I had become the high school outcast, bitter that I'd strived to belong.

I excused myself, hoping to fade into the shadows of diners like me who'd come to Beretta and lost their souls. I choked out the line, "Need a smoke," and approached the bar. Here, I should be happy. Wasn't this success? Wonderful, isolating success—a real New York show. And, on top of that, the possibility of my first sale. Thousands of girls would do anything to be in my place; I knew it. I should have been having the time of my life, but something felt off. This gnawing in my gut was disrupting my equilibrium. I felt like I was riding in one of those bumper cars at the amusement park, where everyone keeps slamming into you and you're supposed to be having fun.

"Darling." A hand grazed my back and I turned around to find Alex standing behind me with two lit cigarettes. "Here, I've got you."

"Thanks," I said.

"What ever could be wrong?"

"Nothing."

Smoothing hair from my face, she said, "Nothing? Jodi, don't play coy with me. I won't have you sulking when there's vino flowing. I just ordered a vintage grappa that's out of this world. You wouldn't want to miss it."

"Wouldn't I?"

She swooped in and slid an ashtray on the bar in front of us. "Don't let Jan bother you. He may be a pretentious asshole, but he's hot, hot, hot right now. Dig me?"

I breathed a sigh of relief. "I feel so much better knowing that's what you think."

"Of course, darling. And I don't want you worrying your head off wondering about stuff like who's interested in buying your work. That's my job."

"You mean?"

"Yes. I'm willing to represent you officially. If you accept the offer." She leaned in close, as if I needed consideration. "I'm on the Guggenheim committee this year."

I took a drag of the cigarette Alex had given me. She smoked French cigarettes that gave you a strong head rush. There was something glamorously sinister about them that made me crave them like no cigarette I'd ever smoked before.

"You know, we're not even eating off the menu." She surveyed the room, cocked her spiked hairdo up to the ceiling. "How many of these prim bitches buttoned tight into Chanel suits can say the same?"

"Let me guess," I joked, "Prim bitches whose freedoms you won?"

"I knew I liked you. And those wonderful statues of yours are going to make you a star. Just you watch." She snuffed her cigarette out and gestured for me to do the same. I could smell the mélange of sweet Italian table wine and salted fish on her breath. I wanted to believe her. I wanted more than anything to stop fighting the tide and let myself get carried away. "Let's not neglect the others. We don't want to be rude."

By the time we got back, talk had turned to Latin American politics. Frederick and Vlad lamented the corruption of land reform and collective farming. Every once in a while, Jan would interject with some lame comment, proving his limited understanding of world affairs. Finally, thank God, our food came.

Chapter Nineteen

Sometimes Monika sniffed drugs. I didn't do much except drink and smoke dope. Everything was easy to get, and people were so open to it. When Monika and I got to Racket Room, chaos had already broken out because someone had dropped an eight ball of coke on the floor. Sure enough, there was a pack of girls crawling and fighting over who got to lick up the dance floor.

We sort of knew the bartender, a rail-thin, multi-pierced chick named Syd. She was loud and bossy and intimidated me, but Monika liked her.

"You know Jodi, right?"

Syd looked me over and nodded.

"Sure," I said. "We've seen each other around."

Syd hooked up shots that tasted like Hi-C. Some noise band was playing that I'd never heard of. The speakers were shitty, but it didn't really matter because the music was thumping a coarse beat.

"Jodi and I want to go dancing," Monika began, thumbing the spike of Syd's earring.

"There's dancing right here..." Syd hopped on top of the bar to the hooting and hollering of a group of guys sharing a pitcher. Gyrating her hips and sucking her fingers, she began a spontaneous striptease, and the bar was packed within seconds. She dropped to her knees for some guy to slide a ten between her tits, and while she was down there she grabbed both my and Monika's heads and whispered, "I get off at two. Go to the Savior; Carlos is doing the door. Tell him I put you on my V.I.P. list, and don't forget to snag a couple drink tickets."

"Definitely," said Monika. "Thanks."

I echoed Monika's gratitude.

"Hey, wait!" Syd grabbed a bottle of vodka by its spout. "Open wide," she demanded, and poured a shot of vodka down each of our throats.

"Shit!" I said, wiping my mouth. "What was that? I nearly choked."

"That's top-shelf shit right there, girl," said Syd. "And don't you forget where you got it."

✷

The Savior was the winter's most exclusive nightclub. Housed in an abandoned synagogue, with its revolving dance floor and dazzling light displays, it was a temple of sinful trance. It set the standard for underground dance parties. Everyone wanted to go.

The music thumped and looped. "Syd seems like a total bitch," I shouted.

"She got us into the Savior. Hey! There's Cookie."

Cookie danced at a topless joint on 42nd Street. She was tall and thin and could've modeled if she wanted to. She had the face for it: sloping cheekbones, pouty lips, and huge green eyes. The type of face that had an alien look to it that could be reproduced like a silk screen without tiring.

"Hello girls!" she called when she saw us, sifting her way through the crowd. People moved out of her way because she was beautiful, despite the hideous wig she wore to parties.

"You made it," she said, kissing us on each cheek. "Did you come to see the Plastics? There are so many people tonight—come sit with us; we have a booth. You should meet Paula, she's a genius painter. I should put you two on her waiting list to have your portraits done. Believe me, you won't regret it—in ten years, you may end up on the walls of the Modern's permanent collection."

We followed her through a series of hallways until we reached her booth. In the center of the room, a nude woman with live birds nesting in her headpiece danced on a grand piano.

"There goes Priscilla, rising to the ceiling with those freakin' turtledoves," Cookie said. "She says she does burlesque. Thinks she's so much better than me."

"Still dancing, Cookie?"

"Yeah. Every night I say it's the last time. But those pigs just can't get enough of this." With that, she tore open her cropped fur jacket and gave the room a twirl. She had very small breasts for a stripper. They looked like dollops of sour cream. Her nipples were covered with black sequined pasties in the shape of diamonds. "Eat your heart out, Priscilla!" she screamed, her fur jacket cocked at her hip. "Have you ever met Paula?"

Paula fanned us over with long, synthetic nails that were painted black and decorated with rhinestone chips. She wasn't as pretty as Cookie, but possessed an enchanting stare that immediately raised her status. Cookie had been dating her exclusively for over a year.

"You'll paint their portraits, won't you, baby? And don't charge any of your uptown prices either. These are very dear friends of mine."

Truth was, I'd only met Cookie once or twice, and wasn't exactly in the financial position to be commissioning portraits. But I felt myself powerless to protest.

"Jodi here is Alex's new girl."

I nudged Monika, curious how the news had spread so fast. "I have two pieces in her next show, that's all."

Paula looked suddenly and immediately interested. "You mean Alex's *newest* girl. Good for you. You know, my first important sale was pioneered by that cow. So, Cookie, listen to this. I'm walking Mr. Last Night down St. Mark's, and I stop because there's this gaping hole in the sidewalk. I have to look inside because I'm drunk and stoned, and I see this enormous rat looking up at me like, '*Bitch, get away from my hole!*'"

Monika looked at me and I looked at her and we burst out laughing. As Paula and Cookie engulfed each other, Monika gestured for us to get out of there.

"What about the drinks?"

"Who the fuck cares? Let's dance."

Then I could see only color. Everything had lost its form. Dancing was the most wonderful thing in the world. And Monika was so beautiful.

"I love this night," I said. "I love you."

It got later. The crowd thinned.

"I'm not even tired," I said.

"I know. Isn't it great? Syd has good stuff."

"What stuff?"

"Pure MDMA. Isn't it the best high?"

"What are you talking about?"

"Don't you remember…we took them back at the other bar. With Syd. I'm really messed up."

She tried to talk but couldn't. All she could get out were garbled bouts of giggles.

Could I have taken a tablet of MDMA and forgotten? That would explain the trails and intense feeling of euphoria.

"Jodi," Monika shook my hand. "Jodi… Jodi!" She opened her mouth and a stream of vomit projected across the room. It was hilarious. Some queen started yelling at me to get her off the dance floor.

"Okay, okay," I yelled. "Where's the bathroom?"

"How am I supposed to know?"

"Just get out of my way."

A skinny go-go dancer tapped me on the shoulder and pointed me in the direction of the ladies room. "That way, baby."

Stop spinning and see clearly. See clearly.

"Monika, shut up a second. Drink this." I palmed her some water and she gargled it up and then spat it on the floor. She'd stopped laughing, and, transfixed in front of the mirror, began caressing the laugh lines at the slope of her cheek.

"Oh my God! What's wrong with me? What happened to my face?" she asked me. Suddenly terrified, "What are these cracks? You see them? Jodi, do you see them? What's wrong with me? How did I get so old?"

"You're not old. Just drink some water. It helps."

I knew she was seeing tricks because just moments ago an entire village had erupted out of my arm. A secret village, like Los Alamos. A town guarded by its inhabitants. There they were: the Calutron Girls watching meters and adjusting dials all day, then knocking off at five to retire to the living quarters, just east of my elbow.

"But Jodi, how did this happen? How did this happen to my face?"

"What's going on here?" It was Syd. She pushed by me to get to Monika. "Why is she crying?"

"She's fine," I said. "Help me get her cleaned up." I wet a paper towel and washed around Monika's mouth. "I don't know about that stuff you gave us."

Syd lit a joint. "Here," she said. I must've given her a look like I didn't trust her. "It's just herb," she said. Syd hit the joint and tried to look casual. "It must be candy-flipped—I haven't tried them out myself, but I heard they were out of this world."

I didn't know what candy-flipped meant, but it didn't sound so bad, so I decided to just *go with the flow.*

"I wanna dance," I yelled. "Let's get out of the bathroom."

Syd and Monika looked at each other.

"She's with me," Monika said to Syd. "It will be fine."

"Whatever you say," said Syd. Then to me, "You can dance at this other party."

"What party?"

"There's always another party. But come on; a car's waiting."

Syd didn't seem like the type of girl to have a car waiting. It turned out to be a stretch limousine.

She told the driver where to go and then took out a snuff-box. "Want a bump?"

"She's had enough. Syd, I'm serious. You don't need that, Monika."

"But I want more!"

"Of course you do," said Syd.

We came to a stop. The driver opened the door and Syd led us into a high-rise with gold-plated elevators. We rode the elevator to the penthouse.

"Where are we?"

Syd opened this fancy alligator clutch and rummaged inside for a compact. You expected a girl like her to sling a wallet from a chain off her belt. As she powdered her face, she said, "His name is Rudyard Hamilton. She's Heather McBride, married to the poet Charles Bartleby. This is Sammy's place; he's seeing Maria, my best friend. They'll have everything you could ever want here: booze, uppers, downers, and wealthy men."

"Rudyard Hamilton, like the department store?" I had an awkward feeling in my stomach. Remembering the man in the porkpie hat who'd taken Monika to the Mark Hotel, I couldn't pretend any longer.

"That's the one," Syd giggled. She put on a coat of mauve lipstick. "Want a breath mint?"

Both Monika and I took mints.

"Let me get another bump," said Monika.

"Inside."

"Wait," I said, grabbing Monika's forearm. "Do we really have to go?"

"You said you wanted to party."

And just like that, everything would change. I knew it and so did she. I squirmed as we waited for the door to open, wondering about the significance of the unsaid.

We stepped into a den of iniquity. We'd been to places like this before, but not like this. I wouldn't have missed it for anything. It was like we'd stepped into an Arabian castle: high pillars and long silk curtains, Oriental carpets, gem-encrusted statues. The film *Lawrence of Arabia* was being projected onto a screen in black and white, and there was at least one person filming and interviewing guests. Some had come in costume. Queen of Sheba burned a cone of frankincense in a wooden case she held in her palm. A genie sashayed by with a lamp. By the bar, an Arabian knight stood casually with a live snake around his neck.

Whoever Sammy was, I didn't see him with Maria, who Syd began gabbing with as soon as she dumped us. It didn't really matter who he was; he sure knew the meaning of decadence.

The dizziness returned and I embraced it. I ate candied figs and Monika and I drank a bottle of champagne while dancing intimately on the parquet floor. I figured I'd moved on to a different stage of the high because my legs felt like Jell-O. Then I realized I was writhing and gyrating all alone.

A crowd of people were gathering around a hookah. Monika was one of them, sucking a hose. The crowd shushed as a couple I assumed was Rudyard Hamilton with the lady married to the poet sauntered in. On either side of them, on hand and foot, crawled two young boys dressed in nothing but loincloths. Syd whispered something in Monika's ear, but I was distracted by the grand entrance of this bizarre entourage. So this was Rudyard Hamilton. Heir apparent to a long line of department stores. Mom bought her linens at the Hamilton's in Danbury.

My legs then gave and I slumped down onto the floor. A wall crept up behind me. Syd was laughing. Monika was topless, and the poet's wife was tracing her silver-dollar nipples with some kind of antique pointing device. Rudyard Hamilton let out a full-bellied laugh and the poet's wife exclaimed, "She's darling!" All the while, the loincloth boys remained on all fours.

Rudyard wanted to know, "I thought you'd said there were two. Where's the other?" But Syd just gave him a key-bump of blow.

The poet's wife seemed to enjoy fondling Monika. The loin-cloth boys hoisted her up and over Rudyard Hamilton's shoulders, and then he was making off with her. I wondered what it meant to be taken like that. But I knew... I'd had Vincent Frand... Monika's breasts bounced like flounces of ruffles attached to her torso. She looked so lovely up there, like this was the life she was meant for.

"Hey," I managed, "Where you going with my best friend? That's my girl..." It didn't matter what I said; she was already gone. Monika was a girl who refused to be contained.

Chapter Twenty

I knew I was going to pass out right here, with a cloud of cumin sifting over me and the bejeweled belly dancer clicking castanets in the corner. Vulnerable and helpless, the thought of Walter watching TV alone in his hotel room popped into my mind. Drifting… This feeling of helplessness that came up wasn't because of Walter; the feeling was for Isla.

Finally, I get Isla out of my mom's condo. "We'll figure this out," I tell her. Her stepdad's on a camping trip with his buddies, and her mom, she says, stays at the salon for hours. I tell her to go home and watch TV, act normal.

"I feel better now that you know," she says. Then, she touches her stomach and looks down at her belly. Her eyes get this kind of crazy look.

I'm practically pushing her out the door.

I watch her walk away from my house. The whole time, she keeps her hand on her stomach. She looks like a zombie with a stomachache. I wait another fifteen minutes, until I know she's turned off the main road, then dig around in the garage for my bike. I'm moving quickly now, pumped up with adrenaline for what I'm about to do. I've had enough of Isla's secrets. Everyone is going to know.

I ride to the high school, where I know Winters leaves the art room unlocked. I've got a half-hour before the main doors lock. No one's there. Maybe practice on the field—but that can be a diversion. I ride faster and faster. A car almost hits me, but

I keep riding. I laugh. When I make it there, I leave my bike at the back exit where the janitor keeps his cart. Then I'm in the art room and my heart is pounding. I can take anything; I can do anything. I choose a can of red spray paint. It's cold in my hand. I shake it, getting it primed.

In the halls, I scan the lockers for Isla's. I hear the faint sound of the janitor's cart rolling down the linoleum floor. I don't have much time. For a moment, I wonder if I'm really capable of this. That day, the boy didn't deserve being humiliated. I should've stood up to Isla. But I laughed; I egged her on; I shouted commands. I got excited. I uncap the spray can and shake it once more, hard, to make sure the paint sprays out evenly. As I paint, I use my whole body to spell the letters so that they cover Isla's locker: WHORE.

After the final "E" I drizzle a little red for effect. Then it's done. I swallow and feel sick to my stomach, like I'm going to throw up, but there's no time. I put the cap back on the can and toss it behind a bush. Then I get on my bike and start riding again. The highway home is a blur. I know I've done something bad and part of me does feel guilty, but another part is pure exhilaration.

Once I'm home, I crash out and sleep for hours. Mom tries to wake me for school the next morning, but I won't budge.

"Baby girl, you okay?"

I barely stir. "Hot."

Mom feels my head and tells me I'm burning up.

"Fluids and Tylenol will bring down the fever. You don't need me to stay home with you, but just call if you need anything. Stay in bed and rest." Before she leaves, she puts a cold compress on my forehead.

I groan, swallow some pills. Then drift. Her voice trails off, "Lots of fluids."

Sleep. When I wake, the fever seems to have broken. I feel an odd relief. I eat a ham sandwich and then take a quick shower.

It's 6:30 p.m. I haven't left the house the entire day. School has been out for over three hours.

I wonder why Mom isn't home, but then think what a good idea a walk would be. The breeze outside feels crisp in my lungs. I let the air circulate, trying for a feeling of expansiveness. But every time I try to let go, something pulls me down. It's a road I know well, the road to Isla's house.

A pulse draws me there, strongly, like a magnetic pull. Suddenly, I'm running. A cop car and ambulance are parked diagonally across Isla's driveway. A crowd is growing and hushed speculations are beginning to fly around.

"You can't come near here, Miss," a cop says to me.

"Huh? What's happening?"

The cop turns to a neighbor in the crowd. "Bill, take her out of here, and try to keep it under control here. Tell your wife to get off the horn."

My stomach drops. "What's going on?"

The cop walks away into Isla's house with the rest of the cops. I turn to Bill. "What happened?"

"It's Isla."

"What about her? What's going on? Where are her parents?"

Someone else in the crowd nudges in. "Have they been reached?"

Silence comes over the crowd as four men carry Isla out of the house on a stretcher. I can't really see what's happening. As she's hoisted into the ambulance, the doors close with acute precision. When the ambulance pulls away, its lights blinking down the narrow road, the crowd starts rambling again.

"How terrible! Unbelievable."

"What?" I ask. "What happened?"

"She cut her wrists!"

I freeze. This is a moment I'll know forever.

Isla dies on the way to the hospital. We find out later she wasn't conscious when the housekeeper found her in the tub, just as it began to overflow.

Chapter
Twenty-one

Once I opened my eyes to witness a monkey wearing a crown and eating grape leaves with a toothpick. When I woke up again, he was gone. The party had died down. Monika was nowhere in sight. Also gone were all traces of Arabia. It had become a regular New York apartment with cliques of people I didn't recognize talking quietly on little couches. They acted like I was invisible. I'd passed out in the living room. It led into an open kitchen that looked like something out of the movies, with stainless-steel appliances and large marble countertops.

I scratched my head. I felt bugs crawling all over me. All I could think about was Monika's bed back at the loft. My mouth was dry and tasted sour. I picked up a half-empty glass that had been resting on a wall sconce and took a swig. It tasted like someone had ashed in it but I was too afraid to check. Stumbling into the kitchen, I tripped over a sylph sleeping in front of the sink. I put my mouth to the faucet and could've drank for hours. There was a plate of pastries on the counter. I noticed the faint light of dawn. I ate a croissant. My chest was tight. I was sad, but didn't know why.

All that mattered was that I get back to the loft. Monika's whereabouts, the nymph sleeping at my feet, the man in the top hat who called to me, "Dottie, get me a glass of water, will you?" were irrelevant. I had to get home.

I made my way to the door, and, when I stuck my hand in my pocket, was surprised by a fifty-dollar bill that had found its way there somehow. I was still high and jittery as hell. But the fifty would get me home.

I stepped outside and squinted at the sun. I had foresight enough to change the fifty before catching a cab. I bought a paper and a can of orange soda from a deli. I tried to play it off like I was straight before it struck me that the cashier couldn't care less about my sobriety.

It was a strange feeling, stumbling into the loft alone. Disorienting. Something inside me was shaking ferociously, as though at any second I might be ripped apart and no one would be here to save me. My stomach flipped, but it was more than that: I could feel my guts in my throat. I told myself I was nervous about Alex's show; it was coming up.

A car screeched outside on the road. Someone's high heels tapped down the stairwell and I realized there were others like me. The pieces of trash accumulating in the hallway —a plastic ring from a BB gun, a Coke bottle, lipstick, balls of lint, sandwich wrappers—were remnants of life. Once inside the loft, I locked the door and turned on all the lights. Then, as Monika would've done, I went to the bathroom to wash my face.

Searching through the soap basket, I came across a photograph of her and Walter sitting on the fire escape. I ripped it up and threw it in the garbage.

As I was washing my face with her face mousse, I was overcome with the horrible feeling that Monika was slipping away. I thought about what Mom had said the day Dad left: "Don't feel that sweet love or you'll lose it."

Then I remembered I was on drugs and shouldn't trust my feelings. The worst of my high was over, and what lingered could be cured by sleep. When my head hit the pillow, all I could think about was that fifty-dollar bill and the fact that

Monika still wasn't home. I couldn't pretend I didn't know what she was up to anymore. Facing her about it was another story.

✳

It's a funny thing, watching people at an art show. You're looking at people as much as you're looking at the art.

There were six of us in the show, which Alex had called "Consortium of Form." I was joined by a light and space artist, a painter who decorated his canvas with dashes and splotches of color, and a sculptor who'd recreated the floor map to the child's game Candyland. K.T. and Jan, who I'd met that night at Beretta, also had pieces in the show. Of course Jan's piece, a phallic volcano that could've been straight out of a high school science fair, had the best placement. The final artist had the closest approximation to my style, a painter of nudes who replaced his models' heads with faces of well-known porn stars.

"Congratulations!" As Alex made her way through the crowd, her thighs chimed and vibrated. "Your pieces look brilliant. I really mean it." As she kissed me hello, a flashbulb went off somewhere.

The piece with the potential buyer, *Persephone Weeps*, was a bust, a literal rendering of the underworld goddess crying at the sound of music. The second piece was *Lyre*.

"I hear you're the creator of the frescoes. Tell me, what are you going after?" The question belonged to an older man with a European accent and huge birthmark across his forehead.

"Dr. Kustav is a professor of anthropology at Columbia," said Alex. "And also an old lover of mine."

"Of course by old, she means former," he said, offering his hand. He wore a smoking jacket, the kind a man might have worn to a Knights of Columbus meeting. "It's nice to see someone of your generation with an appreciation for classical form."

"Generation veneration," I smiled. We shared a laugh.

"I'm so proud of you, Tony," said Alex, caressing the silk

arm patch of his jacket. To me, "He barely ever ventures down past 57th."

"What can I say? I'm slumming!"

I waited a beat or two for Alex to remember the arts reporter she'd promised to take me to, but she wasn't giving up her Tony just yet.

I swished a mouthful of champagne, the bubbles caressing my tongue. Tony was staring at me, and I had to admit, the attention was nice.

"It seems, judging by the work of your contemporaries, that you're the odd one out."

"Oh, now, Tony," Alex began. "That's so easy. Too easy for one of my shows. Wouldn't you say? Besides, you can't forget Alice Neel; she was never in step, and she was underappreciated, I'd say." Then Tony and Alex shared a transient moment of loss, as the painter Alice Neel had died of cancer that October.

Dr. Kustav coughed. "Jodi hasn't answered my query, so I can't quite say if it's that easy." Turning to me, "Young lady, you haven't yet told me what it is you're going after."

"Integrity?"

"I see you're deploying that awfully popular feminine discourse—making a claim in the form of a question."

Before I could respond with another question, he went on. "Figurative. By definition, all that's around you," he said gesturing at Jan's exploding penis, the blobs of color, reclining nudes. "These *dis*-figured nudes, the figurative snubs entirely. What is figurative if not a rejection of the abstract?"

"It's about form," I said. "Not some projected desire. Not some *latent bullshit* or whatever that's so popular in abstract work these days."

"Are you suggesting that AbEx is just a psychological indulgence?"

Alex coyly sipped her wine. I suspected she was very good at pitting artists against one another, and that usually, the game benefited everyone involved.

"*By definition*," I countered, "abstraction is supposed to be about the possibility of something else, but that something else inevitably comes back to the artist."

Dr. Kustav laughed. "Let me ask, what's your relationship with your father?"

I waited for Alex to jump to my defense, but she said nothing. She knew the truth; I couldn't lie.

"I don't see what that has to do with anything. Certainly not my piece."

"I'm not talking about your piece. This is about more than you."

Still, Alex played mute. So I went on, "I think perhaps you're taking too literal a standpoint of what it is to be figurative."

"What *does* it mean?"

"I mean," I began, "people like Kenny Scharf, Mark Kostabi, Keith Haring, and even Basquiat all work with the human figure in their work, in different ways."

"Of course," added Alex, "but they're all men."

"Figurative is what art has always been to me," I said.

"Ah, so it's about you."

I began to glean that my role in this scene would be as an outsider. The avant-gardes would accept me because I was doing something different—and therefore bold. But they wouldn't accept me all the way because of our fundamental differences. Or rather, the fundamental differences in structures: me, figurative, them, abstract. At this moment, I felt like I could be content with this role, never fully ensconced in their world, but rather imposing on it like an irregular guest. But I also believed in moving the figurative to a place that was more intimately aware of itself, a place that suggested divides like figurative versus abstract were generally useless, silly constructions.

"When I think of figurative, I think of the body. That the body is the basis for all form. The foot is a bridge, the body a cathedral, and so on and so forth. The body is the basis of beauty and truth."

Suddenly, I am nine years old again, a little girl

transfixed by a nude in a *Playboy*. My father's final gift to me. The basis for beauty: yes. The basis for truth: hardly. I could feel myself unraveling. Don't let that little girl creep in, Jodi. Not now.

"Well," said Dr. Kustav. "That's all very well and good. But you may—to your detractors, of course—come off as limited."

When Dr. Kustav moved on, Alex whispered in my ear that I'd handled myself exceedingly well. "All great artists are even better politicians," she told me. I thought about the Greeks, how in their world, art and politics were nearly one and the same.

✶

Meanwhile, Monika was getting loaded with Walter over a tray of dim sum.

This is delicious," she said. "Usually it's just cheese and crackers. Come here, let me fix your blouse."

I was wearing a silk tunic over a pair of jeans. "That blouse makes your tits look spectacular."

"Thanks."

We were both avoiding talking about the other night with Syd at the party, which was fine by me. She looked her usual siren-like self, her hair swept away from her face, accenting the slope of her cheekbones. Her dress was demure, vintage, black, and frock-like, with a full skirt. Earlier, she told me she'd decided against her original outfit because she wanted it to be my night, and that if she wore the gold lamé Mackie jumpsuit, "It'd be all about Lady M."

"You mean it's not always?" Walter had teased. He was looking gaunt. He'd taken a turn for the worse. A filmy, sweat-like residue covered him head to toe. Dressed sharply in a white pinstripe suit with a bowtie, Walter tried to play off his dramatic reduction like it wasn't important.

"Killer suit," I said. "Is that from your debutante days?"

"You know it!" He puffed out his chest. "You look good

talking to me. Maybe people think I'm Andy Warhol. By the way, you didn't comment on my new hair. What do you think?"

It'd been hard for me to look at him with that thing on his head. "Hairpieces," I laughed. "Never a good thing."

"Tell me how you really feel, bitch."

Monika wanted to know, "Who was that guy you were talking to?"

"Oh, him. Some Professor at Columbia."

"He looked arrogant as hell."

"He is. Doesn't it piss you off how men like that think they can talk to you and demand things, like your entire soul?"

Walter interrupted, "This is still an art show, is it not? You should be able to discuss your artistic vision. People expect it of you."

"Expectations," I said, "are silly and useless."

"That," Monika agreed, pointing to Jan's eruption, "is silly and useless."

"That," Walter added, "is shit spread thin enough, people think it's caviar."

"Maybe you are Andy Warhol," I said.

"You should mingle," Walter said. "Shoot the shit with us some other time."

I clutched Monika's hand feverishly. "I don't want to leave you."

"Darling, you must." A waitress came by with a tray of champagne. Monika grabbed two flutes, one for her and one for Walter. "Go. Shoo."

"Wait. You don't think I'm making a fool out of myself, I mean, that my pieces are…"

"Why second-guess yourself now?" Walter said. I was a real shit for hating him. He really was a decent person.

Monika was downing champagne and pretending not to notice me. "Go on," she said. "Thank me later, when you're rich and famous."

Chapter Twenty-two

After Isla dies, I notice a strange calm around me. I'm not calm. I'm wound so tight I clench my fists in my sleep. The calm is bigger than me. It's everywhere. Everyone is somehow affected by this beautiful, talented, popular girl's suicide. The grief is crippling. Mom's beside herself; she keeps saying, "Those poor people."

I picture Isla's stepdad comforting Isla's mother, and it makes me sick. I can hardly breathe. All I can think is, he better be sorry. This is his fault, not mine.

What he did to Isla is a sick perversion of life. Still, it's she who suffered, she who paid the price. I think about the part I played, but it feels like it's not really happening, and everything is a bad dream that tortures me relentlessly, day and night.

The whole town is inconsolable. No one can understand— and then the autopsy results come out. There's a special assembly at school. Some lady takes the stage and gives a speech about teen pregnancy, how it's an epidemic. Then another lady gives a speech about teen suicide and hands out pamphlets for a hotline. The whole time I'm imagining Isla. I see the blade against her skin. The water is beginning to rise. The water is warm. It has to be warm. Her slices are quick and precise, her skilled hand steady. Knowing this gives little comfort.

"And remember," says the woman giving the speech about teen suicide, "you are not alone."

I picture Isla in the tub, the water around her body engulfing her, beginning to tint. She's alone. As she bleeds into warm water, her body opens up. As the gash grows, she slips further and further away until there's no blood left. I wonder how it feels to be her in those final moments. I can't stand to know. I can't stand not to know.

We observe a moment of silence for Isla, and then the principal takes the mic.

"School vandalism of any kind is unacceptable at Danbury High. We will find out who is responsible for Isla's locker, and that person will be punished. We are a community," he went on. "Now more than ever, we're a community where vicious acts of disrespect will not go unpunished. If someone in this room is responsible for the graffiti, know this—you will not get away with what you've done."

My hand is on my stomach and I'm retching. Everyone's looking at me but I don't care. I can feel vomit in the back of my throat. It's a struggle to get out of my row, but I manage to make it out of the auditorium without puking. I get all the way to the girl's room, where I'm sick in the toilet.

After I wash my mouth out, I turn to leave but notice the school nurse standing in the doorway. She's a gnome of a woman who's always given me the creeps. Suddenly she's hugging me, and I'm letting her.

"It's okay," she says. "There, there." She looks at me sympathetically and it's a huge relief. Then, "You should come with me."

Chapter Twenty-three

A hand had suddenly found my shoulder. It belonged to a cocky member of the downtown intelligentsia, the type that call people "Sport." He had robust hands, hands that demanded perfection. There was a decisiveness about his hands. He wore a fitted maroon turtleneck and thick black Buddy Holly glasses.

"Mac Frank," he said, introducing himself. "Nice show."

"Oh," I blurted. "The reporter."

Macaffery Frank, Arts and Style editor at the *News*. As for looks, he was average: huge, ice-blue eyes, too widely set apart, cagey smile, and dominating forehead. Each of these features alone was unattractive. Somehow, the sum of his parts had become something else entirely.

At once, I looked down at his hand, now on my waist, with a blush of nervousness. His grip told me that he was the type of man who went after women like prey. I was excited as hell.

"Thanks. Jodi Plum. But I guess you know that."

"Yup."

"What I meant was, I was supposed to meet you earlier. Alex was bringing me over; you know how it is at these things."

"We're meeting now."

"I just met a man in the crowd with a miniature television

set, portable, with a long antenna. He's over there somewhere, watching the news."

"What's happening?"

"On the news?"

"Yes."

"There was a shooting on the IRT." He looked alarmed. "That's a good line. What happened?"

"Some guy was being robbed by a gang of thugs. He shot them. They're calling him the Subway Vigilante. They're saying he just walked right off the tracks into the night."

"He should run for mayor."

We smiled. Then he said, "Tell me, what's the inspiration for your work?"

"On the record?"

"What record?"

I nodded. "Right. You must get tired of that question."

"Secretly love it. What's the question everybody asks you?"

"Nobody really asks me questions."

"That's about to change. Let me be the first to say, you've got a lot of guts going figurative, I mean, when everything considered important these days is abstract. Like, you've got to confuse people, give them something intangible for them to get you. No doubt, you'll get railed by the press. They're not going to get you. What I can't figure out is if you're ultra-modern or ultra-pretentious."

I didn't care that he might have just insulted me. I was insanely attracted to him.

"Ciao, Jodi!" It was Cookie, who was wearing a pink bobbed wig and yellow dress with sequins. "Fantastic party. Have you met Paula?"

"Thanks for coming."

"You should really get Paula to paint your portrait now that you've had such a successful opening."

I turned to introduce the reporter, but he'd vanished. I looked around, but he was nowhere to be found.

"Would you stop? You're such a pimp. She's always trying to

sell me," said Paula, gesturing toward her. "Don't pay her any mind. But if you're thinking about it," she paused to give me her card, "call me. Congrats on the show. All you can do now is pray for buzz."

"Did you see where that reporter went?"

★

A red sticker was affixed next to my sculpture, which sat catty-corner to a defunct washer-dryer combo. A call had come in from my mysterious buyer. He'd been unable to attend the show, but had been following the circuit and was waiting until tonight to cement his patronage. He bought *Persephone Weeps* for $1,000. Alex demanded that we drive up to Connecticut immediately, where, I'd told her, my studio was filled floor to ceiling with fresco pieces. "Given tonight's performance, a solo show's not far behind."

The night kept turning. One moment I'd feel sick to my stomach, and the next, elated to be alive. I needed a minute to myself. I needed to wash my hands.

Monika ambushed me in the bathroom. "Holy shit!" Her face was white as a ghost. "We have to leave immediately."

"What is it?"

"A man is here. And we have to scram."

"What man? What are you talking about?"

"Rudyard Hamilton."

Chapter Twenty-four

"Who's Rudyard Hamilton?"

"That night at the party. The john that Syd arranged."

I knew I hated Syd, and for good reason.

"So, it's finally coming out," I said. "Tonight of all nights. Well, let's have it then. What exactly are you telling me?"

She shrugged and folded her arms across her chest. "Are you really that naïve? Honestly, Jodi. How long must we play the coy game? It's exhausting."

"That you're a whore? You don't need the money. Why?"

Monika laughed dramatically. "And what about Vincent Frand? You slept with him, and *everyone* knows he's a total womanizer, but *you* slept with him to advance your career. What does that make you, besides a bad businesswoman?"

That was enough. I turned around and made for the door.

"Wait!" she called. "I'm sorry! Please, Jodi, that was mean. I've had a million Vincent Frands in my day, believe me, we all have. Don't be mad. I love you, but you make such a big deal out of everything, and it wasn't like I could come right out and tell you."

"Why not? It's not like I'm dumb. I had my suspicions."

"Good."

"And about Vincent Frand, until him, I thought I was one of those 'locked up' women."

"What are you talking about?" she laughed. "Who even says that anymore? Of course you're not 'locked up!' And if he is the only guy who's ever given you... well, then honey, what are we sticking around here for? The night is young!"

"Monika, I'm not some..."

"*Whore*? Madonna, whore, what's the difference? You of all people are always saying that these divides are silly, useless constructions."

"I know, but..."

"But what?"

"I was talking about art."

"Of course you were," she sighed. "Always talking about art."

"This coming from my patron?" I smiled and sat next to her on a little pink couch in the corner of the powder room.

She offered me a fag. I accepted.

"What about your photos?"

"Pictures are just images," she said. "I would never commit to them. And another thing: don't think you have the right to ask me questions, like *Oh, Monika, what's it like?* This isn't some free-for-all. When I'm ready to publish my memoir, I'll hire Manhattan's top writer. Until then, I don't want to talk about it. It's just something to do. Got it?"

"I just wish you'd been straight with me."

"And," she went on, "I wish you hadn't been so seemingly oblivious. It's like half the time you're not even there—you're going on about myths and neoclassical walls, but you've been putting up walls between you and me. *You* made it hard for me to be straight with you."

"I hate when you call me a child," I said.

"That's your problem. Don't think so much about every little thing anyone says to you. You'll never get anywhere with that attitude. Don't get me wrong, I know you'll get what you want one day. It's already in motion. Look around. Can't you feel it? Remember the first night we met? I said I knew you were somebody. Maybe you're not quite there yet. But you're on your way. If you stop thinking so goddamn much."

"But Monika, do we really have to leave now?" I said. "We haven't even been here that long. And Alex just sold something."

"How much?"

"One thousand."

She snickered. "That's how much Rudyard Hamilton paid me that night."

This irritated me. "Really? Seems a little insulting."

Monika laughed. "I suppose I can't call you a child, but, honey, please."

"That was really rude what you said about Vincent Frand. You make me feel so prudish and naïve, when really I'm not. I have experience with men you don't know about…"

"Jodi, please. It's charming. Just tone it down a notch and stop putting all your eggs in one basket. Who cares about Vincent Frand? Let it go, stop obsessing over him all the time. It was silly of me to bring him up. I'm always telling you there are a million men in Manhattan."

Rolling my eyes, "Look, if you really don't care about silly distinctions, why do you need to leave this party all upset over Rudyard Hamilton?"

"I'm not upset, I'm just not up for the performance tonight. You can't understand—about being a call girl, that is. I become another version of myself: *Monika, paid escort, enchanté*. I said I don't want to talk about it."

Her eyes began to water. She rolled them and dabbed beneath her lids with a finger. I noticed her hand was shaking. "I will not be embarrassed at a party," she stammered. All of a sudden, I felt immense pity for her. Of all people, she was the last person I'd expect to care about how she looked in public. I realized her embarrassment was a reflection of who she was.

"Monika, please." I went for her hand, but she flinched and pulled it away.

Then, with a deep breath, "Besides, this party's about to

be beat. No need for you to stick around for that. Leave now, while it's happening."

"I don't want to leave. It's my opening."

"Stay if you want to, but," she said, "I'm out of dolls, and a louse I know is hosting a giant party at Del Mar. If you're smart, you'll come along."

"Wait…"

Chapter
Twenty-five

Something was beginning. I'd arrived. And the success was like a drug.

It started when Alex borrowed a purple VW Bug from her friend and we went to Connecticut for the day, when I knew my mother would be working.

"This is so charming," Alex said, as we drove north through Bethel to the city of Danbury.

When I cranked the garage door open, she removed her thick, red-framed glasses and demanded to use my phone immediately.

"Holy mother of God. What the fuck?! There are over a hundred pieces in here!"

"I told you."

"Artists are always telling me things."

"I've had this stuff for years. You think any of it's saleable?"

"You just showed two pieces," she said in her drawn-out Lower East Side drawl, "when you're sitting on all this."

"I thought we were working with a theme."

"Darling, there are themes all around us. Pick a fucking theme and call it a day."

Minutes later, Alex was on the phone with her art handlers,

and I was feeding her directions from the Tri-Boro Expressway to Oak Drive.

"I need crates, boxes, and blankets," she said. "And I need you here yesterday!"

✶

People started buying my figurines and painted frescoes. At first, Alex sold them exclusively to her decorator friends. They liked them so much, they called back to order pieces by the dozens. Of course, that's when Alex raised the prices. That only made people want more. She sold them to her friends who owned restaurants. She commissioned sales to private buyers, clients of her CPA or real-estate friends.

Plaster castings were so out-of-fashion, they became avant-garde. An article here, a photograph there, and it was easy enough to prove my legitimacy as a downtown B-girl who had breathed new life into a forgotten art form. This was what Alex loved best, proving her prowess at transubstantiation. She introduced me to a slew of people who found me hip and nubile, and allowed me to feel like I was riding bareback through the Bois de Boulogne.

No one was doing figurative. "It's always been about creating a fantasy, the life you wish you were living. But for me, it's really the life." I said things like that at parties thrown for me in champagne bars. One night, a television producer hosted a silent auction in his town house, and I was the guest of honor. I was getting used to how to conduct myself at these types of events, but every time I figured out which fork to use or what a profiterole was, whose name to drop, and whom to avoid, the rules would change on me.

"That's port. It's a dessert wine. Here, let me get you a Pinot Noir, goes marvelously with the oysters." Mac Frank, arts editor from the *News,* suddenly had an interest in which types of red I drank. He was handsomer than I'd remembered, and all of a sudden I had an urge to stand close to him.

"Thanks," I said. I had a feeling in me like Mac was a chance at something—exploring the pleasure principle—and I'd be happy to oblige.

He swished the wine around the glass before handing it to me. "There's a catch, though."

"Oh?" I quickly surveyed the room. He was alone. I wondered what such a good-looking man-about-town was doing without a date.

"Come with me to the back bedroom," he said.

I checked to see if my breath smelled. I was relieved I hadn't eaten any of the oysters. I took a long gulp of wine. As I said the words, "If you insist," I felt myself tighten down there, and an intense pulsing began. Here we go…

I followed Mac down a candlelit hallway and brushed shoulders with a girl named Minnie, a seventeen-year-old model and the new face of COVERGIRL Cosmetics. Her picture was everywhere. Mac led me to the bedroom, and I thought, *This is it*; I couldn't believe my luck. He turned on the light and sat on the bed. On the wall hung an intricately woven Afghan rug. As I looked closely at the design, I could make out two machine guns, ready to fire, as well as tanks and helicopters bearing the letters U.S.S.R.

"Sit," he said. "Make yourself comfortable."

"Sure. The wine is nice, by the way; you have good taste."

"This is true." He opened an attaché case and took out a mini tape-recorder.

"What's this?"

"An interview."

"Oh."

"I told you there's a catch. What do you say? How about we bang this out."

The sting of sexual rejection burned a hole in my stomach and I prayed Mac wouldn't notice I was on fire. Ugh! Why was this always happening to me with guys? When the interview ran three days later in the *News*, I changed my mind and decided that good PR was better than sex.

Beautiful Garbage

Jodi Plum draws from Greek mythology and Roman architecture to create her one-of-a-kind statues and fresco pieces, a departure from her contemporaries, who, she says, "Mimic personal tragedy in modern media forms." Her turn towards the classical aesthetic marks her style, at least for now. Under the direction of powerhouse dealer Alexsandra Czekinsky, Ms. Plum has quickly garnered buzz on the downtown circuit and in select circles that collect unique *objets d'art*. "Everything happened so quickly," she explains, "But this is New York, and you feel like you're just keeping up." New York indeed. For Jodi Plum, it's a far cry from the middle-class suburban enclave in Danbury, Connecticut that she called home. But it's one thing to get the art world's attention, another thing entirely to keep it.

Finally, I was getting somewhere. However, something was bothering me. Alex wouldn't tell me the identity of my mysterious first buyer, and the secret felt sordid, unprofessional. Who was this person who'd taken an interest in me, and why? And, more importantly, why wouldn't Alex tell me? It irked me, nagging just beneath the surface, like frogs caught inside a winter pond.

Chapter Twenty-six

Sickened with the feeling that I'd be found out as the vandal, I hold the vomit in my throat. Just hold on, I keep telling myself, and follow the nurse as she takes me into her office. On the wall behind an examining table hangs a poster that says: "Sharing is Caring." The room is decorated with other posters, anti-tobacco ads mostly, but also colorful illustrations of the food pyramid. She hands me a tissue and then sits me down on the examining table.

"Do you have a temperature?"

"No."

"Virus?"

"No," I say. "I'm fine. It's just…"

"Is there something you'd like to tell me?"

I shake my head.

The nurse sighs. "I'd like you to take a test. It won't hurt, just pee in this cup." She opens a drawer and takes out a plastic cup, a plastic test tube, and a medicine dropper. "It will take two hours for the results to show; you can stay here and wait with me."

"You don't understand," I begin. It's no use; her mind is made up.

"It's okay, dear," she says. "Wouldn't you rather know?"

After my puke fest, she thinks that I'm pregnant. Everything is still. Then the nurse unwraps an indicator stick; the wrapper reads "ACU-Test." If only she had some kind of test that would reveal what a lousy person I was, then maybe I'd have a chance of getting better. But I'm too much of a coward to admit what I've done, that I'm the vandal. Only Isla knows the truth. My stomach gurgles, and I can feel the acrid bile spiraling through my throat. I bring all my focus to the ball at the tip of the nurse's nose.

She walks to a filing cabinet, opens it, and flips through a row of manila folders until she comes to mine. I wonder what's in there; I never even knew I had a file. "It says here your mother works?"

"Yeah, at the Danbury Historical Society."

"I see."

"Your dad isn't listed as a contact. He's not on any of these forms; is he deceased?"

"Divorced."

"I see."

I use the private toilet in the back of the nurse's office for the pee test. Then we begin the waiting process.

"You're not going to write anything down about me, are you?"

"Don't worry, dear. All this is confidential. It's the law."

The nurse tells me to make myself comfortable. She hands me a Dixie cup with some water, and a magazine, and takes a seat at her desk, where she opens a book of crossword puzzles. I begin to think that she's not so bad.

"Something's wrong with me."

"Whatever the test says, God will give you the strength to deal with it."

"No," I say. "You don't understand."

She wraps her arm around my shoulder. "It's okay, dear, all you need is time. When things like this happen, you tend to think the whole world is out of whack, and that's somewhat true. But things will swing the other way. It's God's plan."

But God has nothing to do with it. Now that she's dead, Isla becomes larger than life. She becomes a legend. She becomes everybody's daughter. I picture her punctured body floating in the tub and wonder if this is how everybody else pictures her, as well.

"I didn't mean for any of this to happen." I can feel myself unraveling. My jaw goes slack, my face collapses. "It's not what I wanted. You have to believe me! It's not what I wanted at all!"

"Of course, dear. You know what? I'm just taking all the necessary precautions. The school just wants to be responsible, especially for children like you whose families—it's probably just a bug, no cause for alarm."

But it's more than a bug, it's an epidemic like the lady in the assembly said. I wanted Isla gone, and now she is. She's never getting out of that tub.

Chapter
Twenty-seven

Now that Monika's secret life had been exposed, there was a minor shift in the way we acted towards each other. She was the call girl, but I, too, was living off these men, even if I wasn't directly fucking them.

"Your money is no good here. Besides, I've got rent covered. Don't worry about a thing. I'm your patron, same as before."

But it wasn't the same. She'd let down that guard she fought so hard to conceal. There were times when I'd come home and she'd be sobbing into a pillow.

"Let me see your face," I'd demand.

"I'm not beaten, just battered."

"That's not funny, Monika."

"You'll look after me, won't you, Jodi?" Her eyes were puffy and bloodshot. As if she could read my mind, "I've been on the verge of tears all afternoon. Then I just exploded. It's chemical. Coming off of the dolls."

"Why do you do this to yourself? You don't have to, you know. You're smart, and funny, and talented. You don't have to…"

"What? Degrade myself? Is that what you think of me? What you think I do?"

"No. I admire you. You're beautiful."

"What do you know."

I understood she wasn't really being mean. It was just her way of dealing with the fact that I knew—and that she knew I didn't wholly approve, though I didn't wholly disapprove, either.

"I'll be fine. Always am. But Jodi, do you think you can hold me? Just until I fall asleep?"

I untied my shoes and got under the blanket and hummed what I could remember of "Mr. Wonderful."

Nights we'd pass like this were an odd mix of comfort and inelegance. Strangely, this is how I grew to love her.

✶

Alex had insisted that I quit the hat shop. She said it wasn't good for my reputation to work in retail. One night when Monika was getting ready for a date, I pursed my lips and tried to look sexy. Curious to see what she'd say, I suggested, "You could take me with you."

But she arched her eyebrows and said, "There's a big difference between being charming and being dumb. And you're a real smart girl, smarter than half the city."

"You don't think I can do what you do?"

"Darling, you already do. The whole art world's your john."

"So…"

"Now you're just insulting me," said Monika, applying a coat of lipstick.

"But you just said…"

"Do you think you're better than me, Jodi?"

"No, not at all. I worry about you, that's all."

She cocked her head and said under her breath, "Really. There's always some girl who wants me to bring her in. Don't be that girl. Besides, I never do."

"But what am I supposed to do *tonight*?"

She kissed me on the forehead, brushing my chin with her angora sweater. She grabbed her keys and purse. "Aren't you supposed to be making stuff?"

I was. And sometimes I did. But I couldn't help but wonder what made a woman capable of selling herself for money. Sometimes I thought of Monika as a walking time bomb, but others, she was so put together and poised. Feminists wanted us to think that prostitutes had low self-esteem, but Monika could be a cocky bitch. I thought back to that day I saw her by the Met with the john in the porkpie hat. Even then, I had suspected a secret life, a secret history that excited me to no end. But I'd been granted this opportunity, what I'd been waiting an eternity for: to make art, a name for myself. And I was doing it, even though I goofed around a lot reading magazines, smoking pot, and doing weird experiments with dried flowers, tea leaves, and different types of adhesives. I'd also go out and look for Mac at gallery openings and bars I knew he frequented.

When I got home, Monika would usually be in bed because she rarely stayed the night with any of them. I noticed that she slept in a tight, fetal ball. I'd tried to pry her open, but Monika was a stubborn girl, even in her sleep. For some reason, it bothered me to no end when she slept all knotted up like that. It was like she was never fully at peace. Other times, she'd sleep all day. I knew she took sleeping pills, or whatever those blue dolls were that she kept in her purse. One time I found her stash and flushed them down the toilet. I'd never seen her so livid. But it did no good. A phone call later she had what she needed and gave me the silent treatment for three days.

Then, she forgave me and wanted to take me out for authentic *puttanesca* at her favorite restaurant.

"No one's cared enough to do that before," she told me. "Even if it's none of your business what I put in my body."

The way she said that made me feel awkward. I didn't really know how she wanted me to react. "Nothing is going to happen to you, Monika; do you understand that? But you have to work with me. You have to take better care of yourself."

"I know, I know. Starting this week, no dolls, no booze, and only fresh juices and hot water with lemon. But tonight, we eat, we drink, we make merry."

In the streets of Little Italy, the Catholics had strung lights from street posts. Bags of trash lined the curbs, and I wondered if the garbagemen were still on strike or what. Walking off dinner and two bottles of red, I felt good about being with Monika. I wanted to believe that she would take care of herself; I wanted it so badly to be true, and then things would be right again. But as we turned onto our block, we were met by a barricade of police cars. Monika's face went white. "What is it?"

It could have been straight out of a science fiction movie. Blood on the pavement, and men in rubber biohazard suits were spraying the stain with a hose marked decontamination.

"What's going on?" Monika pushed her way through the crowd.

Chapter Twenty-eight

It's happening again. I can't tell what is real and what is… that tightening sensation that happens when you're compelled to remember. You're moving backwards into a fracture, a crack in the mold.

We all feel it tightening like a vise: me, Isla, Joe Smite and the other girls he tormented, even our art club teacher, Mr. Winters. Only Isla gave in. She wouldn't let herself be swallowed by a life that wasn't worth living. Dying was better than being an invisible person; it was better than being another knocked-up teen who'd never make it out. She wouldn't let the grip take over, so she made the first cut.

Of course, the pastor doesn't say any of this at her funeral, a day when the sun is unseasonably strong and there isn't a cloud in the sky. Light reflects off the lake, about fifty yards south from the cemetery at St. Agnes where Isla's body makes its descent into the earth. We can all smell the lake; it smells alive. It's the season of the Mayflies, or *Ephemeroptera*, as Mr. Ambrosio, our biology teacher, calls them. They come up by the handful from the murky depths of the lake long enough to mate, lay eggs, shed their wings, and die. Most of their lives are spent as nymphs underwater. Once they emerge, their days are numbered. This is how, Mr. Ambrosio explains, they get their name. They are an ephemeral order, and the only insects that molt once they get their wings.

For a moment, the reflection of the sun off the lake is blinding. Then I can see. We're all here: the prep school kids and the truck children; their parents who sell everything from Avon to real estate; 7-Eleven clerks and pageant girls; teachers, nurses, cops, housewives, do-gooders, drunks, and garbagemen. No one in town has missed it.

Isla's mom can barely stand straight. Her weight is too much for her husband, so he lets the women of the St. Agnes choir take over and slinks away behind the crowd. I stay intently focused on Isla's mom, her face swollen beneath a black veil. In that face, I search for Isla.

Isla's stepdad wears a fancy suit and shakes people's hands. He makes arrangements for afterwards, when neighbors will come to their house with Tupperware filled with cold salads. There's a brief moment of confusion when it comes to light that both Mrs. Penny and Mrs. Ted have prepared egg salad. Isla's stepdad assures them that the duplication is fine.

Mom clutches my arm hard. She's shaking, sobbing uncontrollably.

"I must find Jane and tell her… Oh, Jodi, I don't know what to say."

A bunch of guys smoke cigarettes behind the church. I can hear them talking. Everyone agrees that what happened is horrible. Isla was beautiful, talented, and came from a comfortable suburban home. No one says the word sin, but the word hangs over us all, even the non-believers.

The church bell tolls a final time and I help Mom into the car. As I slam the sedan door behind her, one of the popular girls grabs me by the sleeve of my coat.

"Hi," she says. "I didn't really know her. But you were friends. What was she like? I mean, *really*?"

I don't know how to answer, so I just say, "She would've made it out of here."

Then someone says, "I don't understand all this fuss. It's not like it can bring her back."

Chapter Twenty-nine

"Jodi!" Monika screamed. "Something's terribly wrong!"

"Hold up," said a cop, stopping her. "Stay clear of the area."

"But we live here."

The head cop approached us, brandishing his nightstick. "You got somewhere else to stay? The area is under quarantine for twenty-four hours."

Monika clutched my arm and her face waned. "What is it? A jumper?"

"You get them all the time in places like this," confirmed the cop. "This ain't no place for girls like you to live."

"Who is it?" she said. Frantically, "Who?"

"We're trying to determine identity. Anything you might be able to tell us would help. The clerk at the hotel don't got a name; says the guy only paid cash. Guess in a place like this it's best not to ask too many questions. You girls think you'd be able to recognize the body if we showed you a picture? It ain't gonna be pretty."

"What happened?"

"Sorry," I said.

"I ask the questions," said the cop. "Yes or no, girls? I got a photo, one of them, what do you call them? Those instant pictures?"

"Yes!"

The cop opened a black steno pad from the palm of his hand. "All right. From what you can tell, do you know this guy?"

Monika collapsed into my arms.

"His name is Walter," she said. "I don't know his last name."

I added, "He's from Tennessee."

"Did he leave a note?"

"Thanks, that's very helpful." Turning his back to us, the cop finished writing something in his book. He mumbled, "Fucking queers," and was gone.

Poor Walter. I'd forgotten about him. We both had. And just like that, he'd become an invisible person.

Monika kicked a pile of garbage. "Why?" she demanded. "Why tonight?"

✶

The next day, she was dressed by the time I got out of bed.

"You're up early."

Guilt permeated the morning, but I had a crazy notion that somehow the fact that we'd both witnessed this tragedy would connect me to my friend again.

"I'm leaving," she said.

"What?"

"Heading west to fulfill my manifest destiny."

She was dressed in a trench coat I'd never seen before. Two coordinating red suitcases lay at her feet.

"I'm going to California. For restoration."

"California? Where'd that come from? Can't you restore here?"

"I'm leaving this morning. You'll take care of the loft, won't you, Jodi?"

"What? When did you decide all this?"

"I'm no good at planning things, and no good at goodbyes, so it's just better that I do things my way."

"But you can't go, you can't just leave like this. At least let's have breakfast, talk about it like normal people."

"We're not normal people. And besides, I've already ordered a car. I must leave now if I'm going to catch my flight."

"What about Walter?"

"Don't go there, Jodi. Don't say his name to me."

"We can't just pretend it didn't happen," I pleaded.

"Did you know he had an excellent knowledge of presidents—not just the famous ones, all of them. It was sick how he'd come up with the strangest details. I suppose it was his last grasp at... why am I even telling you this?" She turned her head so I couldn't see her cry. "You never liked him anyway."

"That's a horrible thing to say."

"It's true, isn't it?"

"Death makes you do crazy things. You're acting rashly."

"What can you possibly know about death, Jodi? Oh, please, darling, don't give me any more grief."

"How long are you going for? Where are you going? How am I supposed to keep up with the rent? It's *your* place!"

"Shh..." she said. "I'll call you as soon as I get settled. You have a career to worry about, and frankly, you haven't been treating it as seriously as you should be. You don't work enough. I'm too much of a distraction. Don't be such a sourpuss all the time..."

"How can you say that after last night? After Walter?"

"I told you not to say his name. Damn it, Jodi. I thought you were smarter than this. You actually have what you've always wanted. And if I could've played a tiny role in making that happen, then I am so happy."

"Of course you played a role in all this."

"I think it's good that we spend some time apart," she said. "I'll be back. Take care of yourself."

And just like that, she pecked me on the cheek, staining it with her red lipstick. She picked up her two suitcases, turned, and was gone. I watched her teeter towards the town car, the camera that hung from her neck swinging with each step.

Chapter Thirty

The leaves on the fern had yellowed. I dipped my finger into the potting soil, but couldn't determine the source of trouble. Too much water; not enough light? Ferns are agreeable houseplants, why couldn't I get this right? Already I missed Monika, and felt alone more than ever before.

I poured myself another bourbon. The bottle had cost over three hundred dollars. I'd needed it. It was the same brand Matisse drank while attending sculpture classes at the *Ecole Municipale* in Paris.

I looked around me, trying to idolize an everyday object, perhaps one without a solid center, like a guitar. I was copying Picasso, but every artist imitates to find inspiration. I wanted something to open up new contours, rearrange structures. This was good bourbon.

After the bourbon, what I needed was a purifying beverage. I searched for the wheatgrass juicer in the cabinet that harbored a set of pans and two dishrags, then under the sink, where a leaky pipe made its home. I looked in the pantry, among dozens of little jars filled with spices like saffron and rue. Then I realized she must've taken it with her in her set of red suitcases.

I tried to work on the latest centaur Alex had commissioned. Head of a man, trunk of a beast. The mold was old, ready to go. This centaur had been commissioned for a bond trader known for lavish bacchanal orgies, and although it was the sixth centaur Alex had ordered this month, this one in particular seemed to befit its proprietor. The task of casting it filled me with a sense of order. Each maneuver made tangible an electrical impulse in my brain.

I lay my hands in the sink and let the warm tap run over them. Slowly, the plaster setting in ridges behind my nails rinsed away.

I wondered why she'd bothered to take the wheatgrass juicer with her and what else had found its way into her luggage.

For the rest of the day, I cast molds mechanically. My success was wonderful, being noticed, special; but something was missing.

Then the phone rang.

"I'm staying in Venice Beach. I was here years ago but don't remember it being so terrific. It's so California: people hanging out in backyards, drinking beer, bumping reggae. Did I tell you the chick I'm staying with is a photographer? Tatum O'Neil just bought two of her prints. We met her, Tatum, at my friend's show last night just after I arrived. Very thin and blonde. She's really nice. Very L.A. My friend was showing in this gallery that was really camp, and in the back, which had nothing to do with her show, there was this exhibit of Coke bottle caps made to look like a mausoleum. Don't ask me to explain; it was cool."

Wistfully, "So you're having fun?"

"A blast, so far. Because of the time difference I've already had, like, a whole lifetime out here, well really one night, but in L.A. everything's in movie time. I haven't even been here long enough to miss you yet. I just wanted to call and tell you that I'm okay. I admit the way I left was a little dramatic."

"I'll say."

"You're not mad at me? Are you, Jodi?"

"You took the juicer, damn it. Of all things."

By nightfall I was stir-crazy. I decided on a walk by the river. The streets were deserted. Even the piers, where queens would throw all-night discos in the snow, were empty except for Robin Hood, the loony bum who fancied himself a champion of gays too poor to party properly.

He called in my direction, "Maid Marian!"

I gave him a cursory wave.

I walked until my fingers and feet were numb, my face chafed from the wind off the river. Then I noticed the sound of footfalls, heavy and male. I was being followed.

Signs of panic began to set in. I'd seen this in movies and in the writings of Poe and Sir Arthur Conan Doyle. Someone had been lying in wait, lurking at the river's edge for a foolish girl who wanders alone at night. I started to run and heard the footsteps behind me gather pace. I could scream, but there was no one but the mermaids to hear me. Then the hand on my shoulder, his hand, jerking me back, until I could feel his hot breath on my neck. I could face him, fight him with all my might, or I could save him the trouble and run headlong into the river.

I tried to scream but couldn't. This was a familiar sensation. Now that I was feeling it again, I realized that it was a sensation that had been haunting me—the urge to cry out and be heard and not being able to breathe.

He grasped my shoulders and, in one swoop, spun me so we were face to face.

✶

"You!" I roared. "Oh, God! Way to sneak up on a girl. There are killers out here."

It was Mac Frank, Arts and Style editor for the *News*.

"Hey—I didn't mean to upset you. I wasn't even sure it was you, and then you started running, and I thought I should stop you, and fuck, man, I'm out of shape."

I laughed and gave him a chance to catch his breath. "What are you doing out here?"

"I could ask you the same thing."

"Touché," I replied. "And I think I'll take the fifth. It sounds ridiculously and desperately dangerous to say I was taking a walk."

"Yeah," he agreed. "But now that we're here together, it's the kind of thing that passes off as romance. Moonlit walk by the river…"

I felt myself blushing and was thankful my face was already windblown.

"So I have to ask, what did you think? About the article."

"I liked it. Except for that last part."

"What can I say?" Then, with exacting arrogance, "I knew I was going to run into you again soon, I just didn't think it'd be like this. Let's get out of here, catch a cab and warm up with some bourbon. I know a tavern not far from here with a wood-burning fireplace."

"I don't think so," I said. "I mean, I'm just not up for another party."

"Who said anything about a party?"

"Do you mind if we just walk awhile?"

"Yes, I mind. It's like 20 below, and I'm not leaving you here. We'll walk up to Broadway and I'll put you in cab home if you won't drink with me."

I couldn't tell if he liked me or was like this with all women. After the last letdown, I didn't want to make any assumptions. "I just don't want you thinking I need to be rescued."

"Says the girl who I chased down a pier. I mean, how's that for romance? I think we definitely need to toast to that."

He had the type of old-fashioned, rugged handsomeness that was hard to put into words, the type that made women swoon.

I hooked my arm inside his, and, clinging to the wool of his overcoat, let him help me take on the night—until Broadway, at least.

*

One month had passed since Monika had abandoned me for the open air of California. Outside, a lone truck carrying fresh bread trolled the avenue below. Thank God for the truck driver, the hardened kind, the kind who takes night shifts, who rolls down the window to holler at pretty young things. Thank God for the black El Camino blasting Brazilian disco, the queen inside cruising. Even for drunk models, dumbfounded at how they wound up all the way down in Chinatown. Thank God for rows of apartment windows, figures inside dancing to Dizzy Gillespie, their bodies illuminated in mysterious twilight. So kinetic was this city, it was famous for rejecting the basic necessity of sleep. I wasn't sleeping because I had real problems. Monika had left months of unpaid utility bills behind, but I didn't know this until the power got yanked. She could have said something, but it was just like her to "forget" about those kinds of details. It cost $800 just to get power restored. When I sat down and put pencil to paper, I realized I had a lot less cash than I thought. Alex owed me for a ton of work, and was being irregular with payment. Then it dawned on me: I hadn't even secured a contract.

.

Chapter Thirty-one

Alex had this idea that I do Laocoon's scream.

"Just as he's being engulfed by the serpent." She went on over dinner at *21*. "You know the story, don't you? He's the priest who warned the Trojans about the Wooden Horse."

"*Laocoon and His Sons*," I said. "And I know the marble statue, the one that's in the Vatican. Excuse me, waiter —" I signaled that we needed another bottle for the table. "I'm not so sure about Laocoon."

"What," said Alex. "You don't like Laocoon?"

"I like Laocoon. It's just that his scream has been turned into such a cliché on how to read history, how to understand the past. Is he groaning? Bellowing? Silent? Who cares?"

"That scream represents the most terrible silence in human conflict," argued Alex. "When the outcry of terror is squelched in exertion, when it is suppressed."

I continued in an affected voice, "What is permissible in the visual representation of pain? What is sadistic? This whole debate is two hundred years old. I want to try something new."

The waiter brought us our bottle. After he opened it and poured us our glasses, I asked for the dessert menu. "And I'd like to order the cheese plate."

"Yes, Madame, whatever you like."

I took a swig of wine and gathered my courage. "Alex, I hate to bring this up, but it's about my contract. I don't have one. And, well, I'm a tad strapped these days."

"Details, details. I'll take care of everything. Don't I always?"

"I suppose. It's just that there are bills I need to pay."

"It's brilliant. You'd be a fool not to do Laocoon."

✷

Back at the loft, I began the process of casting Laocoon. I started with my sketchbook. I put it down. Longing for Monika's company, her shenanigans, even the grey hairs I got worrying about her, I said to the mass of crispy spindles dangling out of a terra cotta pot on the mantle, "What if there isn't anything new, except this? You used to be a fern."

I felt around in my pocket for the rest of a joint I'd stolen from a party. After paying the utility bills, I hadn't been able to afford my own supply of pot for a couple weeks, but I was an expert in mooching and late-night sleight of hand. I lit up and continued to talk to the dead plant. "Alex is wrong about Laocoon's scream. It's not suppressed; it's the feeling you get when you're being choked. When you're choking, you're not trying to scream, you're trying to breathe."

The phone rang and I jumped.

"Now I'm in Malibu. Fucking Tatum never paid my friend. What a total cunt, right?"

"Speaking of not paying, when were you planning on telling me about the power bills? You must've stopped paying them for months even before you left. The whole place went dead the other day, and it cost almost a thousand to get it turned back on."

"Oh, Jodi, I'm terribly sorry! You know I never remember to pay those things. There's some cash in my jewelry box. That ought to cover some of it."

"That's not the point. The point is that you didn't tell me. When are you coming home?"

"Soon," she said. "I promise. I'm still restoring. Aren't you living the life of a fabulous New York artist? You're so much more talented than anyone I've met out here. You're not best friends with Sierra Walker or anything crazy like that, are you? God, I'd have to kill you both."

Monika kept talking, but I began to think about the beach.

I'm five years old. We've rented a bungalow on the seaside, Mom, Dad, and me. The three of us play along the shore, where the tide makes its line. Someone gets the idea to make a drip castle. We dig a pit until we hit the wet, moist, formless sand just beneath the surface. I grab a handful, letting the wet grains run through my fingers. The sand's malleability is so fierce I can't help but start working with it. I'm getting in and tunneling; there's no going back now. Dad eases a handful onto the dry sand. Mom pats the form with a cupped hand. It solidifies almost instantly into ornate, organic spires. We look at each other and smile in amazement. It is all about solidifying the gesture.

"Jodi, are you there?"

They say you never forget, but the truth is you do forget. But when you remember, it hits you like a flash flood.

"I'm here."

"Good. I'd hate to start all over again. That's all that ever happens here in L.A.—introductions. You should meet so-and-so; he's a friend of so-and-so. And did you know so-and-so, the artist who used to have a studio just up the street and whose roommate can smoke a cigarette in her twat."

It was just like her to make me miss her and act like she was having the time of her life without me, like I didn't even matter.

"Monika, I have to go."

"You can't go yet. Can you believe Tatum? Can you believe I've been in L.A. long enough to make enemies?"

After I hung up, I opened her jewelry box, but found nothing inside except a load of jewelry that looked worthless. I had no idea what to do.

Chapter
Thirty-two

At the Botanic Garden, Mac had been waiting for me.

"Hello!" I called as I made my way from the subway. Mac, bundled up in his overcoat and scarf, stood there shivering.

"Christ," he said. "You had to pick a place outdoors?" He kissed me on the cheek and paid my admission.

We began along a trail that overlooked a bluff of Prospect Park. It was an uphill trail, dotted with winter shrubs, evergreens, and Christmas Cacti. Tiny pewter markers designated the species and genus names. Here and there a ring of daffodils—always among the first to bloom—had sprouted from the hard, winter earth, anticipating the thaw.

"I have to talk to you," I said. "I think I've got a big problem."

"Oh?"

"Alex is selling my pieces to anyone who'll buy them. She's got me casting from molds I haven't used in years. But how can I possibly be complaining, because this is all I've ever wanted."

"The recognition factor."

"She keeps promising that the next show I'll have complete creative control, but right now I've got to make what people want to buy. I don't want to piss her off after everything she's done for me. But I've been thinking lately that what I'm after is a kind of sculpture that breaks the mold, not relies on it."

He looked at me curiously. "And how does one do that?"

"I don't know. Some kind of figurative sculpture that thinks abstractly? I'm still working it out."

"Well," he said, "If you play it right, that may very well happen. Stranger things have."

"Thanks a lot," I laughed. "But seriously. There's something else."

"How much does she owe you?"

I looked at him, amazed. "That predictable, huh?"

"I'd be surprised if you were getting paid. It's not you; it's the game."

"So how does one live this incredible life if nobody's getting paid?"

His laugh was somewhat grunt-like. "Oh, *someone's* getting paid. The trick is to be that somebody."

I shook my head. "Well, I don't want to think about all this. It's too depressing. Let's talk about something else. Tell me about your interview."

"What interview?"

"You know what interview. What was he like, Andy?"

"You know what he's like."

"I mean the small, unimportant things."

"It's all creation with people like that. There are no unimportant details."

The gravel path had ended and we circled back. I heard in the distance the sound of water and I ran ahead. "Look!" I shouted. "A stream. Isn't this amazing? In a couple months the ground will be covered in petals, when the cherry blossoms are in full bloom. But I think it's so beautiful now."

"You really do play the part of the ingénue." He laughed and lit a cigarette.

"I grew up in Connecticut. The trees, flowers, and flowing streams aren't new to me. It's just the juxtaposition, you know? Like in ten minutes we could be back underground on the subway, checking out some epic graffiti piece."

As we exited the Garden, I overheard a skateboarder talking to his girlfriend.

"You gotta know when to bail," he said, raising his shirt. Grinning, he showed off the purple bruise above his hip.

She said, "That looks like it hurts."

"You get used to it."

✳

Mac and I walked along Ocean Parkway and stood out like sore thumbs among the throngs of Hasid, the women with their long skirts, the men with their yarmulkes and wooly beards. We stopped at a kosher bakery and ordered knish with spicy mustard. The baker took her time, carefully wrapping our knish in silver foil. It seemed sacrilegious to eat and walk at the same time, so we stood outside, under the bakery awning, until we were through.

"Clean nail beds."

"What?"

"Andy," he said. "He had the cleanest nail beds. Not manicured, they just looked, naturally, I don't know, perfect."

I smiled. I'd think about this later: Andy's clean nail beds.

"You know, Jodi, there's two types of art out there. Art that makes you remember and art that makes you forget. You just have to figure out what type of art you make, and make it. One's not better than the other. The only sin is art that doesn't know what it is—that mistakes itself for something it isn't. What? What's so funny?"

"You've got mustard on your lip."

"Aw, come on now. I'm trying to have a moment," he said, wiping it off with his handkerchief.

I nodded, "I know. I know. What now?"

"It's about to be dark in an hour, isn't it? I've got to get back to the paper. Deadline. Time flies when you're freezing your ass off in the Botanic Garden."

"Sorry if you thought it was a drag. I had fun."

"Are you kidding? I haven't had this much fun since—I can't remember. Thank you for inviting me to a garden, Jodi Plum."

I tried to flirt with my eyes and lips, the way Monika had down to a science. "You're welcome."

"Well, it's the end of the line, so to speak. That's the subway over there. I think I'm going to walk some more till I find a car service. We're in Brooklyn: no way I'm going to catch a cab. But car services, they've got tons in Brooklyn."

"Can I ask you something?"

"Go for it," he said.

"Are we going to be friends?"

His eyes were so dark blue they could've been black. "Well, now, I wouldn't make a very good friend. See, I've got to be honest. All I can think about is what I would do to you in the backseat of a cab if you rode to the city with me."

"Car service," I corrected. "Let's go find one."

✶

That was how it was that winter, into the spring. Together, we shared the newness of blooming romance, exploring each other as uncharted territories. We devoured the secrets of the city. Old things: museums I'd never known about, like the Transit Museum with its turn-of-the-century steam engines. New things: a play performed with no dialogue, only sound and light. It didn't matter if the things we saw were old or new, because we were new, and we were seeing things together for the first time. After we'd make love, I'd lie there, wanting to say something but not knowing what to say, and he'd read my mind and tell me it was okay, that we were just getting used to each other.

"No," I demanded. "It's more than that. And it's not because we made love in the afternoon."

Covering my lanky body with a sheet from a set Monika's mother had sent from Egypt, he said, "Isn't it?"

"Questions, questions. Always questions. Why can't you stay?"

He said, "Deadline."

"But you never stay."

"It isn't my bed. My bed's in the Village. Besides, I can't stay here. I feel like I'm sleeping with a ghost watching over us. The mysterious Monika and her five-thousand-dollar bedding."

"Well, let me come back with you then. I don't mind."

"Jodi, I have to work. You know how it is. Don't give me a hard time. I thought you liked the way things were between us. Let's not ruin this with lofty bourgeois expectations."

"You're right," I sighed. "Boyfriend/girlfriend are just meaningless labels."

He grabbed my breast, and roughly cupped it in his hand. "Come here, you sexy woman; that's what I love about you. How would you like it if I took you to the opera next month? Opening night of *La Bohème* at the Met. I've got two tickets, and I'd be honored if you'd accompany me."

"Wouldn't that be lofty and bourgeois of us?"

Chapter Thirty-three

"Americans didn't invent the concept of freedom, though its boiled-down, mythical landscape has become a hook upon which we've hung our hats. Freedom, a trope of American artists, has always been a point of departure. Unlike art, from, say, Communist Russia, American art embodies abstract expression. We are free agents, drunk on the excesses of freedom and the unbridled heat on streets paved with gold. Bohemia, smoking dope in roadside motels, New York Fucking City. We breathe the city, its putrid air; thick with trash because Sanitation's on strike, and we think if only we can escape New York, we'll find our Eden. When we do escape, all we can think about is getting back. Back to the grind, because the city is not just in our blood, it is our blood."

The room filled with applause, and the slight, balding lecturer, Clement Greenberg, nodded in appreciation.

Alex was seated next to me; it was she who'd paid for my ticket, which had cost an exorbitant fifty dollars. In all honesty, I would've preferred the cash, but it had been weeks since she'd had any time for me, and to make up for it, she'd promised me the afternoon.

"Of course I have money for you," she said. "I haven't forgotten." She clutched her leather shoulder bag. "It's all in here.

But do come with me to a friend's studio. I have to make the rounds, and you're not doing anything, are you?"

I shrugged.

"Good. I hate walking alone in the afternoon."

It was half past four and the sunlight was flattering and forgiving, so I walked with Alex to a Soho studio. When we arrived, I was less than pleased to find out it was Jan's studio, which was in complete shambles.

"Mind the broken glass," he said as we entered. Mason jars overflowed with crunchy paintbrushes, rolls of insulation laid haphazardly on the floor, stacks upon stacks of magazines and cereal boxes piled up against the walls—no sense of order at all.

Jan's head was freshly shaved, but his beard was long and wild. He was wearing a tank top and I noticed on his puny, freckled bicep a tattoo of a heart inscribed with the word "Mother." Alex sat down on an expensive-looking Danish chair and took out her checkbook.

"I'll show you around," Jan said to me. "This is what I'm working on today." He said it matter-of-factly, ashing his cigarette on the floor. "I think I'm going to call her *Jodi*."

"Oh?" I said.

"The name just came to me." After he said it he snickered, and I wanted to punch him.

The portrait was of a gamine girl, a sepia nude, in an oblong-shaped frame. She was bent over a divan, her body forming a figure "n." She wore—for decorative purposes only—a black blouse, blown open, and pointy, high-heeled shoes. She had a gloomy complexion, overcast by the sepia tint of the photograph. Her face was lovely and expressive, and beckoned: *By invitation only, you may view me within this frame.*

"It's okay," said Jan, who'd been watching my expression. "You're not intruding. She's happy to have us."

"Did you take the photo?"

"Oh, no," he replied. "I found her. Now that she's mine, I'm going to decorate her."

"With ejaculate? That's a stretch."

"And glitter," he added. "In fact, I was just about to embark on an artistic journey, and would like to invite you to collaborate."

I was disgusted. "Can I use your bathroom?"

When I got inside the bathroom, I realized someone was lying inside an empty bathtub.

Flashback. Dizzy. Nauseous. Evil little bitch that I am. I wanted to scream; I wanted to cry; I wanted out of my body. I wretched and thank God my puke made it into the sink. Fuck it. God had nothing to do with it.

"Are you okay?" asked the girl in the tub.

"Where am I?" I wiped my face.

From the tub the girl asked rudely, "Do I *know* you?"

It took me a moment to come back, but when I did, I realized the girl in the tub was Sierra Walker, naked except for a lace bra and garter. She looked at me with a glazed, quizzical smile and repeated, "Do I know you? You look like someone I know." Then she turned her head and addressed some imaginary figure. "Do I *know* her?"

Then I remembered why I was in the bathroom. "I need to pee."

As I urinated, I caught a glimpse of the moon in the late-afternoon sky. The light from the moon cast a misty, enchanted glow that denied the movement of the sun and the succession of day to night.

Sierra burst into a fit of saccharine giggles. "Go right ahead. Since we're such old acquaintances."

I closed my eyes, sat on the toilet, and prayed to get it together. I couldn't let these people sense the slightest bit of weakness; I'd come too far.

When I got back out there, Jan was opening up a little baggie and spilling out a pile of powder onto a rectangular black Formica table. He used the outer flap of a matchbook to cut up a couple rails. Alex declined with a wave of the hand, and directed her attention to me for the moment.

"I've told my friend Ludwig all about you. He and I are on the

Guggenheim committee. And I've gone ahead and sung your praises. I'm telling you, honey, keep those statuettes coming."

For the time being, I let myself be free of Isla. "You really think they'll consider me?"

Jan looked up from his pile of drugs and flashed me those green eyes.

"*Do you really think they'll consider me?*" he mocked.

I waited for Alex to say something. Jan went back to his drugs.

Then Alex said, "Who's 'they'? I've told you, *I'm* on that committee."

"With an award like that," I began, making my best pitch, "I'd be able to pursue a new figurative or a new abstract, that beyond space we were talking about the other day. Like in that Sontag essay you gave me, which I loved, by the way."

"Oh, I nearly forgot," she said and handed me an envelope. "This came for you." It was an envelope postmarked San Francisco. I gave it little thought and stuffed it into my jacket pocket. "Also, I've arranged for an invitation to the Coppersmith benefit to be sent to the loft, so be on the lookout for that. It's the season's most exclusive party. Everyone in the art world who's worth knowing will be there. Now, if I don't get on the West Side Highway in ten minutes, I'll never make my party. Pray for me, Jodi. Pray there's not a four-car pileup like the last time the poet Charles Bartleby decided to throw one of his soirees."

Charles Bartleby... the name sounded familiar, but I couldn't place it.

"You're leaving?"

Wonderful. Alex got up, kissed us both, and flew out the door.

I looked down at the check. She'd only paid a quarter of what she owed me. "Damn!" I said, but she'd already disappeared into a taxi.

Jan licked his finger and cleaned the table of cocaine crumbs. "What's that 'new figurative or new abstract' you were talking about? Is there something going on I don't know about?"

I shrugged obnoxiously. "I haven't figured it out yet."

"You know, abstract art isn't an invention of the twentieth century. Jewish and Islamic religions didn't allow the depiction of humans. Hieroglyphics, calligraphy, these predate Rothko, good ol' boy, by centuries. Did you know that?"

"What? Of course."

Jan smiled. "I think we're alone now."

"Isn't Sierra back there?"

"We might as well be alone. So, what do you say we make some art?"

I looked at the amount on my check. It would be irresponsible but worth it to buy a bottle of Chardonnay and some decadent pastry on Spring Street. I looked up at Jan. He embodied everything I hated about the abstract art scene, how everything boiled down to a hard dick and a wad of come.

"I don't think so."

Down to his "Mother" tattoo, he was such a cliché of himself it would be laughable, if only he weren't so successful.

✳

Beneath me, the subway roared and whirred. The hot air that emanated from the grate had a foul smell to it. I realized the smell was from the homeless people who lived underground. I felt like a brat. The night wind picked up. A chill entered my marrow that left my skin piqued with goose bumps. I hurried my step until I was jogging lightly. A scrap of newspaper blew up from the street into my face.

When I got home, I realized Mac had left his pack of Marlboros on the table. I thought it might be nice to have a smoke on the fire escape, bottle of Chardonnay in hand. When I got out there, I realized that Monika had been right. This was what I'd always imagined for myself. Even though Alex only paid me part of what she owed me, I was still here making art, and that was a way out. Then I remembered the letter in my jacket pocket.

Chapter Thirty-four

The envelope Alex had given me in Jan's studio was postmarked San Francisco. I opened it and it went something like this:

Dear Jodi,

I saw your name in the paper; actually, a friend alerted me to the fact, and I am writing to offer my congratulations and tell you how proud I am of you. Please don't tell your mother that I've written you. I'd like this to be about you and me. Sometimes my work brings me to New York. I will be staying at the Decameron the week of the 20th in May. I'd like it very much if you'd look me up and come by for a visit. Of course I understand how things have played out, that you may not want to see me. However, in hopes that you do, I will keep an extra nice bottle on ice for us; I'd say it's about time we shared a drink, being that you're a grown woman these days. I'm due back in the Bay the 30th. I live in San Francisco now. Regrettably the spring visit will be a short one, but inevitably, I will visit again soon.

Your loving father,
Dad

I read it again in disbelief. When I was finally getting somewhere, he had to drag me back. I guess that's how things happen. You give up striving to be the center of his world, and then suddenly he sees you, and it's like you've been discovered. But Dad discovering me now... I felt nauseated. A fluttering sensation began in my stomach, and I thought, *This is the feeling of things catching up to you.* Then a stray tabby that'd been picking through the trash leapt onto the fire escape. Its rank orange fur grazed my bare foot and I shot back to the open window. The creature meowed at me, glaring with fierce, beady, yellow eyes that reminded me of Monika's.

"Scat, cat!" I yelled, hopped inside the loft, and slammed shut the window.

✱

I was meeting Mom for lunch. She'd insisted we meet someplace other than the Saloon, and had suggested a health-food restaurant in the East Village.

"Since when do you know about the East Village?" I asked upon her arrival.

"How about asking me why it is that I can meet for lunch in the middle of the week?"

"Okay," I said. "How can you?"

"I quit my job."

"What?"

My mother did look different. She wore a blazer, loose jeans, and a pair of black cowboy boots.

"How are you, darling?" she asked. "You have a hug for your mother?"

We went inside and were seated. My mother took the liberty of ordering two shots of wheatgrass juice. When the putrid-smelling drinks arrived, she raised hers in toast.

I smiled, stunned and also a bit relieved to find my mother in such strong spirits. I wouldn't mention the letter from Dad, at least not right away.

She took off her blazer and smoothed it across her lap. The capped sleeves of her blouse exposed diesel arms. The breadth of her shoulders seemed to have increased two-fold since I'd last seen her. Her biceps bulged with mass.

"Your arms, you look like a man."

"I've been working out. Jane Fonda tapes. If you'd stopped by the house lately, you'd know that I'm transforming your former studio into a gym. After you cleared out all your art stuff, I found boxes and boxes of your father's old shit. It's about time I got rid of that, don't you think?"

"I guess."

"You guess? Well, too late anyway, because the Salvation Army has it now. And I got a great deal on some machinery from a YMCA that was upgrading equipment."

"Who buys equipment from the Y?"

"Lots of people. Besides, I think my arms look good, just like Tina Turner's. The Sunshine Burger is terrific. I think I'm going to have the yucca fritters with lima bean paste."

"Come here often?"

"I have to tell you. I'm a new woman, and my new job really keeps me moving."

"New job?" I said. "Don't you have a pension?"

"Retired, is that what you think of me?"

"No, sorry. Of course I don't think you're ready to retire. I just thought, I mean, Dad sends you checks, alimony or whatever, right?"

"Dad? My dad's dead. And if you were talking about your father, I'd rather not discuss him. Aren't you curious about my new job?"

"Of course."

"I'm teaching a Jazzercise class. I'm an apprentice right now, but in three weeks I take the test for my certification. Isn't that exciting?"

I pictured her in tights and a leotard, leading a group of suburban housewives in a jazzed-up version of *Fever*. Suddenly, I felt her slipping away, and it was the most jarring feeling in the world.

"If you were in the city, how come you didn't call me? Stop by for a visit?"

"For one thing," she started, pumping her mahogany curls with the lift of a hand. "I did call you. But the line was disconnected."

"I forgot to pay that bill," I said, trying to sound casual. "It should be back on by now though."

"I read that some artists take the phone off the hook during their work time. Do you do that? You should give it a try. Turn off the world, you know."

This was strange; she wasn't even listening. She used to hang on my every word.

"Oh, and did I tell you? Along with the gym equipment, I've bought a tanning bed and have already made my money back selling tanning sessions to the women in the condo."

"That's great, Mom."

"So when can I meet this Monika I keep hearing so much about? I was hoping she'd join us for lunch."

"Maybe next time," I said.

"Well that's fine. I'd love to meet her. It's just so nice that you have someone to keep you company in the city. If I had to do it over again, I'd be a New Yorker. Could you imagine that? Anything is possible. You'd be surprised what diet, exercise, and a little old-fashioned entrepreneurial spirit can do for the psyche. Really, Jodi, I have to tell you, the day I quit my job and stepped into that leotard, I swear, ten years just melted off my face. Can you tell?"

As she went on, I tried to decide if I would see Dad.

"More wheatgrass?" The waiter wanted to know if he could bring us anything else.

Chapter Thirty-five

It was getting hot. Mac and I sprawled naked in bed. The hotel was his idea. Like Gatsby and Daisy, he'd said. "Let's get a room for the afternoon." Instead of the Plaza, we'd checked into the Palace, a psychic parlor and tearoom that served fine whiskeys and bourbon. I'd been craving mint juleps, and it was just our luck to have stumbled upon this treasure. It was an old rooming house from the twenties, and the proprietress, Jewel, had been in the business for over sixty years. She'd made our drinks, and when Mac and I asked her to sit down, tell us stories of days gone by, speakeasy adventures, and prohibition, the drinks had kept coming. Jewel liked Mac and me very much. She'd given us a great rate and promised that when the clairvoyant came in, she'd arrange a reading on the house.

*

"Did you know," I said, "that in French, the word *hôte* means both a host and guest?"

Mac looked at me, not amused. He cracked open a walnut and tossed the shell under the bed.

"You're littering in Jewel's establishment?"

"Maid will clean it up."

"Everything in this room is made of velvet."

"You sure are an odd one. How'd we even end up here?"

"It was your idea, remember?"

We passed out for a while in the afternoon sun. Before the sun set it changed direction, moving westward and casting a rogue twilight into our room. I awoke for a couple seconds, registering the imminent change from day to night, and gasped a longing, bourbon-scented breath before drifting off, comfortable within the nook of Mac's chest.

In sleep, our bodies found cover under hotel sheets. We slept uninterrupted.

The clairvoyant hadn't come.

"What time is it?"

I turned on the light. He asked the question too casually, like he had somewhere else to be.

I swung myself over the side of the bed and checked the clock, a gaudy pendulum Lux replica in the shape of a sunflower.

"Just past eleven."

"Boy, did we sleep. Those bourbons were strong."

I pinned the bedding to my chest and asked where the smokes were.

He answered, "In my pants pocket. But where do you think you're going?"

"I'm thirsty. There's an ice machine down the hall. Let's get a bottle. They were selling malt whiskey novelty bottles in the parlor."

"You're a pistol," he laughed.

"I'm serious."

"We're only paid up for another hour."

"So? Jewel won't mind."

He reached for my ass. "I've got to check in with the paper."

"The paper? You're the arts editor. Hardly news-breaking stuff."

"I feel like eating a meal. You feel like dinner? I bet there's some greasy diner around here; that's just what we need."

"If you want to go, just go. I get it."

"Come here," he said. He reached a hand around my hips. "Today was amazing."

"It was," I agreed. "Getting a smoke." I pushed him off me, got out of bed and started putting on my pants. I balled my panties and put them in my pocket.

I said, "Should get going now if I'm gonna take the subway."

"Don't be silly. I'll give you carfare. You're in no condition to ride the subway."

I suddenly thought of Vincent Frand paying Ostrich Girl carfare so he could fuck me in the bathroom of the club. "I'm fine," I said. "I do want one of those bottles from the parlor. To remember this afternoon."

He stretched his arms above his head. "You don't need a novelty bottle of malt whiskey to remember this afternoon, do you?" He smiled curiously.

I found my undershirt, a pink, ribbed child size. I slipped it on. I felt better fully dressed while he was still naked.

"We've got another hour," he said.

I lit a smoke and tossed him the pack from his pocket.

"I'm already dressed."

Suddenly, there wasn't much to talk about. He got out of bed and the sheet fell from his body. His flaccid penis stuck out like a pink worm between his legs. His sack just hung. He found his shorts and put them on. I stood there smoking and sobering up. He asked me to hand him his pants. I took my time about it. He put them on and opened his wallet. I stubbed out my smoke and let him hold me close. We rubbed up against each other, touching and sniffing like a couple of animals. Then he stuffed a bill into my back pocket and told me to be careful out there, and to be sure to take a cab.

Of course I kept the money and walked three blocks to the subway, where I went underground and bought a token for a buck.

I was embarrassed to check the amount in my back pocket but didn't want money sticking out of my clothes while I was riding the subway. Fifty—less than what Ostrich Girl had gotten, but she was a pro. Besides, maybe Mac did really have to work. It wasn't that much of a stretch. The money was a good turn of luck, though; I'd use it to pay the phone company to turn the service back on. The subway came quickly and I got on.

There were actually a couple of normal-looking people on board. I sat down next to a black lady who was robustly eating a coffee cake, bite by bite, from a brown paper bag. She had her hair tied up like Aunt Jemima but didn't have Aunt Jemima's friendly, fawning smile. I wondered what she was so angry about. She was really letting that coffee cake have it.

A trail of white-powdered crumbs littered the front of her jacket and she didn't even care to brush them off. The subway hissed and swayed. I could see through the little window into the last car, where a posse of club kids held court. Their colored afros and chain links bobbed and clinked. I wondered where the party was. What would Monika think of Mac? Her dates never stuck around either, but they were johns. It didn't seem like what I had with Mac was so different. Did everyone feel so empty after sex, or was it just me? Orgasms were great, but after they were over, you were left alone with fifty bucks and not much else but the memory of being fucked.

The kids with the colored afros and gold links were walking through the cars, getting closer. Even in the darkness, I could tell they were an eclectic bunch. I picked out a Mexican with a red bandana around his neck and sweaty arms that bulged out of a cut-up jean jacket. His hair was slicked back and greasy. As he got closer, I noticed he wore a patch over one eye. I imagined he was a passionate lay. I pictured him grabbing me by the hair and shoving his cock in from behind. His friend wasn't bad-looking either. He carried a boom box on his shoulders, but it must've been busted or something because it wasn't playing any music. Still, the kids had a pulse to their step and they were free-styling. The lone girl of the bunch twirled a feather boa and exploded with laughter. I wondered what it meant to have fantasies of orgies and rape.

Chapter Thirty-six

"Hello," I said. He looked thin and tired. "You look well."

"You can call me Dad. Let me hold you, look at you."

The hug was awkward. This is what it felt to have a strange man's hands on your body, holding you, as though he knew where you began and ended. He looked me up and down and seemed pleased with himself. "And tell me, how is your mother?"

"She's been working out."

Before inquiring about the details of my life: *Am I happy? Involved? Well-adjusted? Fully functional?* he felt obliged to relay the circumstances of his existence. There were certain things you could tell just by looking at him. He'd aged. He was neither here nor there. Slight frame, olive skin. The shade of skin was the same as I'd remembered. Hair greyed, fully intact. I guess that was something to be proud of for a man his age. I tried not to stare, but there was something wrong with his eyes. A thin, milky film sheathed his eyeballs. When he saw me notice, he reached for his spectacles, which concealed the cataracts slightly. He nervously fondled the loose skin of his gullet. I turned my head and focused on a spot in the carpet where the stitching had come undone. He went on to say that when he'd first moved to San Francisco, he'd lived off Market

Street—near a Safeway, he added, as if this detail were significant. With no possessions of his own, he'd rented a furnished room cluttered with tacky 1950s throwbacks.

"Amazing," he said, making room for me on the chintz hotel sofa, "what you learn to live with." He paused nervously for a moment, and then continued. "I'm very glad you came to see me. I didn't want to admit it, but I'd have been disappointed if you hadn't. This hotel, it's not much, but my firm pays for the whole thing."

"I don't care about the hotel."

"I thought I'd know what to say when you got here," he said.

"And?"

He shrugged. I wanted to tell him about the starfish I collected with Monika. How she loved them because they were migratory creatures, following the tides to eventual shore. Something stopped me. I felt myself shutting down. I hiccupped.

"Of course, things are much better now. I've got a nice house in Marin County with a garden overlooking the ocean. There's a guest room, in case you ever want to come out west."

"I just got used to calling myself a New Yorker."

"They say you've got to live here ten years before you can do that," he laughed. "I only meant for a visit. New Yorkers do leave the city, don't they?"

"Not the diehard ones. I mean everything one could possibly want is right here, all day, every day. There's really no need to leave."

He looked at me quizzically, as if I were speaking some tribal language he didn't understand because he was an elder, and I, young clanswoman, had recently been to the river.

Adjusting thin, wiry spectacles, "Shall we open the bottle—Stolichnaya, for martinis. You do drink martinis, don't you?"

"Actually, I don't drink." I felt like that girl at a party who boasts about her sobriety, but every time she says it she's holding a margarita. "I'll have mine on the rocks."

"All right." As he opened the bottle, I noticed that his hands were shaking. Then he said, "I'll have mine on the rocks, too. Saves me the trouble of mixing a martini. I made reservations at the restaurant downstairs. We'll eat in a half-hour. I hope that's okay with you. Oh, I nearly forgot. Here," he said, handing me a box of chocolates. "These are for you."

I looked at the box of candy tied neatly with a gold ribbon. There was so much I wanted to know, but what do you say to someone who just walked out on you like that, without even a second thought? He was my dad. I didn't just love him; he was everything. And nothing. Suddenly, I remembered how he found me with the *Playboy* and got an invasive feeling of awkwardness. I still couldn't figure exactly what my father wanted with the centerfold and why it bugged me so much. Of course I had *some* idea of what he wanted. But it had to be more complicated than that.

A silence grew between us until finally he said, "I love this city. It's wonderful that you're here. You've done so well for yourself."

I thought about the fact that Alex owed me thousands of dollars and I was living on canned goods. "I have," I said.

He said, "I hope you're being careful," and handed me a highball. "You don't ride the subway, do you?"

"Of course I do. How else am I supposed to get around?"

"Oh, dear," he groaned.

"The subway isn't as bad as everyone thinks."

"Does your mother know you ride the subway?"

I didn't answer.

"She loves a dry vodka martini. I'll bet that hasn't changed."

I took a swig of my drink. "I thought you didn't want to talk about her. I thought you wanted this to be about you and me."

He coughed, and said, "Of course, I'm sorry. I guess old habits; well, you know what they say about those. I did want this to be about you and me. About how proud I am of you."

"You read about my show?"

"Yes. As I said, I often come to New York on business, or my, well, I guess you'd say, colleague, does. And this particular colleague brought me back a paper with your picture in it."

"That was considerate of him."

"*Her*, well, yes. She's a very considerate person. I hope you'll meet her."

"Your colleague?"

"Perhaps next time."

"Yeah."

"And," he continued, "it pleased me to no end to see the types of statues you make… remember how I used to read to you from that giant book of Greek mythology?"

"*You* never read to me. That was Mom. *She* was the one who read to me. Not you."

"Sure I did. Your favorite story was about Persephone. You'd beg me to read it again and again. I think the ending never sat right with you, and somehow you wished it would turn out differently."

"Well…"

"And when I saw your sculpture, your Persephone has the same human features as the one in the book. Amazing, isn't it?"

"The article didn't run a picture of that piece."

He crossed and uncrossed his legs, sipping nervously from his glass. "I must've seen it somewhere else."

"Wait a minute. What are you saying?" All of a sudden, I flooded with anger. "It was you who bought my first piece, wasn't it?"

"Technically, the buyer is my colleague. She's got extraordinary taste, and, well, we did it for you."

"For me?"

"Adele and I, we really like your work."

"Adele?"

"Yes." His lip turned up in a timid smile.

I couldn't believe it. I knew seeing Dad would expose me as a fraud, that lost little girl from suburbia, but I never imagined this.

"Don't you dare say her name to me. I don't want to know these things."

"I'm sure if you met Adele, the two of you would get on."

My heart turned to stone. It seemed I would never be his chosen one. Colleague, whore—weren't they one and the same? I slammed my drink onto the credenza, hoping my glass would leave a mark. "What a farce."

"Calm down, Jodi. I thought this would make you happy. We were helping you out; it's tough out there to get your name known, and well, Adele's connected to the downtown scene. She heard about you from a friend of hers, Aleksandra something."

"I don't want your charity."

"It's not charity. We're so proud of you."

The last thing he needed was to see me cry. "I shouldn't have come here. I never want to see you again."

"Don't say that."

"It feels lousy, doesn't it?"

In front of me was an old man who I had no ties to.

"I'm no whore," I said, digging in my pocket for a subway token. At once, I regretted saying the word "whore" aloud to my father, but it hung there.

It's the worst feeling in the world to just stand there waiting for someone to love you.

He said nothing, but looked into the bottom of his glass. There, vodka was melting a lone chip of ice. It was my turn to leave.

Beautiful Garbage

179

Chapter Thirty-seven

"Earlier today, Lebanese terrorists believed to be part of the radical organization Party of God hijacked a jetliner en route to Rome. Over one hundred Americans are believed to be on board flight 847 out of Athens."

The set, aglow with the static of live broadcast, unmasked the horror. I switched channels to watch hours of soap operas and stuffed my face with violet cream bon-bons that had arrived in a care package from Monika's mother.

The television station had gotten footage of terrified passengers on a plane. A man in a ski mask brandished a weapon and, in broken English, instructed passengers to keep their hands hooked behind their necks while placing their heads between their knees.

Then the serious voice of a newscaster boomed, "There were no reports of violence more severe than beatings, though the hijackers, reportedly armed with grenades, threatened to blow up the plane if prohibited to land in Beirut."

I thought about Monika. It was the small things I missed the most: her stupid jokes, the way she always left lipstick marks on coffee mugs, the random snot rag in the seat cushion. Amid distant reports of political violence, she donned halos of sunshine. In her absence, I realized how far we'd grown apart, how differently we saw the world, but nonetheless, how a girl like her needed me as much as I needed her. I hadn't heard from her since the day she called me from a phone booth at a swap meet, when I'd just been so happy at the sound of her voice.

"Tell me," I began. "Tell me all about some bungalow off Sunset you stumbled on. Or some bonfire where you toasted marshmallows and crazy crystals."

"Well," she said. I heard her reach into her cigarette pack (I wondered what brand she'd been smoking lately), draw out a smoke, and light it:

"The other day I did a photo shoot. Very editorial. Amazing. My whole crew was amazing; we're like this totally dysfunctional family that just gets each other. Shep, he does hair and makeup. Bobby's this totally rad stylist *and* a stone fox; she found the gear. We used this teen model, Holly, who goes by the name Lo, and shot the whole thing in that abandoned house I was telling you about."

"I have news too. I've been seeing someone."

She just went on talking:

"All day, we kept switching rooms, chasing the sun. At dusk, we quit and partied, but were up at nine the next morning eating greasy food at an old Hollywood diner. Our waitress was dressed like Marilyn Monroe. We tried to get her to come back with us but she wouldn't. Wouldn't that have been so cool?"

"Don't you want to hear about this guy I've been seeing? What's the point of having a boyfriend if you can't talk about him with your girlfriends?"

"Just listen! We went back and finished up the shots and by the end of it all we were all so tired. Shep had another job, Bobby had to fly to Miami, and Lo should've been home days ago. So, we all went our separate ways. They're really the best people ever. And the photos came out so great!"

"Images," I corrected. "You call them images." She didn't want to hear anything about anyone but herself. I couldn't take any more, so I slammed down the phone. She wasn't changing; I was. Monika was a constant, still babbling away.

✱

Despite my sour feelings towards Monika, life without my cohort was growing lonelier by the day. Then there was the problem with Alex. I'd stood her up for dinner at *21* and a midtown opening. I avoided calling her back, not thinking her calls would taper off so quickly. It was my turn to call, but every time I picked up the phone, I got so mad thinking about her doing business with my father and his *colleague.*

Along with the bon-bons, Monika's mother had also sent a case of port. In a drunken state, I passed out then woke up and for a moment thought Isla was still alive and that what we'd done to the boy had just been a bad dream.

For a week I followed the hijacking story on TV, and I felt a great weight lift when the hostages were released. The tearful reunion with family followed, and so did the return to normalcy. For them, it was over; they were safe, but my relief was temporary. As the broadcast continued, I became increasingly worried but couldn't put my finger on the source.

Mac came to visit. I told him to bring food. When he crossed the threshold, he tripped on a pile of mail. Recovering, he handed it to me. "I'm your personal postman. Here," he said. "I've also brought sandwiches. Come back to the world, Jodi. You've got to eat something besides chocolate and wine."

I shushed him. "Watching something."

"Don't you want to check the mail? Some of this stuff looks important."

"Leave it over there. I'll get to it later."

"Over where?" he said.

"Wherever."

He said, "I know what you want from me."

"Not now."

"You're acting like this because you want me to take care of you."

He persisted, wanted to talk about art. He wanted to talk about Ray Johnson and his bodiless bunny. But Ray Johnson had nothing to do with me.

The one that had been shot had been thrown from the plane. The news never gave details, like where and how the body had landed. I wondered if such a fall to earth would leave the body intact, or if it resulted in gruesome dismemberment, legs and arms scattered spontaneously in Greek maritime towns. The newscaster reported on what type of soup the hijackers had ordered, as the hostages—minus the one—dined with their captors at a seaside restaurant in Beirut. Even though I'd seen the footage numerous times, the oddity of this deliverance disturbed me greatly.

I kept coming back to that one. He had died, but the rest, they went on living.

✴

Snacking on little more than olives, garbanzo beans, and pickled beets, I'd run out of fuel. I'd eaten tuna from the can and a tin box of smoked salmon. I bought groceries on the cheap—bundles of bok choy and fried noodles that came in paper sacks from the Chinese merchants outside my doorstep. I smoked cigarette butts out of ashtrays and, when the opportunity presented itself, bummed a whole one and saved it for a special moment. This is what it's like to be poor, so not glam.

Tonight was the Coppersmith benefit, a lavish soiree thrown by Marla Thorpe Coppersmith, an octogenarian philanthropist. In her heyday, she was the alleged mistress of Max Ernst. The woman was undoubtedly somebody's daughter; you just don't have that kind of money on your own. In misguided acts of benevolence, she threw parties for the upwardly mobile to raise money for the less fortunate. A select group of guests received invitations personally from Marla. Invitations were coveted, as they entitled you to a free pass on the evening. Everyone else bought tickets to the event, rumored to cost a thousand a head, with all proceeds going to a cause worthy of Marla's choice. Tonight's cause was the construction of libraries in Johannesburg. My invitation sat on the table next to an open bottle of port, one of the last.

Of course I had to go. It was a warm, late spring evening and I'd left the window to the fire escape open for the breeze. I'd wear something fabulous from Monika's closet—she'd left rows and rows of her best dresses—and I'd stand up to Alex and let her know that from now on I was to be paid on time, and to be consulted on all potential buyers. Like that I began to thumb through hangers, until I pulled out a clingy black sheath dress, trimmed with horsehair, zippers, and metal studs. I stripped down and slipped it on. The weight of the dress surprised me; it was heavy. I stood before the full-length mirror and looked at myself. It wasn't quite right. Carefully, I removed the dress and put it back where it came from. Next, I pulled out a modern version of a boned Victorian crinoline. The skirt was beaded with gemstones; the waistline was a thick elastic with a tartan print. It would look outrageous with a pair of fishnets, heels, and one of the pink child-size undershirts I'd been so fond of lately. Naturally, it was roomy on the waist, but I fixed that by cinching it with a couple of safety pins. My crude alteration worked with the ensemble, and gave it personality. I felt like a million bucks and would be eating caviar tonight.

The party was nothing like I'd imagined. When the parlor doors opened, there must've been hundreds of people, dressed to the nines and bopping about with forced grace like exquisitely fashioned marionettes. Some gathered by a champagne waterfall that was flanked by two life-size elephant ice statues. Some danced in measured step to the orchestra. Before

I knew it, I was raising a glass, *salut!* with a party of Italians. I accepted a dance from a distinguished Cuban who kissed my hand when the dance was over. I sipped a grapefruit martini from the glass of a munificent Czech debutante and forgot all about the hostages eating soup with their captors.

The black-curtained stage lit up, and a stream of children arrived, naked except for skirts printed with brightly colored African patterns. Their bodies were adorned with beads and paint, and in their hands they carried small instruments. A couple of African drummers joined the orchestra, and the band began to serenade the child performers. The whole scene could've been straight out of Kipling's *Kim*, except with South Africans in place of Indians. Every once in a while, the music would crescendo, and the children would yell out in English, "Freedom!"

Dripping with food, the parlor offered an endless array of delicacies. Waiters waltzed by with trays of mushrooms, rum, and candied truffles. Towers of bread topped the tables, which were covered in silver plates of meat, seafood, cheeses, and fruits. Another table offered only pâté; one served chocolate-covered grasshoppers.

Then I saw him. He was with a smoky blond whose supple mouth could swallow you whole. It was Mac Frank, wearing a debonair tux with tails. He caught my glimpse and started straight towards me, arm in arm with his date.

"Hello, Jodi." His date wore a blue evening dress and matching arm-length gloves. She looked like a superhero.

"Hello."

"I didn't know you'd been invited," he said. "Is this your first time?" As he spoke to me, his date feigned interest with a polite smile. He spoke in a self-assured, belittling tone. It was apparent that they were a couple and I was just a girl at a party.

All I could manage was, "The elephants, have you seen the elephants?"

Mac and the other woman agreed that yes, the elephants were spectacular. Then, by chance, a woman rushed upon her. This woman was also wearing a satin evening gown with matching arm-length gloves.

"Honey, I've been looking for you," she said. "I must steal you away for a second. You don't mind if I take her, do you, Mac?" She'd elbowed her way in between the two of them and had her arms around each of their waists.

"I'll only be a moment, darling."

"Of course, and hello to you, Natalie," Mac said to the other woman. "You're a bolt of lightning as always."

I just stood there absorbing the exchange of pleasantries that suggested a whole separate life my lover had with these people, women nothing like me.

When it was just us, standing in the amber stage light, the inane echo of flutes played by African babes somewhere off behind us, Mac turned to me and said, "You must've known."

All the signs were there. Somehow, I allowed myself to be too naïve again. I shook it off with a nimble laugh.

"Yes, yes, of course."

I couldn't look at him. I didn't know where to place my eyes without coming off unsettled. Then a flash bulb went off. A photographer had snapped our picture. I was horrified that this moment would be included among Marla Thorpe Coppersmith's party photos. I wanted to shake him. I wanted answers. I wanted to know if he didn't love me because I'd never be able to pull off arm-length gloves, or for some other inane reason.

I'd played the part of the ingénue again. My next thought was to get sauced as efficiently as possible.

As I made my way to the bar, I noticed Cookie and her painter-friend Paula having a drink. They waved me over. A whole crew of punk artists and downtown fashion people were holding court in a candlelit enclave. I recognized a lot of them. This whole Coppersmith cult of exclusivity was such a crock. I couldn't believe the people who'd been invited.

Every time I saw her, Cookie was rocking a spectacular new wig. Tonight, she wore a short-cut platinum piece beneath a velvet cloche cap. Her green eyes were lined with gold pencil. Her eyelashes were big, black, fake, and dotted with gold sparkles.

She kissed me with a warm mouth. "Hello, Jodi. I love this girl," she said to her friends. "But I never see her!"

"Here we are."

"Yes, darling, that we are. Where's Monika?"

"I don't know." It was the truth.

"You look pissed off," she said.

"Men are scum."

"Despicable pigs."

"I should've known you'd be hanging out at the bar."

She said, "You remember Paula, don't you?"

"When am I going to paint your picture?" Paula said.

I stood there feeling like a decent human being for having people to talk to. Cookie giggled sloppily. "I guess I've had a couple. *And* some Percodan."

"Cookie knows how to party," Paula mocked.

"Want one, Jodi? I've got a whole bottle in my purse. You look a little down. What's wrong?"

Paula answered for me. "She's heard about that hack Jan. Don't worry, darling, you're not the only one disturbed by the news. I should start working with hardcore pornography. It's the one thing a woman artist won't touch these days. I'd probably end up with ten Guggenheims."

"What are you talking about?"

"I thought for sure you knew."

"Knew what?"

"About Jan's Guggenheim. Jan is the anointed one, Alex's *artiste du jour*. I hear she's arranged his show at the Whitney, and of course she's bringing the rank prick to Peggy's white party. God, am I really the one telling you this? I thought *you* were Alex's protégée."

"Jan has a Guggenheim?"

"We thought you knew," Cookie said. "But fuck it. Who cares anyway?"

I couldn't believe it. "I just got the biggest headache."

"Here, take a Percodan. You'll feel better."

I swallowed the pill with a kamikaze shot. Then the bartender poured another. Cookie proffered more pills. We partied on. By midnight, I'd vomited up pills in a frothy mixture of champagne and black truffles. In the fancy bathroom the smell of the mess was putrid. I decided to be a lady and flushed it away.

I continued to get drunk with Cookie. Paula got jealous and spent the rest of the night pouting with someone called Baroness d' Amanda. Cookie and I ate lobster or some sea creature with feelers. She fed me icebox cake. At some point, Alex came over. I was shit-faced. She said something like, "Darling, how are you?" Then she told me she had a check for me. She said it like it was the most normal thing in the world. I gave her the finger, threw up on her ridiculously expensive-looking shoes. Then I hit the floor. Blackness.

✶

"It's Saturday night and I'm doing what I always do, spinning records and telling stories of times gone by. 7 to 10, every Saturday night. Remember a time called the swinging twenties? I do. Call in with your stories; I want to hear from you, listeners, on WKSU Radio."

When I woke up, I found myself sprawled on a leather couch, covered with an orange fleece blanket. Monika's skirt hung from the back of a chair. Cookie was smoking a joint and listening to the radio.

"It's Vivienne Westwood," she said, pointing to the skirt. "Didn't want you to sleep in it."

Her apartment had the feel of a gingerbread house, with candied neon light fixtures hanging from the ceiling. The walls were plastered with portraits of Cookie, all painted by the same hand, and framed in maudlin, mismatched bejeweled frames.

"Last night," I began. "I don't remember anything."

Cookie told me everything. "I have to hand it to you," she said, "you sure came up with the most creative way of firing your dealer. And you should've seen her face. She was so pissed."

"I'm mortified."

"Oh, please. At the end of the day, she's the one covered in puke!"

"Yeah, and Jan has my Guggenheim."

"Who cares about trophies? I mean, that's not what you're in it for. Sure, the money is nice. But it's just money. There's lots of ways to make money."

"What am I going to do now?"

"Pray the art world develops amnesia." This from Paula, who'd emerged from the toilet with a paper folded under her arm. She tossed back her raven hair and chuckled like a little kid. "That was some funny shit, though."

I'd never seen her outside a club or party, without her ghoulish makeup and spiked hair. She was actually pretty when she allowed herself to be natural.

"Everybody's stupid," she continued. "Some people are stupider than others. When you're making art, your job is to elicit a response. Otherwise, you're not an artist; you're a decorator."

"It's just that I was trying to *do* something. And I thought Alex understood that. I thought she was in it with me."

"What were you trying to do?"

"She kept saying that if I played the game, gave people what they wanted with those figurative pieces that were starting to give me a name—then I could work towards what I'm really after, a space that's beyond figurative or abstract."

"If you're talking abstract, Jan is the abstract movement right now."

"These labels! They're so silly."

"But darling, how long do you think that will last? Even with his Guggenheim… So he got rewarded for being the asshole with the biggest dick. So what? Maybe Alex doesn't have as much sway as she used to. Let the fallout from last night die down; there are other dealers."

"I should never have let Alex sell those pieces all around town. They're years old; that's not me anymore."

"You need to toughen up."

Cookie looked apologetic. "Can I pour you a cup of coffee? I've got brioche." She got up and went into the kitchen.

"I'll just have some water," I said. She ignored me; began making up a coffee tray, filling a porcelain creamer, laying out sugar cubes.

"The art scene is fake," Paula went on. "Beyond superficial."

Cookie said, "You're not telling her anything she doesn't already know."

"Take Cookie, here," Paula continued. "Cookie is art. She uses her body to elicit pleasure. Sure, some women look down on her, call her a whore, but they're part of the problem, not the solution. Cookie's got the power to turn appearances in on themselves, to play with the body's appearances. Day in, day out, she is—no—her whole essence is a work of art."

Cookie nodded. "I'm not pretentious; I don't call myself a performance artist. I'm just living life."

"Now that's fucking purity."

I asked Paula, "What about your paintings?"

"What about them? I'm not going to stop painting portraits. It's what I do. That doesn't change the fact that my paintings are imitation. I wasn't born for that purity like Cookie was. She's walking beauty."

"Walking beauty?"

"Yes. Walking beauty—the latest frontier in artistic integrity."

Chapter Thirty-eight

Scouring the pantry for something to eat, I feared I'd crossed the line from charmingly neurotic to obsessively troubled. Who cares that she sold my art to Dad's whore and I barfed on her Ferragamos? Now Alex wouldn't take my calls. Well fuck her. Fuck her and all of them who ruined this for me.

I could ask Mom for money; she had her tanning beds and gym. But that would be admitting defeat. That would be admitting she'd been right that day when she told me I could never live the life of *That Girl*. Ugh… hungry… headaches.

Isla and I are riding bikes. We're young, but worldly, about ten. It's an afternoon in early August when it's already been summer for a while, long enough that the days have gone from sticky and expansive to languid and bloated. We're probably not supposed to be riding bikes by Concord Lake, so far from home, but we are. I'm tanned and toned from playing outdoors, and though I'm not athletic, my body doesn't register that yet, so I ride unencumbered. I feel the wind in my face and listen for Isla's laughter, which spirals forward like my foot on the pedal. We go fast. We ride past the swimming area and down towards the bog. Beneath the trail, an area of wet, marshy ground springs up. I shout to Isla that we should stick to the gravel path. We ride for what could be another mile.

"Where are we going?"

"There," she points. "The woods."

There's someone ahead in the distance. It's a boy, on foot. He's wearing swim trunks and carrying a towel. As we get closer, I can tell he's younger than we are. Either that or he's small for his age, with a body as gawky and stringy as mine. Isla looks at me and I look at her, and suddenly, we just *know*. We can tell from how he walks: awkwardly and without purpose. He lumbers without a sense of where he is, without understanding of the woods, what can happen when you're shrouded in the density of trees. We're aware of ourselves in a way that eludes this little boy. And, there are two of us.

We speed up. "Yoo-hoo!" She cries.

I laugh. She nudges me. She wants me to say something. So I yell, "I'm talking to you!"

At first, the boy doesn't know what's happening, but because he's alone, he knows enough to run. We chase him, Isla and I, and we laugh. His thin calves are slighter than ours, and we are on bikes. When he realizes that the road suddenly ends, the boy turns his head with a look of fear in his eye. We run him all the way to the dead end. Cornered, he's left to choose: us, or the woods.

∗

So here I was, a smart girl, living rent-free in prime Manhattan real estate. The bubble of my notoriety had burst, but that didn't mean I had to go hungry. What I'd done to the boy was shameful, no denying that. But I was beginning to realize it spoke to a part of me that was ruthless, and as sickening as that may have been, I began to think it was a necessary evil, a survival tactic, especially in this city. I could exist as a pathetic entity, sulk around and starve. Or I could go out and hustle dinner from one of Manhattan's lonely bachelors. If I couldn't accomplish that, I didn't belong in this city, and might as well head back to Connecticut and become a suburban body-builder, like Mom.

The city was filled with men; Monika was always saying that. It was nice to get dressed up—especially with Monika's closet of designer clothing—rim my eyes with liquid blue liner, perfume my neck and wrists with luxury rose oils. I styled my hair in an up-do with lots of lacquer, clipped on a pair of rhinestone and ruby studded earrings, and took a clutch—ornamental only; I literally had no money, but was nonetheless confident that I'd score a meal. It's funny when and how morals decide to kick in—or check out.

I walked two blocks to the corner deli and picked up a *Post*. I turned to Page Six and scanned to see what restaurant the latest starlet had been photographed at. Apothecary—perfect, only a twenty-block walk; I'd intentionally worn Monika's most comfortable pair—a three-inch crocodile pump.

The hostess at Apothecary wore a miniature top hat pinned into her hair. From my days with the milliner, I was able to discern the designer and talk extensively about his Baroque inspiration. Whoever said flattery gets you nowhere never lived in Manhattan. The thing was that you had to trick people into believing you were in on their cult of exclusivity. Name-dropping disguised as a compliment worked every time. The hostess sat me at the bar and told the bartender to take care of me.

"I've never seen you here before, and whenever I'm in town, this is my place." His name was Yassir and he was everything I was looking for that night: debonair, arrogant, foreign, and dripping with cash. He told the bartender to bring me a glass of Dom. I suggested a little tin of caviar to go with, and in no time we were seated at the best table while the chef prepared our dinner. My new friend was a diplomat from Fujairah in the United Arab Emirates (I'd never heard of Fujairah despite taking two classes on the Middle East at Vassar). That night I learned all about the mountainous city.

"When the rains come, it's the most beautiful, seductive time of year. Fog encircles everything, and the ground is steamy and moist. Of course that deters business—but life is too wonderful to be mercenary. Don't you agree?"

"What's your business?" I asked.

"I build hotels."

I must have shown surprise, because before I could say anything, he began, "There's lots of money to be made in the luxury industry in the UAE. People don't think so now, but trust me, no place on earth is immune to hedonistic pleasures. Even the desert." He laughed a deep guttural laugh. "*Especially* the desert."

"But your city is in the mountains?"

"Yes. The only one in the UAE that is almost completely mountainous. Of course precipitation is higher, but so is crop production." He took my hand. "Fertile land in a world of desert is no ordinary commodity. That's the principle I live by."

The champagne, the tang of his musk, the *duck confit*, the way he pronounced his "s's" and hard "c's," all made me feel like I was floating. I couldn't believe everything I'd been missing out on being so serious all the time.

"My estate is bordered by almond trees," he continued. "The scent of the leaves after the rains is unlike anything in the universe."

He didn't care what I had to say; I couldn't be sure he remembered my name. All of that was fine with me. I was content just to soak him all in and eat.

"You must come and see for yourself; or should I say smell: smell is the most powerful of the senses. If I could bottle the scent produced by my glorious almond leaves, I'd have my statue erected in every town in the Middle East, on Park Avenue and Rodeo Drive as well."

The courses kept coming. I ate until I felt my stomach would burst. I considered visiting the ladies room to stick my fingers down my throat, excise some food and return for another course, but didn't want to risk losing anything. Savor the fullness, I told myself. I rubbed my belly, and then ordered dessert.

"Are you hoping a genie will come out?" He laughed. "It's fine; you have not offended me. Our *Jinn* is popular folklore in the West."

"Oh," I said, suddenly self-conscious. Then, "If a genie appeared right now, what'd you wish for?"

"You." He leaned in and kissed me. "Shall I have my driver take us to the hotel?"

In the limousine, we went at it like animals. My new friend stopped briefly to say, "I don't want to leave marks on your skin."

"Mmm," I groaned. "Of course not."

"And," he continued. "I wonder if you'll afford me the same accommodation."

He was so formal; he really cracked me up. I nodded that I understood. He probably had seven wives, none of which he wanted to know about his New York dalliances.

When he laid me on his lush mattress, I let his pliant breath wash over me, excited beyond belief.

In that moment, I thought about the images that Isla made. Her heart-shaped leaves, skeletal palms—these were and were not what plants look like in real life. There was something else. Her dissection of the leaves had duality: the garbage that spilled out, and the shell that had the power to contain life. Her drawings moved towards examining interior and exterior. You were left with nothing but the moment, and in that moment, you felt your heart drop.

✳

The boy gets only a little ways into the woods when he trips on the towel he's been dragging behind him. He hits the ground hard, smashing his leg on an exposed root, which protrudes from the earth. There's no blood, but Isla and I both hear the *snap*. We're now circling him; we ride steadily, she first, I behind. Then we change directions. We're laughing.

"Get up!" I yell.

Clutching his leg, the boy stands up. He still hasn't said a word.

Isla and I continue to encircle him. We ride slowly, deliberately. What game we're playing, I'm not completely sure. All I know is that I'm not afraid of the boy. He fears us, and there are no adults left on earth.

"Where were you going?" I demand.

The boy stutters to speak for the first time. "Huh-ome. Home," he says. His words make him real.

"You shouldn't be walking by yourself," I say. "And how come you don't have a bike?"

The boy looks confused. "I got a bike."

"No you don't," says Isla. "You're too poor and stupid."

Isla and I are playing at being evil. Suddenly, I recognize him. The boy is the son of a Polish immigrant, a single mother who cleans houses.

"Stoopid!" As I hem in around the boy, a tingling sensation creeps through my body. Pulsating between my legs. Taunting the boy triggers powerful pleasure.

We laugh. Then I yawn, an exaggerated gesture that tells Isla I'm bored of talking; I want action.

"Take off your bathing suit," she says.

I stop laughing. We shouldn't be doing this. I want to tell Isla to stop. But I am helpless against her. More than that, I'm helpless against this feeling inside me that makes me curious to see how far we can take this, how far our power goes.

Suddenly, I'm talking. "Take it off," I say. "I'm talking to you!"

"Pussy!"

We laugh because she's said that word, and the boy trembles before us.

He slips off his bathing suit and leaves it at his feet. He's just standing there. We keep circling him with our bikes. Isla dips off hers, snatches up his bathing suit, and flings it to me. We take turns with his swim trunks on our handlebars.

Isla is in charge. She's running the show. She decides to stop her bike. She kicks up a pile of dirt at the boy. The moist dirt and gravel hit the boy's penis. I dismount my bike and start kicking up dirt too. There's lots of kicking and thrashing as the boy crumbles into himself, occasionally letting out a muffled scream. It's not about sex; it's about humiliating the boy. Soon, his little rosy nub is covered in soot; head-to-toe, the boy is filthy. I can taste blood in my mouth.

"What can you do with that thing?" she asks.

The boy looks confused. "What do you mean?"

"You heard her," I say. "That thing between your legs."

"Come closer," Isla directs. "Come closer and show us."

"Don't want to," he says. "I want to go huh-ome. I want to go home."

"Oooh," taunts Isla. "The little baby wants to go home." I laugh.

"We said come closer, or…"

"Or else!" Isla picks up a big rock and makes likes she's going to throw it at him. "Listen to what she told you to do."

The boy creeps forward until he's standing a couple feet before us.

"Closer!" we shout.

He obeys.

"Now you touch that thing," says Isla. "I want to see what happens when you touch it."

"Isla," I say. "What are you doing?"

"He knows what I'm talking about. I know about his mother." She draws out the syllables in the word "mother," long and deliberately. "How *good* she cleans houses."

"Don't talk about my mother," says the boy. It's the first time his voice has some fire to it.

"Shut up," commands Isla. "How big can you make it? You know what I mean."

I have a vague sense of what she's talking about, but not

really. I need to know what she means. It's wrong; I can't help myself.

"Wipe it off," she continues. "It's all dirty. Lick your hand and wipe it off."

I don't know what to say so I glare at him with the meanest look I can muster and stick my face in his and say, "Do it."

His hand is shaking, but he licks it with his thin, pink tongue.

"More saliva," Isla insists. "Get yourself cleaned up so you can make it big."

The boy just stands there and Isla gets frustrated. "God, do I have to do everything myself?" She gathers a mouthful of spit, bends down, and without their bodies touching, she covers his penis with her drool. "There," she says. "Now rub that in."

Something shifts inside me and I know that we've crossed a line. Still, I stay firmly planted in front of the boy, unable to look away.

He starts rubbing himself. The mixture of Isla's saliva and the dirt turn his penis an unnatural color.

Tears stream down his face. "What do you want me to do?"

"Keep rubbing!" Isla demands. "You better not tell anyone about this. I know who you are and I know who your mother is. My stepdad is a real important man who knows lots of people and he can get you and your mom kicked out of this country for being dirty immigrants, and whatever else your mom is."

*

When I awoke, I'd forgotten my nightmares, and Yassir was already dressed and speaking on the phone in Arabic. He noticed me stir, hung up, and came into the bedroom.

"Good morning, sleeping beauty."

"Morning." I smiled. He poured me a glass of orange juice.

Handing it to me he said, "I've got to be in a meeting in fifteen minutes. Stay. Enjoy the suite; I've got it for another night. After my meeting I'm flying to Miami."

I drank my juice and sat up. "No, I should go. Can I use the bathroom?"

He nodded, led the way and when we reached the doorway, he grabbed me one last time. "Thank you for a beautiful evening. See you soon, I hope, in a grove of almond trees."

"Oh," I laughed. "Thanks for dinner. It was delicious."

"Any time. And the next time I'm in town, you know where to find me."

I squinted at him, momentarily confused. How would I know the next time he was in town?

"My driver has to take me now, so promise you'll take a taxi-cab home? I've heard horrible things about the crime in your metro and I can't imagine you riding it in that cocktail dress."

"Don't tell me you've been following the Subway Vigilante?" I smiled.

"Yes, Jodi, I have."

So he did know my name. What a night. I couldn't be happier. Yassir had digressed, tsk-tsking our government's inability to protect its citizens, touting the safety and order of his city. "I've left funds on the credenza. One more kiss?"

We kissed deeply, and then he was gone, back to his life, wherever and whatever that was. Naked, I walked to the credenza to collect my cab fare. I thumbed through the bills three times to be sure: $1,000 cash, slightly more than cab fare. The night of freedom and pleasure, had, in fact, become my first trick.

Chapter
Thirty-nine

Even now, I'm not sure if I would've spent the night with Yassir if he'd offered me the money up front. But it doesn't really matter in the end, because I had. True, I wasn't so naïve as to be *completely* surprised at the transaction. There was something so intoxicating about the anonymity of it all—the lascivious pleasure happening behind closed doors. There was a tremendous excitement in living out the fantasy without getting caught. It tasted delicious on my lips, until I realized that taste was fluid left behind by some Arab hotelier I'd never see again.

Then I felt shameful and repulsive, like that little girl who'd gotten caught by her father. The irony was that after he caught me, I became invisible to him. Suddenly I was filled with contempt for all the men like Yassir who thought that little girls didn't count for more than cash on the credenza. I threw the money on the bed and started jumping on top of it like a madwoman, laughing and laughing with spite. The little girl didn't need anyone. She would fuck the world and everyone who dared to underestimate her.

★

Soon after, Monika returned to the city. She said she'd had enough of L.A. and that she missed walking, although as long as I'd known her, she'd never been much of a walker; she always took taxis. I had the sneaking suspicion she came back because I told her I'd become a tart.

So began the process of shedding skin. It was easy enough to take pumice to body.

"There's no talking me out of it," I insisted. "I'm telling you, it's what I want. I've been having this inner dialogue with myself…"

"Inner dialogue?" Monika interrupted. "You mean like Freud? He was a complete misogynist cokehead, you know."

"What I mean is that I'm tired of living in a state of denial and playing the good girl who never gets what's coming to her. This is Manhattan for chrissake. Everyone else is having the time of their lives. Why shouldn't I?"

The sun had tanned her impossibly pale skin, and she'd shed about ten pounds. Her hair was golden and cut evenly so it fell in soft layers upon her shoulders. Sunshine agreed with her. And so did time away from the combustive clamor of the city. "I've only been trying to tell you that since, like, the night we met. But I guess you had to figure it out on your own." She lit a cigarette with a fancy onyx lighter. "That's partly why I left. Sometimes, I felt like I was taking care of a child. But I never thought you'd grow up and turn tricks." She sighed. "I've never brought someone in before," she said, opening a bottle of cava. The cork flew across the room. "Oh, shit. After as many bottles that I've popped, those suckers still get away from me." She poured two flutes and put on a captain's hat, acquired along her travels. "I don't know how I like being your madam, although any worthwhile courtesan starts out with one."

"Who was yours?"

"A fabulous Italian who called herself Lucia," said Monika, sipping her bubbly and fingering the brim of her hat. "She owned a bordello in the city; the last I heard, it's still around, though she sold her share years ago and moved to Ibiza."

"You worked at a whorehouse?"

"God no! Too much risk and for the fraction of the pay, though I did start out at her house—answering phones. That's how I learned the business, talking to these men: screening them, flirting with them, getting to know exactly what they wanted without flat-out asking. When I was ready, Lucia taught me the art of the out-call. She liked me too much to make me one of her girls. Besides, she recognized my potential. Not everyone can finesse an out-call where the girl is completely protected and accounted for. There are several steps before you even leave the house." As much as she said she didn't like the idea of bringing someone in, there was a pride with which she spoke about tricking that made me think otherwise.

She kept on talking. All of a sudden, the memory of Monika's bloody, broken face popped into my head. Then, as she must have, I developed selective amnesia and finished my drink. "And of course," she continued, "you can't have out-calls without your own client base."

I nodded. She stared me straight in the face.

"I'm sorry about Alex, Jodi. What she did was nasty. You've a right to feel the way you do, and don't listen to anyone who says otherwise. I just never thought a woman like her would screw a woman like you. But I suppose that's what people do."

I smiled coyly. "Isn't that what you bank on?"

"The game is ugly. But life is ugly. It's not some fantasy; it's the complete opposite of it, really. That's why we put so much effort into making things look beautiful. You're an artist, Jodi. I mean, really an artist. I know you are. I shouldn't have left you alone to handle your career. Any good artist can't handle their career for shit. I admit, it's a bit messy right now, but your career isn't over. It *can't* be."

I sighed. "I know it."

She smiled. "Good."

"But," I sighed, "I need a break. Everything just got so heavy. I want to make art, not play some game."

"Darling, everything's a game. The trick is to know it and

outsmart the opponent—which wasn't exactly your strong suit." She placed her hand on top mine, and immediately, I became warm inside. It was like I had the old Monika back, and things felt safe yet thrilling all at once, just like they used to be.

"So, as a courtesan, do I have potential?"

She was silent. Then, "There's a certain logic to you whoring right now. I believe *whoring* was your term, by the way. You should know, that word will offend most girls I know."

"I'm sorry I called you that."

She laughed. "That's just semantics. What matters is what I get paid. *A lot.* To make it back into the precious art scene that means so much to you, you'll need money. And this time, you'll be self-financed, with my backing; that goes without saying, *but* even my lifestyle has limits."

"You'll help me then?"

"In the name of art. Because I do believe in you. And I don't make bad investments."

"Of course." I wrapped my arms around her and squeezed.

She pried me off.

"Jodi, you must let things breathe. In the meanwhile, are you really prepared to do what I do? I have to know that you can handle it."

★

It was a sunny afternoon when I took a taxi over to TriBeca. I looked for a brick building with carriage doors and didn't stop the cab until I saw it. I asked the driver to sit outside for a minute and wait until I was inside the building.

Before I left the loft, I caught sight of myself in the mirror and couldn't believe who was looking back at me. I'd grown out my punk rock hair, buffed my skin, toned my muscles, waxed all surfaces, plucked, primed, and preened my body to perfection. With the right alterations, Monika had made me unrecognizable from my former self. It was work that required money and know-how. For instance, Monika took me to a Russian woman who braided extensions into my scalp, which were artfully dyed, along with my eyebrows, a light shade of brown. Mom had been right all along: black hair *was* too severe for my skin tone.

For my first date, I wore my hair in pin curls at the nape of my neck and slicked my eyebrows with Vaseline. My heart was racing as I slammed the door to the taxi and approached the buzzer, which was gold-plated and engraved with two butterflies in flight. I was wearing a black pencil skirt, silk blouse, bolero jacket, sheer pantyhose, and heeled Mary Janes.

I'd rehearsed with Monika a hundred times what to say and how to act. It was like memorizing a script. She told me to just keep thinking about the money the whole time and block everything else out: have my mind go entirely blank. Get in and out, just like any other shit job. What I didn't tell her was that I wasn't doing it for the money. I had other reasons. I was filled with a perverse pleasure in feeling contempt for my would-be clients. Remembering the plight of the boy, I could act without remorse. I was a dark little bitch, and it was time to give into those black desires.

I rang the bell.

A bare-footed Asian woman, dressed in a cotton kimono nipped at the waist with a thick brocade sash that formed a bow in back, let me inside. She carried the scent of gardenia. I registered the taxi taking off and the door slamming shut behind me. All of a sudden, I began to question everything. I wondered if I was truly a bad creation, ruthless, calculating, and capable of complete annihilation.

The woman bowed her head and said, "Come in. Take off shoes."

I turned around. The taxi was gone. There was still time for me to turn around, run. But ever since that day I'd seen Monika with the man in the porkpie hat, I'd been curious about what it'd be like to indulge in such recklessness.

"I'm Monika's friend. I've got an appointment with Boris at three."

"Boris," she repeated, smiling. She gestured for me to sit on a small bamboo stool, and to leave my shoes in the rack at the gate.

The woman who greeted me seemed in no hurry to announce my arrival to her employer. I had little experience dealing with maids, so I patiently waited to be given instructions. I remember looking up at the ceiling and noticing a red paper lantern shade, illuminated by a single bulb that hung from a wire. After several moments of silence, she motioned for me to follow her into the corridor.

The floor was incredibly dusty, a detail I found odd considering the impeccable sparseness of the décor. We walked towards the sound of water dripping, what I thought was a fountain. It turned out to be a relaxation tape, my last connection to the outside world.

"Don't be shy," she said with a mischievous grin that embarrassed me. Then she led me into an empty room.

"Sit."

The floors were planked and smelt of cedar. The room was a shell, absent of decoration except for a gong and a scroll hanging on the opposite wall. The maid returned with a stone basin filled with water, a thin mist of steam rising from it.

"So, Boris is a man of the theater. Is he a director, or just a patron?"

The maid looked at me curiously and nodded.

Her face was made up like a Geisha's, painted white with wide red lips and thick black eyelashes. She wore a woven silk headband at the crown of her head, just above her bangs.

"Give hands."

She washed my hands in the basin and dried them with a warm cloth. Her hands were cool and smooth as pebbles.

Just as I was beginning to wonder if my host was ever going to reveal himself, the maid got up and rang the gong.

At the fifth strike, a portly, dark-skinned man with ebony eyes and a pencil-thin Dalí moustache arrived holding a scalding hot Japanese teakettle. The kimono he wore was black silk and embroidered with exquisite gold stitches.

He said something in Japanese to the maid. She bowed her head and exited without looking in my direction. I could hear laughter as she slunk down the hallway.

"I'm Boris." His voice carried a heavy Eastern European accent.

"Jodi," I said, forgetting to give the stage name "Blanche," which Monika had concocted. As he looked me up and down, I felt worried and excited all at once. He seemed pleased.

"Come," he said. "We will drink tea in the tearoom."

He led me to another room, the steaming kettle hissing in his hand. The tearoom was just as sparse as the room we'd just left, with a latticed screen dissecting it.

Besides the screen, the only other furnishing was a rectangular mat, raised off the floor with lifts, where I was told to sit. A larger, more majestic stone basin holding steaming water rested on the floor by the mat, where small teacups had been set up on a wooden tray. Boris poured the tea, set down the kettle, and joined me on the mat. As I reached for my teacup, he grabbed my hand.

"To drink tea, you must wear kimono. There is one waiting for you behind the screen."

"Oh. You want me to put it on now?"

"Yes, please."

His politeness set me aback, especially considering his stodgy build and slipperiness. His voice was low and had a fragility about it.

As promised, the kimono he'd left me hung behind the screen. Red silk embroidered with multicolored thread.

"I see you've left on your stockings. That's all right. Leave for now. I will enjoy to watch you take them off. It surprises me that a woman wears stockings in this heat." Amused, he smiled. "You can drink now."

"Thank you."

"You like it, yes? Then I am glad. You know, I keep the hall dusty because I like to wash my visitors' feet. You don't find that strange, do you?"

"No."

"Good. But one thing troubles me. Because you're wearing these stockings, your feet have not collected my dust."

"Well," I began, "you can wash them for me anyway. My feet get hot and sticky in these stockings."

"Ah, yes," he said. "Your feet are filthy and require me to wash them."

"That would be very nice."

"Tell me to wash your feet."

"Wash them. Wash…"

He interrupted, "Do not look at me when speaking. Now take off the stockings."

Then he touched me for the first time.

Cupping my foot, "Beautiful feet. Size seven, yes."

It was not a question, but rather an appraisal.

"Toes are symmetrical, well kept. Look at this freckle here on the pinky. Don't look, please don't look. If I say look, I don't want you to look."

I turned away. "You better scrub my dirty toes." I started to feel unsure of what he wanted from me.

"Relax. Relax your foot. Yes, like that." He stretched my foot out toe by toe over the stone basin. "Now I will wash your feet in my *Tsukubai*."

With one hand, he held my foot. With the other, he raised the ladle and poured on the warm water. His hands were still filmy. I imagined it was his maid who was touching me, and the feel of her pebble-like fingers on my skin. He took great pleasure washing my feet. The process went on for about fifteen minutes. When he was done, he said, "Your feet were dirty. I can never drink tea around such vile feet. If you noticed, I haven't had one sip."

"I'm sorry they were so dirty."

"You should thank me because now they are clean."

I thanked him, understanding: he wanted to be dominated but also remain in control.

"Drink your tea. Don't let it cool; that would be wasteful of you."

"Of course, thank you," I said, pouting my lips. "But you haven't touched yours yet."

"I'll drink it, but you must stir it for me. There's still warm water at the bottom of my cup."

Certain I knew what he wanted, I thrust my big toe into his teacup. He moaned with pleasure.

"Now lap it up!"

As he brought his mouth to the cup, his lip grazed my toe.

"What else can you do with your foot?"

"The question is: What else can you do to my foot."

"Oh?"

"Start with the freckled one. Tease me with your lips…that's right…give a nibble. That feels so good. You make me feel so good."

"Look away!"

I had been looking away. I kept repeating, "You make me feel so good."

I could hear him touching himself, slowly at first, then faster.

"Jodi," he called.

I felt like an amateur for giving him my real name. He wanted me to look at him now. He was lying face down on the mat, nude. "You've got me so excited. I will finish, and that's not so easy of a task," he said. "I'm not as young as I look. Do you know what I want you to do?"

Silence. Then, "Climb on top, and trample me."

Tearing open my robe, I climbed atop my host's fleshy back, and let the kimono fall to the floor. It was a thrilling feeling being naked with this complete stranger, and I noticed a subtle tingling sensation between my legs. I was aroused, a fact that surprised me. Faintly at first, I trampled until I found my stride, and then went at him with unbridled force.

I couldn't help but go here: just as the figurative artist would argue that her work is about much more than the body's imitation, the abstract artist would argue that his work is about much more than unmasking the disguise. What I was making with this john was something else—exactly what remained to be seen.

As soon as he came, I hopped off. He dealt with the mess and I fumbled with the sash of my robe. Together, we shared a moment of awkwardness.

After he dressed, he invited me to sit against the wall with him so we could finish our tea. The look on his face told me he had enjoyed our time together, that I had pleased him.

He said, "I practice the Japanese aesthetic of *wasbi-sabi*, that celebrates the beauty found in decay and impermanence."

My host rose and bowed, and told me his maid would pay me well. With no further gestures of intimacy, he said, "The principle behind the Japanese tea ceremony is that each encounter in life is unique," and departed.

In the taxi back to the loft, I opened the envelope the maid had given me and counted my money. I rolled down the window, and thumbed through the wad, watching the hundreds scatter in the wind. The driver didn't say a word.

Chapter Forty

At seven years old, I get my first marriage proposal. Daniel Holden pops the question. We're equals, Daniel and me. Equally novice, equally inquisitive, equally playful. I say yes. We consummate with a ceremony beneath a lacy maple, its mauve leaves tickling our foreheads, and we stare into the white sunlight together, where a future awaits us. We are the best of friends.

Married life is simple. We ride bikes down a gravel road and find a patch of smooth ground. There, we go fast. I rise out of my seat, legs pedaling with the force of a whirligig beetle. I experience the sensation of speed. Also, I experience what it's like to navigate the world with another.

When I tell Mom and Dad, they aren't pleased by the news. Instead, they frown and say in the same breath, "You can't wear that skirt, and you can't ride your bike anymore after 4 p.m."

They are always taking things from me.

Without my bike, I become an unappealing bride. Daniel soon loses interest. I take this rejection to heart, and blame Mom and Dad for their unfair rules.

We find each other again, Daniel and me, ten years later, the fall after Isla dies. As devastated as everyone was, the town has forgotten about her by now. The school board decides the vandal must have been a Lion, the wide receiver from our rival team who Isla was dating. It's an easy answer, and everyone seems to be relieved that the source of trouble is not internal.

Daniel and I go out a couple times. Now he's called Dan. Daniel, or, God forbid, Danny, won't do. I'm trying things. We hold hands in public; kiss. That is, after all, the healthy thing to do. He's terribly excited to touch my body, which gives me a rush. This is normal for a seventeen-year-old girl. But there's something else. I let him spank me.

Bare bottomed, bent at the waist, I thrust my head between my legs so I can watch him hit me. Sometimes he retracts when I watch, so I try to keep my eyes closed. The thud of his hand on my flesh stings, and I tell him to hit me harder. Harder. Until my skin is pink, raw. The whole while I keep thinking: "I've been a bad little girl!"

I don't need to know his reasons for complying. Or for agreeing to use the brush next time. I don't care if this is why he likes me. It has started. It starts with an innocent tap on the bum in the hall on the way to the science lab.

The attention is a shock at first. But I can get used to this: I can love this. When he hits me, I know immediately what I need, and I want more and more. Daniel—to me he's Daniel, he'll always be Daniel—is a willing participant. He doesn't ask questions.

"I want you to spank me."

"Bend over."

There are probably no more than three separate episodes, but they are instantly imprinted on my memory. In this chasm, these episodes multiply. I'm left with a series of afterimages that in time become reality...

He doesn't ask questions because he *does* without *wondering.* I think about how we used to ride our bikes; it was his idea to speed down that gravel road. I never would've thought to do so on my own. I was seven. I *did* without *wondering,* too.

"No, this isn't like that other game we used to play. This is something different. I want you to spank me. That's right. I'm telling you! Play along or else."

We're flirting with a watered-down, suburban version of sadomasochism. Penance for Isla is generic psychology. But

Daniel doesn't know that I was the vandal, the one who spray-painted that word on Isla's locker. How much I wanted to be her—until she left me, when the separation stung so badly I couldn't face it. He doesn't know about the boy. How I lashed everything out on him.

All I'm really after is a pleasant burn, just enough to feel present, for me to feel *there*.

It's exhilarating to feel that smack.

Then there's the pleasure of Daniel to consider, and I feel it slipping away. Spanking me won't keep him satisfied for much longer. "You can touch me, too," he keeps saying, his wet tongue in my ear. I feel the urge to vomit. That's not what I want at all. I'm clearly and utterly on the receiving end.

I put him off and rub my own ass, trying to titillate him. "Hit me!" I say.

I make up an excuse and get out of there quickly, before he can try anything else.

Everyone else may have forgotten her, but I haven't. I can't. Isla has triggered something, and I understand for the first time what it means to be connected to myself. I'm connected, even if I don't fully understand the consequences of my actions.

Relieved to be away from Daniel, I find myself in front of Isla's house; their yard is overgrown. Amid the neighborhood's manicured green, the brusqueness of foliage signifies that some tragedy has befallen this home.

The "For Sale" sign confirms the gossip. Isla's mom has moved down to North Carolina; her husband is packing up the house, and will join her when it sells. So I'm not surprised when I see him through the window, stacking boxes in the hallway.

There's a moment when we look at each other. The look is intent and locked in. I'm very clearly there: a girl with a pixie cut on her bike—around Isla's age, he must think—on the other side of the screen door.

The man in front of me was inside of Isla. He has bushy, arched eyebrows and a strong, prominent jaw. I wonder what it's like to kiss someone with a jaw like that. He's wearing a flannel shirt ripped off at the arms and a black bandana tied around his head. Suddenly, I wonder if I've put myself in danger. The law's definition of what he did to Isla is rape. It's curious, how such distinctions are drawn. I think alternately what it's like to kiss that mouth, have his sharp tongue inside me, a tongue different from Daniel's boy's tongue—a man's tongue; disgusting. The carelessness that he displayed towards Isla's life is unforgivable.

Inside the house, I hear a country rock song playing on the Hi-Fi. He turns and walks away.

When I get back to the condo, Mom's in the kitchen taking a pie out of the oven. She never bakes.

"I'm here," I call, out of sight.

She opens her arms. "My baby girl, I'm so glad you're home."

I let her hug me and try hard to hug her back. Then, suddenly, I'm not trying anymore, I'm holding her; I'm holding on for dear life.

My premonitions are right. Daniel loses interest. It's a familiar feeling that leaves me sick, vacant, and floating. I vow then and there to stop grasping for attention. Some people, people like Isla, are made to be fawned over, and others—it's easier for us to be invisible. Daniel leaves me for his ex-girlfriend, who gives blowjobs and wins him back by burning his initials into her chest with a red-hot razor. I'm stung with that awful, familiar feeling again; there's no way I can compete with that.

Chapter Forty-one

He recklessly plunged into me. It was the part of sex I enjoyed the most—the moment of penetration. I had everyone else fooled into thinking I was doing this for the money. But I couldn't fool myself. If only they knew what I knew, that I needed to feel complete, that somehow being filled up would repair the void.

"And what is it you do?" he said.

"You mean besides fuck?"

"Yes."

"I used to make art."

"I know some people in the art game. I can introduce you."

The perfect john was the one who allowed me to escape completely while in his company. I knew the art world itself was riddled with whores. People were bought and sold all the time. Except no one ever acknowledged this explicitly.

"Oh, thank you," I said. "Now, unbutton your shirt."

★

The first thing Monika told me was not to get carried away with the money or attention.

"It's just a job," she said. "And you better have learned by now, people will take whatever they can from you, so it's up to you to set limitations. As you do it, and the *more* you do it, you'll come to appreciate the power to set limits as one of the perks of the job. Tonight, you have a date with a fourth-year law student—that should tell you all you need to know about him, but he's easy where it counts, not much work in the sack. 9 p.m., Stanhope bar."

She paused for a moment, and it began to make sense. All this time, she'd been torn. She hated herself for the lifestyle she'd undertaken—why, I never really knew, and I couldn't ask now. Especially because I couldn't stop now, not when I'd just gotten into the game. And I certainly couldn't stop her. I had to figure out what it was that entrapped her, held her tight like a vise. We weren't the same, but I had to get into her mind, inside her self. That suddenly seemed to be the key.

✴

"Hello, Harry," I said, pulling up a barstool at the hotel bar.

"You must be Jodi." I'd decided to use my real name because— I don't quite know why—it felt more exciting that way.

"So wonderful to meet you, Harry." I pulled in the stool, resting my alligator clutch on the bar. The bartender immediately brought me a glass of water. I smiled, making limited eye contact.

The first thing Monika taught me was to repeat the john's name upon initial introductions, and not to sit down until he did. This way, I could establish control subtly. She also told me to ask for the envelope, "before you forget" or "to get it out of the way," if he didn't offer it up right away, but most johns did. Harry was no exception.

"Thanks so much, Harry." I slipped the envelope into my clutch inconspicuously. "What are you drinking?"

Step two: Be overly gracious when accepting the envelope. Otherwise, it might seem like you thought there was something sordid about it. And never forget you were in a hotel bar.

A courtesan creates an atmosphere where she runs the show, and she does it because it's fabulous all around. Gratefulness conveys a party mood. But you couldn't be *too* grateful. It was important to act like you *expected* to be treated like a lady, even if you were a lady of the night. The type of men we saw got off on taking a lady out—otherwise, they would've gone to any trollop off the street. Whore, courtesan, maybe it was just semantics. Nevertheless, when it came to business, there was a distinction. And one we were happy to live by: Monika and I were courtesans.

"Scotch and soda. Can I get you one?"

Step three: Strike up relationships with hotel bartenders. For instance, at the Stanhope, Mike would pour us flutes of apple cider that he'd pass off for $400-a-bottle champagne. That way, he made a bar profit off johns, and we stayed sober. In case we wanted a real drink, the code was to say, "You're not out of Veuve like you were last week?"

"You're Monika's friend," Mike said to me, laying down a cocktail napkin. "She called earlier telling me to expect you."

"Hello," I said. "Beautiful night."

"Just got more beautiful." Then to Harry, "Top shelf for this girl, right, Sir?"

"Oh, yes, of course."

"Why, thank you," I said, remembering how Monika taught me that gratefulness conveys a party mood. "Don't think your fine manners go unnoticed."

We sat at the bar for a couple rounds. Harry was a young guy, very attractive, rich, charming, easy to make conversation with, and I couldn't figure out why someone like him would need to hire an escort.

"Would you like to show me your room?" I said after three ciders. I would've been better off with real champagne. But Monika was insistent that I stay sober when I went out these first couple times. The out-call was an art form unto itself, and I was a novice, just learning techniques that Monika had taken a lifetime to perfect.

There was an inherent sense of adventure in meeting a new client, making him feel comfortable, giving him my whole, undivided attention. In my French-cut lingerie and false eyelashes, I gave myself wholly to the performance. That was the most fun of all: I could hate him, and he wouldn't have a clue. Nothing I did was authentic, which meant I didn't have that nagging feeling of need.

It was exhilarating to fulfill the fantasies of so many men. And not all of it was about sex; in fact, that was just one portion of it, and a small one in contrast to the rest of the work I had to do. A lot of the men I saw liked to think of the time we spent together as real dates. That was oddly nice for me, too, I suppose. I'd missed out on all of that in high school, when everyone else was dating and that's what you were supposed to do… When I got to college, all people did was hook up; they never went to hotel bars, four-star restaurants, or nightclubs that made the society pages.

Take Harry. I could tell he preferred to think of me as a date rather than a call girl. When we got upstairs to his room, I unzipped my dress and let it fall to the floor while I stood there in a transparent white corset and lace stockings.

Harry got flustered and spilled the glass of water he'd poured himself. Ugh. Not exactly the reaction I was hoping for.

"What's wrong?" I asked. "Don't you like?"

"Oh, yes," he said, reaching out to touch my waist with the tip of his finger. "This is very nice. It's just, can we talk for a minute?"

"Sure," I said. "I bet there's a robe in the closet. Would you mind checking for me?"

"Of course." He did, and sure enough there was a white terry cloth robe, which he handed to me. I accepted with a smile.

"Thanks, Harry. Hey, let's have something from the minibar. If you don't mind, that is."

"Not at all. My father pays for everything," he said.

"Ah," I said.

He made two drinks, and this time I joined him in a scotch and soda.

"You seem like such a normal girl," he said.

"I am a normal girl." I sipped my drink, and then giggled. "Well, kind of. Actually, not really. I'm just a girl."

"I have a girlfriend," he said. "She's pressuring me to marry her. My father is opposed to it, and, well, I hate to say it, but that seals the deal for me. Does that make me a terrible person?"

"Of course not," I said, leaning into an armchair.

"Well, look who I'm asking." He took a swig of his drink and then said, "Sorry, that probably came off as rude, and I didn't mean it to."

Didn't he know this was a performance? That thought never crossed his mind, the arrogant son-of-a-bitch. Gently nudging his glass from his hand and placing it on the coffee table, I said, "Do you love your girlfriend? I mean, what are we talking about, here?"

"She's a good girl. Gorgeous, sweet, the type who's always partying but when you get her sober the next morning all she wants to do is make you French toast and talk about how she wants to have four babies—two boys and two girls. I'll bet you're not like that."

"If you had me around the next morning, I wouldn't be in the kitchen."

Harry rushed to the armchair and ripped the robe from my body. He carried me to the bed and flung me down. We laughed and I realized: *I was getting good at this.*

He wet my neck with kisses, undid my corset, and kissed my thighs. As he went down on me, my mind drifted off to the Greek myths Mom read to me as a child. The gods were always punishing women for being overtly beautiful and sexy. But that's what real flesh-and-blood men wanted, a beautiful, sexy woman to covet, just like Dad's centerfold.

At first, I'd envisioned dangerous desperation, Charlotte Rampling, topless in suspenders and a general's hat. But Harry and I were just two ordinary people buying into the anonymity of the night together. I switched positions and got on top and rode. I didn't think about anything except the smacking sound our two bodies made as we moistened the bed sheets with our perspiration. Of course, I couldn't help but think about the money. And my contempt for the bastard.

After the shower, I was drying my hair when Harry came up to me and grabbed me from behind. "Thanks for a wonderful time, gorgeous."

"You too."

"You know, I've got an idea, and I'd be willing to pay you to help me out with it."

"Oh?" I said.

"I'm supposed to have dinner with my girlfriend next weekend and then take her to the opening of a new club in TriBeca. If I stand her up, she's bound to come looking for me at the club opening, where I will be with you. A big scene will ensue, and she'll break things off with me."

"You want me to be your hired gun?" I smiled like I was getting away with something. I suppose everyone wants to feel like he or she's getting away with something; it's a real dose of self-esteem. I mean, look at me. This whole thing was an exercise in what I could get away with, without anyone suspecting a thing. God, I could be ruthless, but I had to know that part of me, I mean *really* know it, in order to truly let it go.

Whoring will teach you everything you need to know about human nature. You get to see the underbelly, what no one else wants you to see. This one guy, he got off on being dominated. He dressed up in women's lingerie and heels and told me to make him feel like a woman. I told him to shut the fuck up and give me all his money. He got insulted, wanted to call the whole thing off, and I was like, honey, you said to make you feel like a woman.

Monika got a real kick out of that one. "What a creep!" she said.

We were in the bathroom, sponging off our makeup with amazing, lavender-scented wipe-aways that erased everything from mascara to spooge.

"I don't know," I remarked. "It kind of makes me feel sorry

Jill Di Donato

for him. I mean, having to go through life hiding something that turns you on and shames you at the same time, that's pretty annihilating."

"Jodi, he's a freak-popper."

"He wears a wedding ring. What do you suppose would happen if he told his wife what he was into instead of going to see a prostitute? I mean, if she really loved him, wouldn't she understand it's just a fetish?"

Monika tossed her wipe-away into the garbage. "Would you?"

✶

Bernard Goetz was on trial for attempted murder, and the city was struck with crime-fever. Experts testified to record-high felony rates; officers on horseback started manning corners; ADAs made press trips to tenement housing projects that for years had existed under the radar of normal society.

The trial had nothing to do with me, but there was nothing else to read about in the papers. Bernard Goetz was everywhere and nowhere; I mean, face it, no one really knew anything about Bernie, let alone the teens he shot.

America was focused on Manhattan. Everyone was watching to see what would happen next. If it wasn't crime, it was AIDS. I watched, too. On TV, I'd seen this story about a Park Avenue physician who'd smuggled in experimental drugs from Mexico to treat his patients. "It's taken our president three years to even utter the word," he said. "When an epidemic is festering." The doctor risked losing his license to go public with his story. He said he was fighting for a cause.

Monika and I had a cause of our own. We sought out girls to party with. It wasn't really me so much, but Monika, who thought it'd be a good idea to meet some new people. Our life together wasn't like before, and both of us knew it could never be like that again. Then, all of a sudden, she couldn't stop talking about this circle of girls she knew. "Fabulous courtesans— with the best contacts in town. They're such a tight-knit group, when you first meet them you're going to think they're exclusive as hell. But once you get to know them, they're all really nice."

"You know them?"

"Not really. But we should *get* to know them."

I couldn't fight her. In a way, finding women who did what we did made the whole thing more of a party. So I met these girls who pleasured for profit and cinched their waistlines with gilt belts. Girls who played squash and kept cupboards stocked with cash and rich foods low in nutritional value. It was the sisterhood, and the safety it offered, even if it was just an illusion, that drew Monika and me in.

"I like her," the head courtesan said immediately about Monika, *oohing* and *aahing* over her Bulgari watch and the way she tied her Ungaro scarf around her head.

Monika was an expert at introductions and initiations. I, too, was learning how to make myself appear valuable.

Most of the time, a woman named Blaise held get-togethers at her place. She was the circle's arranger, and had a huge apartment in Union Square with no doorman. Her floors were covered in white shag carpet, and there was a little sign upon entering that instructed guests to kindly remove their shoes. You knew you were in the company of exquisite women by the rows upon rows of high heels.

There was Lela, who barely moved her lips when she talked. Everyone said she looked just like Bianca Jagger. She and Jo Danna were tight like Monika and me. Jo Danna was a perky blonde from Kennesaw, Georgia who played up her accent, especially around men. Sapphire was the only black girl in our circle. She wore her hair in a Black is Beautiful afro and had more ego than any of us.

The circle taught you how to calculate everything and that everything was subject to calculating. Once you were in, you shared phone numbers and liaisons with the other girls, who were happy to set you up with so-and-so, introduce you to so-and-so's friend. That Monika and I could be counted among women with such power gave us a rush of adrenaline. I became beautiful by association, a step above mere beauty.

Each girl got into escorting for a different reason. We didn't talk about those things when we'd get together to perform our beauty rituals and drink pink martinis. The circle fueled our goddess energy. No madams and no strippers. No girls who thought they were above us or could pull a power trip.

The one exception was Blaise, head courtesan. She was older, in her mid-thirties, and worldly. All the girls looked up to Blaise, and she knew it.

To defray the costs of beautification, each girl in the circle offered up her expert service on our weekly maintenance nights. Sapphire did our nails with a filing kit and mini-buffing machine that came in its own suitcase. Jo Danna had a natural talent with hot wax. It was relentless, the way she'd go after every last hair. Monika got us into the most exclusive sample sales so we could spend a hundred dollars on a pair of white go-go boots under the impression that we were getting a bargain. Lela was the pharmaceutical hookup. My talent: I could tell each girl in exactly what position her body looked best and what bedroom poses were most flattering. "Girls like us must know every inch of their body intimately," I said with authority. They adored my suggestions for subtle maneuvers that would alter their entire silhouettes.

"Oh, Jodi, how'd you find a way to make my ass look even better?"

Even in the most wretched situations, beauty of some sort is always possible.

Chapter Forty-two

I can't figure out the void that Isla's left behind. I'm running a lot, in the woods, on the bike trail. I don't know which is stronger, the feeling of guilt or grief. The battle between the two is always with me. So I run. Under the gravel, the earth is firm beneath my feet, and I'm thankful for that. A crow caws. I look up. The sky is filled with birds. It's windy, and my ears are uncovered. I don't feel any need to protect myself.

School will be ending soon for winter recess, and I've just sent away my college applications. Right now, an institution is deciding my fate. I want to build up a sweat. It's hard because of the wind and the December chill. Then comes the sound of something behind me. Faintly at first, but enough for me to register that someone else is out here. It's the sound of tires on gravel, the hum of a motor. I turn around and can see a pick-up creeping towards me. It takes a minute for me to remember that cars aren't allowed on this path. Whoever it is must be a stranger.

I pick up my pace and my legs begin to burn. A stitch forms in my side, and I try to rub it out. This slows me down, and I can hear the truck gaining speed. So I run with the cramp, trying to make up for lost time. It's no use; the truck will soon overtake me. I look behind me and can see a boy wearing a baseball cap behind the steering wheel. He has his foot on the pedal and is headed straight towards me. Panic sets in. He's about to run me off the road. I don't slow my stride. The door swipes my side, right where the cramp is gnawing away at me, and the driver honks his horn loudly. The sound is deafening and, reflexively, I put my hands over my ears.

The near collision has run me off the path; in the slippery dirt, I lose my footing. I'm panting, out of breath. Then I notice the truck has slowed. The driver's window is rolled down. His pace is deliberate. I look around. There's nowhere for me to go except the woods, but that would look strange, like I'm scared, and I don't want the driver to know that yet. I don't know for sure that I'm in danger. The plates are local. My heart beats faster. But it's just some guy, I tell myself, playing a prank. The best thing for me to do is return to the path, keep jogging like nothing's wrong.

In seconds, I'm running again, careful to stay out of the truck's direct path. I find my stride again. In the rearview window, the driver is watching me. I take a deep breath as I pass him. He sticks his head out the window but I keep running like I don't notice. Then, all of a sudden, he speeds off ahead of me. His tires have left an imprint in the gravel, and as I look down, I realize that my pants are torn and my calf has been badly scratched and is bleeding. It's okay, because all I feel is relief. The truck is no longer in my sight. I know for sure that when I passed him, I heard the driver laughing.

Shut up. Shut up. Shut up.

Chapter Forty-three

Harry convinced me to come with him to the opening of *Lola*, a supper club in TriBeca. I was conflicted about playing a part in the deliberate humiliation of Harry's girlfriend, even though his guilt had made him exceedingly generous with my compensation. That was Harry in a nutshell. He paid everyone and got what he wanted. Me, for three pre-paid hours, anyway. In addition, he had a hired entourage and made sure his girlfriend would "find" his booth by slipping the bouncer several bills.

I felt like a shit. Public jilting was so Middle Ages, not to mention humiliating. I couldn't stand the thought that courtesans made a mockery of ordinary women. After all, what we were was anything but ordinary. It wasn't a fair competition by any means; normal women didn't have a chance.

Monika reminded me, "It's just a job. Don't moralize."

"I know," I said. "When you think about it, though, it's for her own good. I mean, the creep was never going to marry her."

"How do I look?" asked Harry, sitting back in the booth.

"Dashing."

"I know, but I mean *how* do I look? Describe me."

Utter fucking idiot. Lower than plankton in the scheme of the universe. I furrowed my brow like I was mulling it over, and said, "Like an Ivy-League crew champion with Lou Reed edge. Is that what you're going for?"

"I guess."

I picked up a menu. "Are we ordering?"

"Oh, yes," said Harry. "Great idea. What should we get?"

"Champagne, oysters, and strawberries are a given. We'll start with those. But we should get something messy, hard to eat."

"Go on…" he said, intrigued.

"I have to think about this." I put down the menu.

"Would you care for anything else?" asked the waiter.

"We'll have the bone marrow."

"Yes! Fantastic idea, Jodi. You sure *are* clever."

I did my tart's duty, rewarding his compliment with a caress on the forearm. He responded with a case of goose bumps and said, "Apple crumble, can we get apple crumble?"

✶

I knew from the expression on Harry's face when his girlfriend, soon to be ex, arrived. I turned my head and registered a blond, thin, birdlike woman, dressed to the nines, wearing fake blue eyelashes. It took a minute, but I recognized her. It was Ostrich Girl from that night at Mudd Club when Vincent Frand fucked me in the toilet. I gulped. Of all the women in New York… Obviously time hadn't done much to improve Ostrich Girl's taste in men. Despite that, you had to hand it to her. She was an impeccably preserved woman who drew the attention of all the men in the room. Unfortunately for her, she was solely focused on one. Harry was now pretending not to notice her, and he poured me a glass of champagne. He stuffed a strawberry in my mouth somewhat violently. I had to pity him; he was clearly nervous. Even worse, he'd remain his father's patsy. If he wanted everything that went along with being Harry, possibly everything *there was* to Harry, then he'd remain chained to his father's whims. He'd never amount to anything more.

"Harry," I whispered. "There's a woman heading straight our way. Is it her? It must be."

"Yes," he said. "Just play it how we talked about."

Ostrich Girl stomped up to our booth and threw her purse on the table. "I knew. I knew you were seeing someone else. But you weren't man enough to say it to my face."

Harry clutched my knee. His hand was shaking.

Ostrich Girl went on. "You made me promises. You asked me to believe in you. What was that? Just lies? Why bother? Why go through all the trouble of lying and covering things up? Why not just be up front? Why not be a man?"

Sure, Ostrich Girl wasn't stupid. She knew exactly where to hit her man.

Poor Harry exploded. He sprang up and lunged for her, but I pulled him back into the booth with a quick arm and calm voice. "Harry, sit down. You *are* a man. You're my man."

That seemed to do the trick. Poor Harry broke into an easy smile and relief flooded his entire body. I hated to face the truth: this was such an ugly business. And yet it paid my bills. "Bastard!" screamed Ostrich Girl. She grabbed her purse and ran into the powder room.

As soon as she was out of sight, Harry sat down and gulped a glass of champagne. "Terrific," he said. Then he motioned to one of his buddies at the bar to have a car come pick him up right away. He turned to me and kissed me. "Sorry," he said as he pulled his mouth from mine. "That is to say… I couldn't have imagined it going any better. Thank you." He reached into his pocket and pulled out an envelope.

"We're all settled up," I reminded him with a smile.

"This is a tip. For handling it with extra class. You really came through." He touched me on the arm and then followed his buddy, who'd already procured a vehicle.

I stood there for a minute, taking it all in. Instead of leaving, I followed Ostrich Girl into the powder room. She was at the mirror trying to fix something. Her tears had messed up her eyelash adhesive, and lashes dotted her cheeks.

"You!" she screamed when I entered the powder room. "Now that you have Harry, can't you go piss somewhere else?"

"Listen," I said. "There's something you should know. I'm a whore."

"No shit," she said.

"No, literally. I'm a call girl Harry paid to come here tonight and make you think we were together now so he didn't have to break it off with you himself."

"That coward. I can't believe I wanted to have his babies. Do you ever start thinking, *I'm going to be that 'end of the line girl'—the girl who's it—the finale*? Well, don't ever start thinking that, because men, they can always sense it, and that's when they drop you. Just when you get comfortable."

"Here," I said. "Let me help you with your eyelashes. I kinda have this trick to get the adhesive sticky again. We can reapply the ones that fell off."

She didn't seem to care. "I just don't understand. I mean, on the surface, things were going so well between us."

"His father…" I began.

"Oh, I knew Daddy wasn't fond of me. What a complete waste of time. And now I'm a year older."

I didn't know what to tell her.

"What's the trick? For the eyelashes?"

"Come here," I said. She brought her face close to mine and I told her to close her eyes. I worked my magic with acrobatic fingers, a lighter, and some Vaseline.

"Be very still," I whispered. "Okay. When that dries, reapply mascara." I paused, then said, "You know what you should do? Give it a day or two. Then go to him and tell him you forgive him. Tell him that you understand he's been going through a rough time and that indiscretions happen to lots of couples and they live through it." I opened my purse, fumbled through my makeup bag, and handed her a tube of mascara. "Say it makes them stronger in the long run, and they can go on to lead happy lives together. Tell him he's worth it—*so* worth it that you want to work it out. He couldn't be serious about a new girl; convince him that he's being rash. Then say you're willing to do anything to work it out. And then..."

Ostrich Girl flashed a smile. "Then it's payday. Wow, smart," she said. "You're not a complete bitch."

"I know you don't recognize me," I said, "but we've actually met before. A while ago, back at Mudd Club. You were dating Vincent Frand, and he was sitting with me at a booth when you came over."

She studied me real closely. "You know what? I do remember."

"You remember me?"

"Sure," she replied. "I'm not bullshitting you. You actually became somewhat successful, didn't you?"

"For a minute, I suppose."

"I remember Vince being pissed he let you get away."

"Really?" I said. "What an asshole."

We both laughed. She let go of my hand.

"So, what happened? How did you go from being an art-ist—I mean, that's got such a serious ring to it—to becom-ing... Never mind. You don't have to tell me what happened. It wouldn't matter anyway, because I don't follow art people any more. Wall Street, like Harry. That's where it's at. No shame in taking money from stockbrokers; after all, their whole lives are based on the 'exchange.' Only, they fuck over entire nations." Then she snickered. "And you want to know the funny part? Just so women like us can take money from them. So I guess we're all part of the greater scheme of things. That must be what you tell yourself, huh?"

She made a lot of intelligent points. I remembered the tip Harry had given me. When I offered her the envelope, she blinked her eyelashes, which were fully dried and intact now.

"Why would I want your money?" she said, looked at me dismissively, and left the powder room without another word.

Chapter Forty-four

It was a night's work. Not just for me, but for the doorman who rang me up to a bachelor's apartment and signed me out exactly one hour later. I was learning to rely on the tacit consent of people who inhabited the murky, in-between spaces when I wasn't fully engaged as a whore but wasn't fully free from it, either. It was like somehow we were in it together, me and the cab driver, who, from his rearview mirror, watched me reapply lipstick and count my money. Here I was, on my way to meet Sapphire, who'd arranged a get-together with two of her favorite clients at the Hotel Emile, but to him, I was just another fare.

"Would you mind pulling over?"

Sapphire was standing on a corner a couple blocks from the hotel. She wore a cream-colored pants suit with a pair of navy stiletto heels that elongated her dancer-like frame. None of the girls in the circle dressed in any way you'd associate with a hooker. They were all too elegant, with their posh suits and satin blouses. Everything was very prim and sleek—except for the high heels. Those were the one tell.

Casually slung on her arm was a Gucci doctor's bag, from which she drew a gold-plated compact. She checked her makeup unapologetically, paying no mind to the two college boys who nearly tripped over each other as they passed by. Some of the girls thought Sapphire was pretentious, but that was exactly what I liked about her.

I rolled down the window. "Want to get in?"

"It's such a nice night. I thought I'd enjoy the fresh air and walk."

"Fine," I said, glancing down at the four-inch heels that pinched my toes. "I guess." As I paid the driver with a twenty from the stack he'd seen me counting earlier, I decided that a permeable membrane separated my two worlds, and it was my job to constantly shift between them both. "Keep the change."

Come to think of it, the process reminded me of casting molds, meticulously concerned with the imprint.

We walked for a block or two, me teetering, still getting used to the skinny heels.

"My feet are killing me. How do you do it? You make it look so easy."

"Easy? Darling, nothing is easy. Look at these heels. You think my feet aren't in agony like yours? Sure, you can think about what kind of sadist designed these contraptions that cost me three hundred, or you can ignore the suffering. Just pay it no attention; that's how I do it. Mind if I have one of your smokes?"

"Sure."

We stopped in front of an electronics store so I could light her cigarette. In the window, a television display caught our attention. The program being broadcast was a talk show with a smartly dressed host and wretched-looking guests.

"That's a nice set," Sapphire said. "Would you look at the size? I wonder how much that would run me."

Couldn't she see what I saw? The gaunt faces staring at us from behind the glass. The sunken eyes, the sloping cheeks. Behind the glass, behind the faces, there were real people who felt compelled to go on national TV and tell their stories.

"The sign says $385," she said. "I bet I could talk the manager down."

For some reason, she really began to piss me off. It was like she had no conscience, no cover story, no depth. As I lit a cigarette for myself, I needed to know the facts behind the faces and how they were connected to me, because, strangely, I felt connected to them. I closed my eyes, but the faces wouldn't disappear. It was like they were trying to tell me something, and I just had to figure out the message. Sure, I felt pity like everyone else, but I wasn't like the doctor who risked everything to treat the terminally ill.

"Wait. Don't you want to know what they're saying?"

"Who?"

"Them!" I screamed, pointing wildly with my cigarette at the screen in the window.

"Darling, I think you've lost it. I don't see anything."

"On the TV."

She squinted and raised her hand to her brow.

"Look," I said. "Look at their faces."

"Now I just don't understand why they have to show AIDS on TV. It's enough to put me off that set, and I was seriously contemplating buying it."

"I bet her friends won't even have her over. She's totally alone."

"Have you seen this?"

I shook my head. "I don't want to see any more." I started to get nauseous. It had been ages since I'd felt that gnawing in my gut. But all of a sudden, I started feeling like the more I fucked the world, the less gratifying it became.

"Then why are we standing here? We have places to be."

We walked in silence to the Hotel Emile. The whole way, not one word passed between us, and I could tell that the faceless images had gotten to her too. In a sense, we were all disposable.

In the lobby, the concierge tipped his hat and Sapphire flashed her smile. Those faces floated up, all sick and bloated, like hot air balloons.

"Wait here," she told me.

Even if she were mad, she looked like a million bucks. It wasn't enough to look beautiful and sexy. We also had to look like we were part of the furniture.

A minute later, she returned with a look of annoyance on her face.

"What's wrong?"

She shrugged, tore the message to bits and deposited the mess into an ashtray. "There's been a change of plans."

"Now what?"

"Now, I sit. Can I have another cigarette?"

I opened my purse, rummaged in it for some change and pulled out a quarter. "Help yourself. I'm going to call Blaise."

Without thinking, I turned to her and asked her if she wanted to go out with me on another call.

"Fantastic," she said, but she shot me a look that said she was mad as hell.

I turned my head and noticed a man seated nonchalantly on one of the couches. He'd been eyeing us and listening the whole time. Immediately, I was ashamed, not because this man knew what we were up to, but because I'd inadvertently placed Sapphire and myself in danger of being exposed. Even though it was a simple, careless mistake, I'd showed my naiveté. We got up and walked towards the hotel bar. Here, survival depended on my ability to navigate the gap between worlds seamlessly, and if I failed to do so we might face unspeakable danger.

"On second thought," said Sapphire, "I think I'll stay here and have a drink. Look! They carry my favorite brand of rose champagne. You know, I heard some girls talking about a call today that would be just perfect for you," she said in a hush tone. "Call Blaise and ask about Arnold. I believe he wanted to see someone tonight."

"Thanks, Sapphire."

"Don't mention it."

*

When I arrived at the Four Seasons, I strutted into the lobby like a power woman. I immediately located the elevator and waited patiently until it came, avoiding all eye contact. Just as Sapphire said, Arnold was looking for an immediate appointment, and Tamara, the girl who answered the phone, didn't even have to get Blaise. I checked in with her from a payphone on the street before I entered the hotel.

"Room 16 G," she'd said. "He's a firm two hours."

"Thanks, Tamara. Oh, is there anything special I need to know?"

"Didn't Sapphire... oh, never mind. No, nothing in particular."

"Okay," I said, hanging up. I checked my compact and was a little excited to finally get to see the inside of the Four.

When I arrived on the sixteenth floor, I found the G line easily and knocked on the door. When it opened, I gasped, and immediately felt shamed. The man behind the door, Arnold, was covered in purple lesions. Uncontrollably, I gasped at the horror of seeing a body in such a state.

He'd noticed my reaction, but pretended not to. I felt like the lowest of the low and mustered the kindest smile I could and said, "Hello. I'm Jodi, I'd love to have a drink with you."

Arnold, a gaunt Hispanic man dressed in a baggy tracksuit, invited me in and took a seat on the sofa.

"I can tell from your face that the girls didn't tell you about me. I will be the easiest call of the night. Money's on the credenza."

"Thank you," I said, collecting the envelope. It was bad form to count the money in front of a client; you did that in the bathroom when you went to freshen up.

Arnold continued, "I just want you to lie with me."

"Oh?"

"In bed. With your arms around me."

"Should we have a drink first?"

"Help yourself," said Arnold. "I'm fine."

I looked at him and thought I might cry. But that's not what he was paying me for. "If you're not drinking, I don't need one either."

We looked at each other in a way I hadn't with any of my johns—or anyone, for that matter—in a long while. Inside, I was trembling; my eyes welled. It was the hardest thing in the world to hold back the fury I felt at universe and its unpredictable injustices.

Then I offered him my hand, "Shall we?"

He rose, cupped my fingers gently, and, as if he could feel what I was feeling, said, "You're a strange one." He took back his hand to cover his cough. "But I like it."

When we arrived at the bed, I asked if he wanted me to take off my clothes.

"No, it's not necessary. Just, if you could…"

"I know," I said, kicking off my heels. "It would be my pleasure to hold you."

He started crying. I wiped his face and he wiped mine. "It's been forever," he began, "since someone offered to hold me."

We settled onto the mattress and Arnold curled like a fetus, my arms encircling his slightness. I knew Sapphire thought she was teaching me a lesson sending me to Arnold, and she wanted me to be pissed. But for the first time on the job, I let myself fall asleep beside a john. And it felt like how home is supposed to feel.

★

One evening, Lela brought in a woman journalist who wanted to write an exposé on us, under assumed names.

"You've got a marvelous place," the journalist told Blaise with a nervous, complimentary smile.

It was true. Blaise's apartment was spectacular, every detail attended to. On its own, the size of the apartment was striking, but beyond size, it served as a backdrop for an impressive antique collection. In the parlor, illuminated by the dazzling light of a crystal chandelier, sat a mod egg chair, a claw foot rocker, a Danish mini bench, a Betty Martin table, and a serpentine console. She liked to mix and match eras, and pulled off the mélange exceedingly well. Always present were vases of fresh flowers—usually tulips, usually white.

"There's no reason for adoration of beauty to be limited to the canvas," said Blaise, offering the journalist a seat. Blaise had huge, almond-shaped eyes framed by sweeping brown eyebrows. Everything about her face was over the top. Big nose, lips, and forehead. She made the scale of her features work for her, and I rarely offered to do her makeup like I would for the other girls; her face was always impeccably styled and beyond suggestion.

The journalist sat down and crossed her legs. Regardless of what we told her, there were things she would never know, like how Jo Danna's friend with the teardrop tattoo suddenly stopped coming around; how Lela refused to eat anything but handfuls of hard candy; how the host at Tabac would grab girls hard on the ass whenever we came in with a date; how Blaise's neighbor had purple lesions on his leg. Everyone in the circle was always coming and going and everyone knew everything: who'd been touched as a kid, whose father was a drunk, who used to model, who had the clap. These things inhabited the world of the unsaid.

The questioning began. I think we were a little curious to see how this would all play out. It wasn't every day that girls in our profession got to brag about their business expertise, branding genius, or marketing plans. Even though secrecy was sacrosanct, the urge to tell everyone what we were getting away with would creep up from time to time.

"Is that an Etruscan vase?" the journalist asked.

"A gift from a royal Saudi family. I had it on the coffee table, but then some john used it as an ashtray."

To show her appreciation for the interview, the journalist opened the conversation with the offer of marijuana cookies. She wore a lousy suit, cheap shoes, and a knock-off bag. Knock-offs were worst when you tried to pass them off as genuine, which, by the way she propped up her purse on the seat cushion, she was trying to do.

Sapphire shook up martinis. Monika and I lounged on our stomachs on the soft white shag, slightly chilled from the blast of the air conditioner. Monika looked completely at ease. After all, this was her world, and I was just along for the ride. And what a ride. When Monika was with me, I was so much more at ease. The faces like the ones I'd seen that night on the TV screens with Sapphire ceased to haunt me as much. I kept wondering what that meant—and if I would ever be an artist again.

"Just act natural," said the journalist. "Pretend like I'm not here and talk amongst yourselves."

"That won't give you a good article," said Blaise. "We wouldn't be sitting around telling each other stuff we already know. If you're going to do this, we're going to have to tell you what it's like."

"How we're living the life you've always dreamed of," someone said.

It would've taken a lot more than pot cookies to get us to open up. We'd already decided the article would be a terrific endorsement of the circle, and like Lela kept saying, "There's no such thing as bad press."

"I was thinking," Monika began. "Isn't it just the same thing as seeing a psychotherapist? Where you're paying someone to divulge your secrets to, someone who won't judge you, make it about themselves."

"My analyst would love that one," said Lela.

"Skin-to-skin contact is nice. It's important," said Jo Danna. "I think if everyone had skin-to-skin contact every day, the world would be a different place."

"Hmmm," I began, breaking off a piece of cookie. I liked to eat the cookie piece by piece, draw out the high. "You should make that your platform and run for president."

"Yeah, you're a lot hotter than Gary Hart."

"Imagine that," said Jo Danna. "Only, I'd feel like such a fake."

Sapphire wanted to know: "You mean to tell me what you

do every night is not fake?" She set a tray of candied martinis on the table. "Cheers, ladies."

"When I meet up for a date, they like to talk a little, have a cup of coffee or tea. I use the real me for that," said Jo Danna. "How couldn't I?"

"I hate how people think you've got to be fake to survive this business," said Lela. "Or more fake than anyone else who uses a persona to do her job. I mean, what about secretaries for big-shot CEOs or waitresses who bring us service with a smile? How come no one accuses them of being fake?"

"Everybody is fake," said Sapphire.

"I think what Jo Danna's saying," Lela began, "is that people act like we're not smart enough to figure out the difference."

Jo Danna went on, "I feel one hundred percent confident in saying that my dates genuinely like me because I'm a charming girl and they know I'm a good person. That's because I'm the real me around them."

Of all the girls, Jo Danna was the most beautiful. Her features were perfectly symmetrical, her body well-proportioned. She had a physical quality that emanated a sense of ease about her appearance. She was also comfortable with being pretty in a way that wasn't haughty or ostentatious. That's not to say she didn't preen herself like the rest of us. Her strawberry blonde hair was long and shiny, and she treated it with a mixture of beer and honey to keep it that way. Still, she didn't need as much upkeep. She never put on a pound, never had complexion problems or hair growing in undesirable places. Of all the girls, her look had the most universal appeal to men. Lela was flashy, Sapphire sophisticated, Blaise had foreign mystique. But Jo Danna had naïve beauty that made her approachable and soft.

"It's still *work*. I hate it when people think the money is so easy," said Sapphire. "But that doesn't mean I can't enjoy my job, that I can't enjoy the sex. Sometimes I do, sometimes I come."

"But the feminists, they don't want to hear that," added Blaise.

"They don't want to hear that you choose this work because you like having sex or you do it because you like rebelling against society. The only reason that is only slightly acceptable is to do it for the money." She paused, sucked the cherry in her martini, and looked around the room pretentiously. "Because you want to become filthy rich."

The journalist scribbled furiously. Blaise allowed her a moment to catch up.

"With some clients," said Lela. "I'm thinking about the money the whole time. Those are the bad times. Times when I have to close my eyes and do everything I can to stop myself from screaming and yelling. But with most of them, it only lasts an hour or two."

"And then all that's left is the money. Beautiful, faithful, sexy cash," said Monika.

Other girls agreed. "Exactly. You forget his face."

The faces... the images hit me straight in the gut. I burped, and, with an embarrassed hand, covered my mouth. What a lie. I remembered all my john's faces. I was different from these beautiful creatures, Blaise, Jo Danna, and the rest of them. There was no use denying it anymore. A part of me connected with the bloated faces of disposable humans—distorted people, the people I saw on TV that night with Sapphire, the terminally ill. Walter.

The journalist looked up from her pad and asked, "How do you negotiate money? And how much do you charge?"

"Well," Blaise explained, "the cardinal rule is always business before pleasure. And none of the girls in the circle see dates for less than the going rate."

"Which is?"

"Look around you, darling. Let's just say, more money than you'll ever see in your life."

I noticed the journalist slightly bite down on her lip, but she handled the truth with sheer professionalism. "Probably," she said. Then pressed, "But I want to know how much a date with you costs."

"And I'm not going to tell you. Not for any other reason than it's bad business to go around publicizing those kinds of things. This topic relies on mystique. Let's move on."

The journalist wrinkled her nose and nodded. I finished the last bite of cookie and was feeling nice. It must've been made with strong weed. I wondered where this mousey journalist, with her crimped hair and ski-slope nose, got such top-shelf stuff, and how she even met Lela in the first place. "In relationships," I began, "at work, people were always fucking me over. I mean, people who are supposed to care. With dates," I went on, "the exchange is so open, so unambiguous. The funny thing is how the feminists insist that this is what's damaging. That this open exchange is the source of all the trouble—that somehow it makes me damaged goods. But sometimes, you know, men are just looking for someone to get drunk with and to listen to them. In a way, it's comforting to know that people still feel things, that they give their hard-earned money to feel things."

Blaise nodded and looked at me like I'd said something wise. You could tell she wanted to make sure the journalist knew that she picked up on everything.

"Do you need a break?"

"No," said the journalist. "Keep going. Tell me how you got into doing this."

"Every woman has got her reason," said Sapphire. "How did you get into journalism?"

"In the seventies," Blaise began, "I was living in Amsterdam. I had a chance to move into an apartment in the Red Light district. At the time, I thought that it sounded exciting but also terrifying. My family was very strict religiously; I had a very sheltered background."

"Hard to believe *that*," said the journalist.

I felt sorry for this journalist. Here she was, theorizing a world she'd never in a million years be a part of. She was that kid, hopelessly trying to fit in.

"I was in Europe," Blaise went on, "backpacking on holiday,

when some Dutch friends offered me a cleric position at their newspaper."

When she said that, Monika and I shared a look that I regretted immediately.

Jo Danna noticed and didn't like it. She said, "What's that to you two?"

"Oh nothing," Monika said. "Just that I think she meant to say a *clerk* position at the paper. A cleric…"

"That's what she said."

I tried to think of something to interject. I didn't want the girls thinking Monika and I thought we were smarter than them. They were very sensitive about that kind of thing. Monika didn't understand fine nuances like I did, no matter how many times I reminded her not to pull any attitude. "It's just that I was seeing this guy," I said. "An editor at the *News* who was a complete asshole. Monika's sick of hearing about it, so it kind of became a little joke between us. That's all."

"Not that guy again." Monika did know how to smile and touch the person she was talking to on the arm at all the right moments. "Ugh. But we're being so rude; Blaise was talking."

"That's how I ended up in Amsterdam, anyhow. The Red Light District sounded so taboo. It was the seventies, though, and sex work had more of a bohemian feel to it than it does now. When I first moved into the neighborhood, the most difficult thing was figuring out how to respond to the women working behind the windows. I'd be on the way to the store to buy a quart of milk, and there they were in their lingerie and wigs. I didn't know if I should look or turn away. Working at a political newspaper, I didn't want to give them the impression that I was ogling them like monkeys in a cage. But then, it was stranger not to look. After a while, if I happened to catch the eye of a working girl, I'd smile and she'd smile back. Of course, the longer I lived there, the more of a fantasy it became to be behind those windows."

"I know you tried it, Blaise."

"Yeah," agreed Lela. "Didn't you rent a window?"

"I did it once, only briefly. For like a couple days. But I tell you, I learned all I needed to know from those couple days."

"Show me what you learned, Blaise," said Lela, hiking her skirt up and taking a seat on Blaise's lap.

"Oh, please," Blaise said, giving Lela a nudge over to a hard white sofa. "I'll tell you one thing: I hated it when women just rushed by, pretending I wasn't there when we both knew I was. It was like, who do you think you are, acting like I don't exist?"

The sound of Blaise's voice reminded me of something sizzling on the stove. It had a maddening effect that I kept telling myself to ignore. When I focused on her voice, the faces of the sick and dying would float up into my brain and make me feel weak in the knees. I couldn't let any of the girls notice. I turned to Monika; I missed when it was just the two of us.

"Back to what you were saying about this being a high-class activity, Blaise," said Sapphire. "I think that is what we bring to it. Because we bring class and refinement and handle the situation in a very glamorous matter. Notice I said glamorous, not delicate, because it shouldn't be delicate, I mean, we're dealing with sex, and who wants delicate sex? But when you hear stories of men who are disrespectful, fault those cheap girls. Addicts, alcoholics, and aliens who work the streets and suck guys off in parked cars. You tell me: is there not a difference between *that* and a sober, healthy girl who serves espresso and can appreciate the value of insider trading?"

That's the thing with escort work, and we all knew it. Even if it was strictly referrals, sometimes a client would be too drunk, or maybe you just didn't like the way he looked. We didn't talk about these things. As wonderful as the circle was, there was an intense pressure to keep up the idea that everyone was always having a fantastic time.

"I charge a lot and I'm not going to lower my rates," said Blaise. She got up, and we knew that the interview was over. It was time for the journalist to go.

We stood up, one by one, and shook the journalist's hand.

Of course when the article came out two weeks later in *New*

York Magazine, the journalist had betrayed us, with some lame title like "Circle of Sin" or something like that. She made us sound pathetic, like a pack of beautiful but desperately delusional airheads.

"That pretentious shrew!"

"She's just jealous," dismissed Blaise. "Couldn't you tell she was one of those jealous types?"

Someone said, "This is so New York. It happens to everyone I know."

No one talked to Lela for a week. Then we forgot about it. That was the beauty of the circle, and the fact that the journalist had missed it made me feel triumphant. It was simple, really: when a group of people forgets a shared event, it ceases to exist.

Chapter
Forty-five

Then came a powerful yearning to be different from all the other girls. Still, I took my clothes off for men—for money, just like the other girls. Wasn't hooking just an artistic exercise that began the night I slept with Vincent Frand? I'd be different because I'd think about things: how abuse and pain can be authority figures, and that the only way to let go is through art. Was I delusional?

What I'd done to Isla was unforgivable. And the boy, he'd taught me the horrible truth that part of being fully human is that we abuse others.

"Good evening, Gabriel."

He opened the door to his suite at the Carlyle. This was our first time meeting, and I was surprised at how tall he was. He must've been at least 6'5," over a foot taller than me. He had very broad shoulders and an athletic build but was dressed like a dandy.

"Jodi, come on in. I'll fix you something from the bar."

Not only did he look like a dandy, he acted the part, moving about the room gallantly.

"If you don't mind," I said, "I have to make a phone call."

"Extension's in there," he said, pointing to the bedroom.

"This will only take a minute."

I'd gotten in the habit of checking in with Monika, though she rarely reciprocated the gesture. "Everything's fine," I'd say. We'd worked out that if there was a problem, I'd say, "Things are groovy."

"Everything's fine."

"Okay, girl. See you later."

Conjuring the most aristocratic walk I could imagine, I found Gabriel at the bar with two Manhattans.

"Why don't you show me the suite?" I said. "But first…"

"Oh, of course," he interrupted. "Where are my manners?" He handed me the envelope, and I tilted my head towards him with an inviting smile.

I nursed my drink for a half-hour while Gabriel got comfortable, having two more and telling me about himself. He was a professor (anthropology? Or was it sociology?) who taught a class at Eugene Lang College every Tuesday and Thursday evening. Then, when I could tell he was ready, I put a hand on his knee and locked him into me with my eyes.

"You have to kiss me now, Professor."

It didn't take long for Gabriel to become a regular, booking me twice a week on Tuesday and Thursday evenings. However, it did take me a while to figure him out—what he desired, what made him tick. The first time we'd met, I'd played the schoolgirl, assuming this would be the natural turn-on. He'd been polite, and obviously, as he became a regular, was pleased with my services. Later on, he told me that the last thing he wanted to do was reenact who he was in real life. What I was to him was a regular distraction. His fantasy was to get as far away from the university as possible. I started to think Gabriel and I had a lot in common. I even started to think of him as a friend. Of course, I couldn't tell this to Monika or the other girls.

I tried leather panties and a horsewhip. I did a 1950s pin-up, then a '70s stewardess, until one Tuesday night he told me to come next time as I would in normal, everyday life. To a call girl, this is a contradiction in terms, but I understood that his fantasy was not founded on reality, and that what he wanted was the girlfriend experience. Some johns were the worst communicators, and would never answer when I'd ask, "Is there something special you want?" Maybe they thought they were being polite; some were awkward; others probably just didn't know what they wanted. Or maybe they didn't know how to say what they wanted. I enjoyed, in a sick, compulsive way, the road to unraveling each john's secret desires. The things he wouldn't dare do with any other woman. And then, one day, Gabriel completely surprised me.

I entered the suite as always, dressed in flats, my faded Calvin Klein jeans, and a taupe cashmere sweater, little makeup. This, for Gabriel, *was* Jodi in real life—how she presented herself to others. Johns always wanted to feel like they were special, though this manifested in different ways. For Gabriel, he wanted to be the john who saw the "real Jodi," and when I "acquiesced," he took it as an emblem of his uniqueness.

"You look nice, Jodi. Can I make you the usual?"

"Certainly," I said. With a kiss on the mouth, "Nice to see you. How was your day?"

"Not bad," he said. "Though the traffic uptown nearly gave me a hernia. This is for you."

Accept the envelope. Smile. "Thanks, darling. I have a feeling tonight will relax you. I think I might have a shower after our cocktail. Care to join me?"

"Actually," said Gabriel, voice suddenly shaking. He was nervous about something.

I sat down next to him, placed my hand on his wrist. "What is it?"

"There's something I'd like you to do for me tonight."

"Oh?"

He took a long gulp of his drink, crossed his legs, and took his hand from mine.

"Ever since I was a kid, I've always had a liking for this certain stench. Lately, it's all I can think about. I've never felt such an intense arousal, but I don't know what it means…"

I stopped him. "You don't have to know what it means; that's besides the point, the point is that it's a turn-on. Tell me what it is and..."

"I want you to take off your clothes and lie on the bathroom floor so I can piss on you and smell the wonderful smell of my urine."

"I'm happy to." I swallowed. "If that's what you like."

He looked away.

I got undressed slowly, hating myself. It's true that pleasure and pain are inextricably linked, but I didn't know how much longer I could go on playing the whore. Contempt for johns was getting boring. That contempt was really a smokescreen for the contempt I felt for myself. That, too, was getting tired. The pleasure I took in humiliating the boy, the pleasure I took in annihilating everything that Isla stood for—it was time to put all that to bed.

✳

"What can you do with that dangly thing?" Isla asks.

"Dangly!" I laugh. "Dangle, dangle that thing."

The boy looks confused. "What do you mean?"

"You heard her," I say. "What's so great about that thing between your legs?"

"Come closer," Isla directs. "Show us."

"Don't want to," he says. "I want to go huh-ome. I want to go home."

"Oooh," taunts Isla. "The little baby wants to go home." I laugh.

"We said come closer, or..."

"Or else!" Isla picks up a big rock and makes likes she's going to throw it at him. "Listen to what she told you to do."

The boy approaches until he's standing a couple feet before us.

"Closer!" we shout.

He obeys.

"Now touch it," says Isla. "I want to see what happens when you rub it and play with it."

"Isla," I say. "What are you doing?"

But it's too late. She has the boy's little pink worm in her mouth and she's sucking at it furiously. Tears stream down the boy's face like he doesn't understand what's happening.

"Now you, Jodi," she tells me, thrusting it my way. I open my mouth and copy how Isla did it. She gets behind the boy and grabs his buttocks, shoving his thing deeper down my throat.

"You're hurting me!" the boy screams. It's unclear if he's talking to me or Isla, who has a manic smile as she digs her nails hard into the boy's behind, hard enough that blood trickles down his legs.

I feel myself gagging and then a putrid taste fills my throat. The milky sludge oozes down either side of my mouth. Isla wipes my face and throws the stuff into the boy's hair. She laughs and laughs.

The boy screams, "I hate you!"

"Come on," she tells me. We mount our bikes without looking in the boy's direction; he doesn't exist any more.

I'm here and she's here. Together, Isla and I are allies. We begin the ride out of the woods and find the trail with ease. Momentarily, I think about what we've done.

"Could you really get his mom thrown out of the country?"

"Of course not," she says. "I was just messing with him. Don't worry, Jodi. He won't tell."

Isla and I ride past the bog, past the lake, and soon we're on the road that connects our two houses. The wind picks up. I'm shouting a little, "Are you sure he won't tell?"

"Of course not. Trust me."

✱

Belly-up on the cold tile of the Carlyle bathroom floor, nude, and drizzled head-to-toe with warm piss, it occurred to me that fetishes might just be ordinary after all. No living with them; no living without them.

"If people like us ruled the world!" Gabriel yelled as he came into a warm washcloth he'd readied for the occasion. "Jodi? Are you crying? What is it? Was it something I did?"

I wiped my face and turned away. "Oh no, of course not. I'm having a fantastic time."

After that night, Gabriel started seeing Jo Danna. He never booked me again.

Chapter
Forty-six

There's an explanation for ruthlessness; it's called frustration. We're all more human than not. The sadistic drive comes from the need to dehumanize. I learn this today in AP Psychology.

The three of us—Isla, the boy, and I—are tangled together. I don't want to be guilty. I want Isla to forgive me. I focus on the teacher's chalk making words on the chalkboard: "Prefrontal cortex: hub of executive functioning, mediator of moral conflicts."

Today the news is good. An acceptance letter arrives all the way from Vassar College in Poughkeepsie, New York. I can't believe it. Full scholarship. First thing, I call Mom at her job, and she goes crazy screaming. Her co-workers must think she's nuts. She comes home with a bouquet of flowers and a cake from Salvino's bakery.

"Baby girl, I'm so proud of you! Not that I doubted for one minute that you would get in. But a scholarship to Vassar College." She pauses to wipe her eyes. "These are tears of joy, you know."

"I know."

So it's decided. This will be my way out. There's a silence between Mom and me, like we've both realized what this means.

Then, "Shit, you know what? We're all out of soda. I forgot to stop—my jacket's still on, I'll just be a minute."

"No," I say. "I'll go. You get dinner ready, and besides, you've done so much already."

She hands me her car keys. "Just look at you."

"You're not going to be corny all night, are you?"

"And what's wrong with that?"

I roll my eyes. "I'll be back."

I'm halfway down the driveway when I hear her call out, as if she can't help herself, "Be careful!"

I take a roundabout route because I want to drive. I want to feel the motion. This is happening, I think. Vassar College is still an abstraction, but soon, the abstract will take form, and in the process, I will escape from myself, the now. Isla, if she were here, would be proud of me; she would be happy. But she's not here. Her form has become an abstraction.

I'm locking the door in the parking lot of the 7-Eleven when I get the sense that someone's watching me. Uneasy, I turn around slowly, casually. It's a boy, about my age, wearing a baseball cap and sitting in the front seat of a pick-up, window rolled down. I stare at the truck. It takes a couple moments to register that it's the guy who ran me off the road that day when I was jogging. By now, he's gotten out of his truck and is standing in front of me, inches away from my face.

"Excuse me," I say quietly, trying hard to sound indifferent.

He doesn't budge. Now my heart begins to flutter.

"You don't recognize me, do you?"

His voice is deep. I look around the parking lot. A mother is buckling her kid into the backseat of a station wagon; two teenage girls, underdressed in cut-offs and sweatshirts, are smoking cigarettes by the partition; a man carrying a bowling ball bag walks towards his sedan.

"Huh?" he repeats.

"Um, no," I say. "Don't think so."

"Think harder."

I pause, make it seem like I'm thinking. "I don't know."

"Do you run on the bike trail by the lake?"

I nod. "Yeah, sometimes. Why?"

"I've seen you running."

"Okay. Well, I've got to get to the store. My mom's waiting on me."

He thinks this is funny. Laughing, "Oh, is your mommy waiting on you?"

Suddenly, my chest tightens, filling with something: shame. I hear, for the first time, the slightest hint of a Polish accent in his voice. He says again, "You don't recognize me, do you? We just got back into town. I spent years in Boston, where my mom had a job with a real nice family. She's retired now." He's taunting me. He knows that I know.

He's grown into a man since that day Isla and I made him strip down so we could torment him. Now, he towers above me. His shoulders are broad, his pecs meaty. The thought of what he's got in his pants, no longer a rosy nub but something sharp and penetrating, sends a chill up my spine.

I cower. There's nothing I can say to make up for what we did. I can pretend I'm someone else, or maybe even that I don't remember, but that look in his eye tells me he's not going to let me get away with that. "We were kids," I say finally.

It's a lousy excuse and both of us know it.

"You wanna go for a drive?" he says.

"I can't. My mom is waiting on me, really. If I'm not home soon, she'll freak."

"I want to take you for a drive."

"Look," I say. "I could tell you I'm sorry, but I don't think that's what you want."

"You're right, that's not what I want."

"Please," I'm fighting the urge to cry. "Just let me go buy a bottle of soda. I promised my mom I'd be home soon."

He just laughs.

The tears are coming down my face. This makes the boy laugh harder.

"I'm sor—rr—sorry."

His laughter deepens, and then all of a sudden he's silent. He makes a gun with his fingers, points it towards me, and pulls the trigger.

We look at each other for a moment until I can't look at him anymore. It's like it would all just be easier if he didn't exist, like Isla.

Then he moves out of my way and lets me pass.

I walk a couple yards in the direction of the store when he calls after me. "I heard about your friend," he says.

I stop in my tracks and turn around.

"How'd she do it? The papers wouldn't say."

"I don't know."

"I bet it was pills. Girls always off themselves with pills. Like cowards."

"It wasn't pills," I say.

"Thought you didn't know."

"I know it wasn't pills."

He's grinning when he says, "You should be careful running by the lake, a little girl like you alone in the woods."

I've stopped crying. I swallow. Now numb. "If you want to take me for a drive, just get on with it already. Let's go to your truck…" I make my body limp and prepare to go with him. "And you can do what you want."

The boy is quiet for a minute, grinning, glaring, fucking me with his eyes. "Nah," he says. "Go home to your mommy."

Chapter Forty-seven

Isn't it funny how the people you try to forget always turn up, just when you think you're done with them forever? Wouldn't you know, I was at Mary Lou's with Monika and Sapphire when we noticed that pimp Syd across the bar. Gone were her body piercings and rocker hair. She'd transformed herself from downtown punk to a 7th-Avenue, champagne-swilling swan. Her manner, though, was still crude. When I noticed her across the bar, she was doing bumps of cocaine off her friend's knuckles. I almost threw up when I saw her. If she didn't exist, all of our lives would be different. I was filled with an arousing hatred.

"Look," I said to Monika. "Look who it is."

"Wow. She looks fantastic."

"That's what you have to say?" I said, kind of pissed. "Come on, let's get out of here."

"No way," said Monika. "We've got drinks coming."

"You know her?" Sapphire asked.

"Not really," I answered. "But she gives me the creeps. I don't trust her."

"Don't blame you," Sapphire agreed. "The nefarious Syd Carpenter. You do know what people are saying about her?"

Her vodka cocktail flashed silver-white in the prism of her hand.

"Stop staring, Jodi. Jeez."

It was too late. Syd had spotted us. Thank God the bar was packed so it would be a while before she and her entourage of drag queens and mediocre-looking girls could make their way over.

I wanted to know what Sapphire was talking about. "What?"

"That she's seeing a man in the Russian mafia, you know, those guys with the pentagram tattoos on their chests and kneecaps."

"So?" said Monika. "I'm sure we've been with lots of guys like that."

Sapphire wrinkled her nose. "I, for one, have not. And no one I associate with, or, for that matter, refer to the circle, has any illegal dealings."

"Go on," I said.

"Well, this so-called Russian boyfriend of hers is a real monster. He lured Mandy Warrick into a room at the Carlyle, but had no intention of meeting her for a date." She lowered her voice. "He told her to get undressed and then burnt her between the legs with a red-hot poker. Revenge because she went out with one of Syd's regulars."

"I've been to the Carlyle recently," I said, shooting Monika a look. "Is this true?"

"Bullshit," Monika said.

Sapphire retorted, "I have it on very good authority. When was the last time you saw Mandy out?"

Monika said dismissively, "That proves nothing."

"I wouldn't trust that girl. I wouldn't trust that girl within an inch of…"

"Monika! It's been forever. How good to see you." Syd swooped in and her long nails grazed Monika's neck.

"You remember Jodi, right?"

"Of course. I just can't believe how posh you two look."

"And do you know Sapphire?"

"Didn't I see you at Johnny Valo's party last week? Oh, who knows! Did you say you call yourself Sapphire? That's exotic.

I'm Syd. Monika and I go way back. She's like a sister to me. My long-lost sister, because I haven't seen her in ages."

"I think I did see you at Johnny Valo's party," Sapphire said. "You were the girl with Peter Gold."

"Oh no, darling. Wasn't me," said Syd. "I haven't talked to Peter Gold since '83."

Sapphire angled her face towards me and said under her breath, "Better watch what I say."

"So," Syd interrupted. "I heard you're all friends with Blaise. Call me," she said, reaching into her purse for a business card and handing it to Monika, "if you ever want to party."

"Still selling acid trips?" I said.

This incited a fit of laughter. She snorted, "Oh, Monika. Your friend is such a riot. I love this girl."

An intense pressure filled my head. I began to envision the faces of all the men I'd been sleeping with. Deans, doctors, a judge, politicians, husbands, some poor old schmuck who'd saved up an entire month's paycheck for a night with me…

One by one, each face became distorted and devilish, growing horns and warts and boils. Noses morphed into beaks, chins into horrendous fangs, eyes into spades that cut you in the deepest of places. I wanted to grab Monika and get as far away from here as possible, but she was paying the bartender for another round of drinks. Someone in Syd's entourage leaned in and whispered into her ear, and Syd began laughing again.

"Nooo way. *That* I can't believe. What a star fucker!" She tossed her double blonde processed 'do and extinguished her cigarette on the bar. Her posse was getting rowdy, dancing to the '70s Italian pop the DJ cranked out of his booth. "Sorry to leave you, all, but I'm expected elsewhere. *Ciao, bellas.*"

"What a piece of work," said Sapphire.

"What's with you?" Monika said to me. "I was just being polite. Do I have to be a bitch to everyone like you?"

"Meow!" purred Sapphire.

"I just don't get why you have to be friends with everybody. Especially people like her," I said. "If it wasn't for her…"

"Okay, girls," began Sapphire. "Are we going to argue about this cunt rag all night, or are we going to party?"

Syd had left behind her vodka cocktail. I couldn't take my eyes from the prints she'd left on the fogged-up highball. Fleeting, dime-sized proof of life.

"I'm not feeling so well," I said. "I have to go home."

*

Lately, I'd been thinking a lot about Walter. His bald, speckled head started floating up behind the faces of johns, behind faces of strangers—the salesgirl at Bloomingdale's who sold me a wrap dress, the pharmacist who filled the prescription for my diaphragm, the bartender who mixed my cocktails. It was his face haunting me, reminding me that I'd known someone who'd had the bug.

Walter had gotten a hold on me and wouldn't let go. We should have been there on the edge of that roof with him. We should have been there to hold him back. I tried to imagine what he saw before the fall: how people can shrink down to the size of a pea, and you can hold them there, between your thumb and forefinger. From this vantage, he'd decided it was the end, his end, that his life was disposable. Sometimes for hours, I'd lie in bed while Monika was out shopping, and I'd think about Walter. Nothing ever came of it.

Then I had a vision. Walter had taken the form of the death figure in the macabre Baldung Grien painting, *Three Ages of the Woman and the Death*, also known as *La Vanité*. The painting is of a woman in the prime of her beauty, admiring her face in a mirror. So absorbed in her reflection, she ignores the world around her: the child at her feet, the forest behind her, the shrew at her side. Even death, given the body of a man whose flesh has been eaten away, cannot get her attention. In one hand, he holds an hourglass above the woman's head. In the other, he holds a scythe. Only in my vision, the emaciated death figure was Walter, and the woman none other than beautiful, talented Isla. A veil hangs over her eyes. Still, she is taken with herself. More than her beauty, she's taken with her earthly existence.

It was about then that I couldn't pretend any longer about the circle. The whole sisterhood thing was a load of crap. How come Jo Danna would be the last girl to get a referral? Some girls would keep clients from her or forget to put her name on the guest list. Even Lela sabotaged her haircut. Subtly, of course, with a smile and compliment: "Oh, Jo Danna, you're so goddamned stunning, and it will grow back."

The other night, we were at Blaise's about to go out, and Jo Danna had forgotten a change of clothes. She asked Blaise to borrow a dress, but Blaise replied, "Sorry darling, none of mine will fit you. I have mine custom tailored," so Jo Danna had to stay in.

And these women were beautiful; they had nothing to feel insecure about. They just couldn't help themselves.

Then Blaise would take you to lunch or for a steam at the bathhouse, make you feel exclusive as hell, talk your ear off about how Sapphire went home with her date. The next night, you'd see Blaise and Sapphire holding court at Mary Lou's, laughing and sharing a bottle like the best of friends.

None of the beef was ever over men. Not in any real, meaningful way. Tangentially, men were involved. Even though they were whores, the women in the circle didn't work for men. More and more, it began to seem like their job was to make ordinary women feel lousy about themselves. In fact, it wasn't that long ago that I'd been paid to do just that. I never told any of them about my encounter with Ostrich Girl. Not even Monika. They wouldn't understand.

*

"Jodi, I have to talk to you." Jo Danna was dressed in a tight black leather skirt with a slit that meant business, an ivory silk blouse, and white lace thigh-high stockings. She pulled me aside from the chatter of the party, where the other girls were busy entertaining.

"What is it?"

"I really need to talk to you about something."

"I'm listening." I poured myself a glass of Pinot and kept an eye on Monika, who was across the room with her hand on some suit's knee.

Jo Danna took a sip of my wine and smiled. "I have trouble with guys, Jodi."

"What are you talking about? You do the best out of all of us."

"That's not what I mean. I mean, with guys in private life. I start thinking about how I can turn him on, how to get him to fall for me, so I start doing things I do when I'm working. And it's so confusing, because I can't tell if I'm having a good time or just pretending."

I took her hand and we sat down.

"I didn't know you were dating anyone."

"I'm not; I mean, no one special. Jodi, are you listening?"

Monika was roaring with laughter, like she was having the time of her life. She and the suit had gotten up from the couch, and were walking arm in arm towards the outdoor balcony.

"What? Yes, I'm listening."

Jo Danna continued, "I did acting in high school, and I was really good. But it's like all I'm doing is acting, trying to get men to play along, and it's like, I'm not in high school any more, but in some ways I still am. You know? I don't want to do this forever."

"Of course you don't, and you won't."

"Don't you ever feel guilty? I mean so many of the men we sleep with are married or have girlfriends…"

"And we're sleeping with them, too. Not exactly, but we're in this triangular relationship with their wives and girlfriends." She looked at me kind of confused. It was like her synapses had stopped firing and the sound of my voice had made an empty echo in her beautifully constructed head. "If it weren't us," I went on, "it'd be some other girl. That's just part of life, Jo Danna."

"I know. I had this date earlier, and we'd already done it twice, but he still had time and wanted to come again, so I gave him a hand job, and he was like, so grateful. It's just…"

"What?"

"Nothing," she said. "You're right. Let's have fun. Let's enjoy the party."

There was a lull in the room when the record stopped. The needle skipped for a moment or two until someone put on a new record. Jo Danna fixed her hair, took in a deep breath, and surveyed the room. "We should probably get back."

"Actually, I'm meeting a date at the suite upstairs."

"That's convenient."

"Lela's friend, Ramón. Do you know him?"

"No," said Jo Danna. "But I've heard Lela talk about him. You better finish that wine; he's not very attractive. But he's all right." She kissed me lightly on the cheek before she got up, and in no time, her hips found the beat of the song.

✶

Ramón was punctual, and for this I was grateful. I hated when they'd make you wait, like your schedule wasn't at all important.

"Coming," I said, as I walked to the door. I checked the peephole. Harmless enough, though Jo Danna was right: he was a troll.

I opened the door and invited him in. Immediately, I could tell something was off. I didn't like it.

He made himself comfortable, at once sitting down on the long, ivory couch. I swallowed hard and tried to put myself at ease. *You've done this plenty of times before; there's nothing to worry about; you're in control.* Besides, he was Lela's friend, and Lela was right downstairs, ready to stake on her reputation that this guy was all right.

He adjusted a thick pair of glasses and said, "Nice. Lela didn't let me down." He couldn't look directly at me when he spoke, but, like a lizard, kept shifting his eyes.

All of a sudden, it hit me. I knew this guy from somewhere.

"So," he continued, "would you like me to pay you now?"

It was Dirty Lonnie, the creep who'd sold Walter dope. He hadn't changed a bit, except now he was Ramón. Who knew? Maybe he still went by Dirty Lonnie, but Lela knew him as Ramón. Just as Mom knew me as an artist and Jo Danna knew me as a whore. I waited a beat or two to see if Dirty Lonnie remembered me.

"Don't you talk? Not that it matters much if you do or don't." He counted out a stack of bills and snickered a low, menacing laugh.

If he were any other guy, I'd be able to stomach a creep like this for the money and the sense of moral superiority. But I didn't like Dirty Lonnie, never did.

"I'm terribly sorry," I said, "but I'm going to have to send myself home. I'm not feeling well."

"Oh come on," he said. "You can do better than that. Sit down; take that off. This won't take long."

"I—I don't want to get you sick. Really, I wanted to cancel earlier, but I thought I'd be fine, but unfortunately I'm not up to it."

"Give me a break."

I had an idea. "Listen, you can still have a wonderful night. Lela's just downstairs, and would be happy to come on up. I'll go get her. And, if you like, I can have her bring a friend."

"Oh?" Suddenly, he was interested.

"Absolutely. I'll take care of it for the inconvenience."

"Well," he said. "Yeah, do that. It's not like you're anything special."

I forced a smile. "No, nothing special. Stay here and I'll send two ladies right up." I returned the envelope. "You can give that to Lela and tell her I'll cover her partner."

There was no contempt; in fact, I pitied him. The contempt was killing me. It wasn't any way to live.

When I shut the door, the sound left a nice thud that echoed as I walked down the hallway. And like that, my career as a call girl was over.

None of this was helping the little girl inside me feel any better. I wasn't getting over any of the guilt I felt about the boy, the longing to see Isla, my impotence to undo what I'd done to her. Maybe there was no getting over things like that. Maybe they just had to sit. Life is sure full of foibles—I was laughing this to myself, and good God, when was the last time I'd laughed? Maybe that sociopath Dirty Lonnie had actually uttered a brilliant truism on modern life: maybe none of us is all that special, and therein lies the beauty.

Chapter Forty-eight

I'd gotten the idea to contact Monika's parents. We needed a vacation. We needed to get far away from the circle and New York City and go someplace exotic and transformative. Monika's mother had to care about her; why else would she send those packages? I found the latest. The postmark on the box read Palma, Majorca. Then I found a map and located the Catalonian island in the Mediterranean. Somehow, I needed to see proof that the place existed. After several hours, I finally tracked down a phone number for the villa on the postmark. The concierge spoke with a British accent. He regretted to inform me that there was no couple by the name of Bond, Monika's last name.

I realized then that there never had been any parents; Monika had lied to me about that too, just like in the beginning she'd lied to me about being a whore. She didn't want me to know she had no one. I suddenly felt very empty.

✱

Isla was gone, but I was here. I had an intense desire to see Mom. Getting a hold of her was tough. She'd opened up her own exercise studio in Danbury, a gym exclusively for women, and was busy all the time. Finally, we arranged a time to meet: at the grand opening of some gym in midtown so she could check out the competition.

"In my day, they said Communism was a disease, an epidemic that spread and brought death. Nowadays, what you kids have to deal with. Your poor friend, Walter, it's terrible that he died so young. Just awful. Must you insist on smoking? For goodness sake, we're about to play a game of racquet ball."

"I'll put it out."

She'd met the manager at some equipment conference, and he'd given her a weeklong free pass and a couple of guest cards. We went inside. As we spun through the revolving doors, I felt like I was entering another universe. The sparkle from shiny dumbbells and the promise of a new, better you kept the facility par excellence. Attendants dressed in white, their shorts matching their veneers, led us to the locker room. It could've been a de Kooning *tableau vivant*.

We found our lockers, and Mom took my purse and cigarettes. "Before I got fit, Jodi, I was petrified of life." She handed me a bottle of water and a towel.

"But then I found the magic of exercise and clean living, and I know I'm doing my best to be the best. And I'm helping others fulfill their potential. I can't tell you how much joy having the studio brings me! It's successful, too; can you even believe it? Did I tell you the Danbury paper is doing an article on me? Spotlighting new businesses, and my fitness studio is one of their features."

"That's terrific."

"I know it's not exciting to you, my downtown daughter. Next to you, I'm small potatoes. Did I mention I'm having them build a juice bar so we can sell protein shakes and shots of wheatgrass?"

"We?"

"Fitness Maven. My friend Judy thinks I should incorporate. So I'm going to see a lawyer about that."

"Good for you."

Really, though, I was happy for her. She seemed so impassioned. Hers was the remarkable transformation; she'd done it all on her own. Maybe that wasn't completely true. Maybe she'd needed me to leave. Maybe my leaving was the catalyst that had gotten things going for her.

"This place is way too flashy for my taste," she said. "But it's good just to see what's out there. Come on, we have to pick up our racquets."

I sat down on the cold locker room bench.

"Do you ever talk to Isla's mom?"

"Jane? God, it's been years. Let's see, that husband of hers moved to the South years ago. Have you been thinking about Isla? Maybe that's what's bothering you. I have to tell you, Jodi, you don't look good. You look different, and it's not just the hair and clothes."

I wondered if the two worlds I inhabited were misaligned, and the whore in me was shining through. Could she tell?

"I actually miss the way you used to look, if you can believe that, the way I'd complain about the punk hair and ghoulish makeup."

"Really?"

"Yeah. I'd always say that about you—that you're a natural beauty. Come on," she said, "you just need to get the blood going. Sweat a little."

Maybe, like a cat, I had eight times to be reborn.

"Do you remember the day I left for college? I had that gigantic suitcase with the wheels that stuck and we had the hardest time dragging it down the driveway. And you were trying so hard not to cry on the drive and we kept playing that one Marvin Gaye cassette over and over. Then we got to the dorms and as soon as you got the suitcase inside I made you turn around and drive home because I just couldn't wait to be alone."

"That's okay," she said. "It was your first day at school—I understood."

"It was rude. I know you wanted to stay and help me unpack,

take me to dinner. Well, when you left I just got into bed and cried and cried. I cried for hours, all alone, scared as hell."

"I cried too. But I was singing along to Marvin Gaye."

"Mom..."

"Jodi, you found your way."

"I want to tell you something. I want you to know that I don't blame you. I don't blame you at all for Dad leaving. For years I did; I don't know, maybe I also blamed myself."

"Oh, sweetie, it had nothing to do with you. I don't mean..."

"No," I said. "It's okay. I know it didn't have anything to do with me. I can accept that."

She took a long drink of water. I went on, "I saw him, you know."

"What? You did? Why didn't you tell me?"

"He looked terrible. And you know, I feel sorry for him."

"Yeah?"

"Yeah. He missed out on so much."

Chapter Forty-nine

The thermometer read 101°, and Randy Valentine was making Bernie sound like a monster. The newest in a string of shock jocks, Randy Valentine was going on about something Bernie had allegedly said to a friend, that the only way to clean up the streets was to get rid of all the garbage, a euphemism for "spics and niggers." Such evidence came out at trial as iron-clad proof of Bernie's guilt. He was an apathetic, racist trash-hater, suspected of burning down a vacant newsstand next to his apartment building because bums would use it to sleep and piss. Witnesses claimed to have seen him sweeping up the mess. They said he'd been obsessed with cleaning up the neighborhood.

Everybody was wondering what Bernie would say for himself when he took the stand. I knew what he was going to tell them. He wasn't born to this; he'd been made. As a child, he'd been teased for asthmatic conditions. His father was a brute disciplinarian who constantly ridiculed Bernie and punished him with a harsh temper. So he got out; went to college, learned engineering. The government hired him to build nuclear submarines, but that didn't last. Bernie couldn't take orders; didn't like being told what to do. He hated how his superiors would cut corners or make ill-informed choices about who to promote and who to leave behind.

Still, there was the problem of his father. Goetz Senior continued to be a hard man to please. Finally, he died. Coincidentally, this was shortly before the subway shooting.

"Would'ya turn that off, Jodi? Enough with this guy. You're driving me nuts with your radio programs and news, if that's what they're calling it."

There was no point in me bringing up what I'd learned about her "parents." And the last thing I wanted to do was talk about the circle or to see any of the girls.

Monika swept the hair off her neck and rummaged for a barrette in her bureau drawer.

"Come on. Let's go out," I said.

"But it's so hot."

"Precisely."

She drew a pack of skinny menthol cigarettes from the freezer, where she also came up with some sunglasses, their lenses frosted over.

I said, "You're so cool."

★

We found ourselves at the flea market, browsing through vintage, sepia-toned photographs, when she came upon a daguerreotype. The image was of a woman at the seashore.

"Ooh…"

"What is it?"

She told me about daguerreotypes, early photographs whose images are exposed directly onto a surface. "There's no negative. No reproduction. Just magic. The image appears by placing the plate over a cup of heated mercury. Then the vapors go to work. Look over here; you can see spots where the mercury vapors condensed because the light was so intense."

It was like old times.

"There are others," I said, fanning through the collection in the merchant's tin. "Other bathing beauties."

"Daguerreotypes were among the first erotic photographs. Look at her." Monika palmed a rectangular portrait of a woman holding a parasol. She wore a bandeau suit with the laces undone, exposing breasts with engorged nipples. Her hair was bobbed and pinned above her ears, and her eyes made up with too much kohl pencil. I imagined her penning a note to her lover: *I've spent the week at the shore.*

"Look at her," I said. "*She* wants to collect all the shells along the shore and bring them home. But she's afraid."

Another. A nude, splayed upon a rock, the froth of the cold sea curling at her feet. Nipples piqued, pointing sunwards. Flesh goose-bumped and young. Fold of thigh covering her mound of pubic hair, perhaps at the photographer's request.

"I miss you," I said suddenly.

"But I'm right here." Then, to the seller, "How much for the whole lot?"

Without her saying another word, I suddenly realized what a game-changer Monika was. She'd let me access this world that, otherwise, I'd never have dared set foot into.

It was at that moment that I got the idea.

✶

Lela and Jo Danna put on these shows. They'd rent out a posh suite at a hotel and sell viewing invitations to a dozen or so of their favorite clientele. Their show involved lots of lace, French cabaret, feathered fans, and strategically placed jewels. Lela insisted they were lucrative, a "free advert," and Jo Danna added, "Men just love to watch us tune each other's knobs."

"Hey Lela," I said one night at one of Blaise's upkeep parties. "When's your next show?"

"We're doing one Thursday night, actually. Why? You interested?"

Jo Danna chimed in, "You and Monika should do it with us. We can double the guest list."

Sapphire was making the rounds with her nail kit. "Looks like you could use a polish change, Jodi."

I wriggled my toes in the furry recesses of Blaise's white shag carpet. She must've spent a small fortune having it professionally cleaned every month.

"Red?" Sapphire wanted to know, holding up a bottle of polish. "Why not."

"Well, get your butt in my chair," said Sapphire. "And Lela, fill up that bowl with warm water."

"Why do I have to do it?"

"Because I'm busy. You want to be here all night, or do you have places to be? Because I have places to go and do *not* want to be doing nails all night."

"Fine, okay," said Lela, grudgingly snatching the bowl.

Sapphire went on, "I'm on the list at The Saint. V.I.P. Some downtown label is throwing a show, which means tons of A&R people. I'm bringing my demo tape because you never know who you might run into."

Blaise said, "Honey, I need a copy of that tape. My friend Halo is the hottest DJ in the zip code. He'll play your cassette at all the top venues."

"I'll get you one," said Sapphire.

I knew she wasn't serious about her music. It was just something to do like a lot of vaguely hip things young social aspirants with an edge did in New York.

"Jodi, these nails need a quick buff while I'm at it."

Monika pulled me aside, "You okay? You've been acting weird all day."

"Great," I said. "I'm just thinking about something. I've got an idea, and I'm going to need you to pull it off."

Sapphire flipped the switch on her buffing machine, and the little pink heads spun round and whirred.

Jo Danna poured herself a flute of champagne. Sloshing bubbly, "You know what *I'm* doing?"

"No, Jo Danna, what is the Georgian princess doing tonight?"

"Me and Lela are partying with Luke Fauchlain. Oh my God, I'm so excited. I swear I'd settle down if he proposed."

Sapphire laughed like Jo Danna had said the funniest thing in the world. "Oh honey, don't delude yourself. Luke Fauchlain isn't the marrying kind."

"Well, we don't have to be married. I'd be happy as a kept woman."

Blaise shook her head. "You know, when I was living in Amsterdam and working at that political paper, the men who ran the show were real bearded Communists. *Free this; free that. Down with the man! Equal rights and justice.* Except they treated all the women like slaves. Not even a thank-you half the time. We had all the bullshit jobs while the men wrote the whole damn paper. They were never up for hearing any of our ideas. My point is that was the first and last time I was a kept woman."

"I don't care," Jo Danna said.

"Even if Luke Fauchlain were the type to get married," Sapphire began. "Jo Danna, do you really think it would be to you?"

Jo Danna rolled her eyes and said, "Never mind you. I've got something special planned for tonight. I know this dentist, and he gave me these tooth caps filled with surgical anesthetic. He said it's like liquid ecstasy. And the best thing is, you can share it with your partner just by kissing." She opened her purse and took out a gilt snuffbox. With a snap of her pearl pink-polished nail, the lid came up and exposed four or five tooth caps.

"Before he knows it, Luke will be madly in love; think I'm the most wonderful woman in the world. One for me, one for Lela. Who else wants one? Anyone but Sapphire, that is."

Sapphire balked, "You think you are going to drug Luke Fauchlain into falling in love with you?"

"Why not?"

"That's messed up," I said.

"Messed up? It's so romantic, like a modern-day love potion."

What was even more messed up was that Jo Danna would probably end up with the guy, too. That was the thing. No one could say no to Jo Danna, even if you saw through her bogus flattery and sophomoric attempts at manipulation.

"I'm always saying there should be more love in the world," she said. "Now, who wants one? I'll consider all requests for barter."

Like harpies, the girls closed in on the kill.

I caught Monika's eye and smiled. She returned the smile and mouthed, "What on earth are you thinking?"

I was thinking that all along, Monika had been my one true benefactor. She may have been flighty—but she'd never changed. She was the constant I needed to balance out the equation.

Chapter Fifty

We'd promised Lela and Jo Danna that we'd go in on the hotel suite with them, and there was no backing out now. Monika and I had been to the suite earlier to work out logistics. It was a risk, and I wasn't sure I'd be able to pull it off, but I had to give it a try.

"You got everything?"

"Yep," said Monika, pointing to a cumbersome shoulder bag. "It's in here."

"Tripod too?"

"All set to go."

"Good," I said. "Now, you're sure you want to do this?"

"We've got nothing to lose."

"Well," I said. "Nothing, and everything."

"And you've set up the meeting with Sam?"

Sam was a friend of Monika's and a video editor whose work, she said, was at "*the* forefront of technology."

She put down the camera bag and handed me the toolbox. "Yes. I've told him all about your idea and he says what you want will be no problem." She paused and smiled. And this was one of Monika's genuine smiles. "I always knew you'd end up here."

"Where?"

"Making something that matters. You're committed. More committed than I could ever be. You're the true artist, though I think these past months you've come to see the artistry with which I live my life. We both know that you're not suited for it, though you had a fantastic run."

"And tonight will be my final performance."

"When the curtain comes up, the whole world is going to check it out—well, New York, anyway, the only place that matters. God, this idea is brilliant. You're going to be a star. I just wish I'd thought of it!"

✱

Later that evening, we arrived back at the suite. Lela was setting up the chairs, and Jo Danna dialed in the proper lighting.

"The show itself will be performed in the parlor," said Lela. "Few props are required."

Those that were remained in the adjoining boudoir. They included rose petals; a long neon light sculpture, the night's obvious phallus; a chest of lingerie; pasties; belly chains; feathered head pieces; and colored plastic gem stones that served a variety of purposes.

We agreed that when it was time, Lela and Jo Danna would open the act while Monika and I served drinks and got acquainted with the clientele. To everyone else but Monika and me, this was just another party.

Jo Danna turned on the Hi-Fi, and we all began to dance a little. Then Lela arranged delivery of a phenomenal dinner, and when it arrived we were treated to oysters on the half-shell, caviar spread on bruschetta, olives, skewers of beef, strawberries, more champagne, and every chocolate dessert on the menu, plus a "soufflé I thought up myself and demanded from the chef. I knew Monika would really enjoy it."

"It's delicious," gushed Monika. You had to hand it to her; she was an incredible performer.

When we were done feasting, Lela called up for the maid, who removed the remains of our meal and, upon Lela's request, touched up the toilet and wiped out the sink.

The maid waited for her tip while Lela rummaged through

her purse and pulled out a crisp bill. Once the maid had gone, Lela opened a case of cigars and let Jo Danna choose which one we'd smoke. She sliced the cigar down its spine with her nail file and filled it with Chronic. We all got stoned and were already giddy from the champagne. Then there was a knock at the door. The first guest had arrived.

✱

He was very good-looking and tastefully dressed, wearing a snug polo shirt, tailored jacket, and loafers. Most of the guys Lela and Jo Danna entertained were wealthy and handsome, the types beautiful women all over Manhattan were vying to date. It kind of made me sick to think of men like that paying for it. At least with someone like Dirty Lonnie I could understand it a bit more. Then, no matter how repulsive he was, it was like you were doing him a favor. These guys, guys like Harry—they just liked to pay for women. It gave them a thrill. They could own the world, one whore at a time.

The first guest didn't need much to relax and seemed to relish the personal attention. After the first, the rest were quick to follow, as Lela had been very specific about time. Lela dimmed the lights and Jo Danna cued the music as the guests mingled.

"Good to see you, Dan," said one.

"How's Patricia?" said another. "We must have you out to the island before it's completely overrun by holiday traffic."

Cocktails were served, the room silenced, and the guests were instructed to take their seats. "Gentlemen," said Lela. "Do enjoy the show." She was so serious about it all. God, it reminded me of how I used to be. I could see how it played on the nerves. Monika really was a saint for putting up with me.

Lela began a solo act with the neon sculpture. It was something to watch her body bend flawlessly in sexy, undulating poses. She was talented at showmanship, and like any diva, she knew it. Piece by piece, her lingerie disappeared from her figure. Soon she was naked and fingering her hole indulgently.

It was at this moment that I made my escape into the boudoir while Monika kept an eye on the guests. Once inside, I unpacked Monika's camera and tripod and set them up like she'd shown me earlier. Then I removed a cheap reproduction of Monet's *Water Lilies* from the bedroom wall and found the peephole that I'd carved out earlier. Precisely the same height as the camera, the peephole gave a perfect view of the show. I pressed the record button on the camera and let the rest ensue.

The men had made a ring on the carpet with their chairs. I made sure that the camera captured them as well, but mainly I was after the girls. With everything ready to go, the only thing left was for me to walk into the circle of light.

✷

It was a strut more than a walk. Oh, yes, Jodi's here, and here to play.

Fondling the silk necktie hanging loosely from my shoulders, I eyed the audience, looking for a willing participant. It wasn't hard to find one, and once I did, I led him to a velvet divan and instructed him to lie down. Then I blindfolded him with the silk necktie. In this small way, I could protect him.

My body started to move to the music. I caressed my breasts and stripped down to panties and garters. I parted my legs and stroked the inside creases of my thighs. I had to wonder just how far I would go. There was no turning back once it was done: no more hiding. Long ago, in a dark, carpeted closet, I had experienced desire that was quickly followed by shame. From then on, the two feelings went together, hand in hand. But they didn't have to. The circle had taught me to give in to desire and also to let myself experience the thrill of being desired. And in the circle, secrecy was sacrosanct. Now it was time to turn all that on its head.

I unbuckled the bachelor's trousers and took his member,

hard, into my mouth. I remembered the waiter I'd blown at his uncle's apartment. I never told anyone that when his shaft touched my throat, I'd had the most intense orgasm.

My john lay back and relaxed in pleasure. I motioned for Monika to join me. She approached the divan, and, turning towards the place where she knew the camera loomed, began her striptease. She fed her breasts, one by one, to the bachelor while I mounted him. He groaned and then found Monika's mouth. The two of them kissed while I rode until he could take no more.

At the end of the night, all the girls agreed that the show had been a wild success. While they tidied the room, I slipped into the boudoir to disassemble the camera before anyone noticed. As I packed away the tripod, I smiled, thinking that I'd have to thank Cookie's friend Paula. She was the one who'd pointed out that hardcore pornography was the one thing a woman artist wouldn't touch.

Chapter
Fifty-one

Valentine was at it again. This time his beef was Central Park. "This city used to have a beautiful park until the perverts and hoodlums took it over doing what they do. Now I'm not advocating vigilantism; you gotta understand, if they acquit Goetz, they're inviting nine million people to arm themselves with handguns on the subway. You want every pissed-off son-of-a-bitch shooting off rounds on the IRT? Whose fault is our current state of disaster? The tree-hugging hippies say just let it be. What do you say? Sound off with Randy Valentine. Callers, I want to hear from you."

I picked up the phone.

"Cookie?"

"Who wants to know?"

"Jodi Plum."

"Why, hello, darling. It's been ages. Tell me, what's new?"

"Listen, how quickly do you think you could find me a venue? I'm putting together a show. Oh, and I'll need high ceilings. I'm working with a very large structure."

"Is that all? You should see some of the shows I've been going to these days! I'd love to help you out; I've always been a big fan, and if you're putting the show together, there's no doubt the work is fantastic. Not like the crap that's been selling—oh, but have you heard about Paula? She just returned from India. Who would've thought she'd be a hit in the Orient? High ceilings, you say? Though, is there really any other kind? I'm thinking of a space that's perfect, and cheap; I just have to make a couple calls."

"Terrific. I knew I could count on you."

"What's terrific is hearing from *you*. I thought you'd fallen off the face of the earth."

"What about a guest list? I need you to invite everyone you know. I need the *crème de la crème*. This is going to be the show of the century. Everyone says that, but I'm telling you. It won't disappoint."

"Who's the artist?"

"Me."

"Why, Jodi, that's the best news I heard all day. I didn't know you were back in the game."

"Never left. I was just working on something."

"Marvelous," she said. "In that case, my and Paula's Rolodexes are yours. Can I ask, what are you calling the show?"

"I'm calling it *Beautiful Garbage*."

✳

Opening night. The structure was complete. With some help, I'd inflated the screen, which resembled a rectangular hot air balloon. To mount the structure took several people to tether the tie-down cords to stakes that had been properly assembled on the floor. There were some creases in the PVC skin that revealed my stitches, but I didn't let the imperfection bother me. Besides, when the light from the projector hit the screen, no one would notice a couple of folds in the membrane.

Sam, Monika's friend who worked with me for hours creating the effects I wanted, had put the finishing edits on the video feed. It was important to me not to reveal the faces of the other girls or the johns. Not even Monika was left in her natural state. This wasn't verisimilitude, nor really fair to them. This was something else. I had Sam distort their heads, not only by blurring out features, but by making the shape of each skull less solid, more fuzzy, balloon-like, and nebulous, like the structure the images themselves were being projected upon. My photographic trick realized the cosmetic modifications we make in memory, and the warped way we see ourselves.

I needed the other girls as well as the men to remain faceless, not only because I thought it was ethical, but because this way, the faceless—the disposable people—became so much more than whores and johns. They became specters of what had been haunting me—they became images breathed onto the transparent plastic ribbon, onto my blow-up structure, images that would pass like the rest of what has passed into the opposite of eternity. I was the only person in the footage to remain unaltered. Self-exposure was critical to the entire piece, almost as critical as the structure itself. There's a weird moment when you realize what an art it is to see yourself as you really are. I was pleased with my progression and allowed myself the satisfaction of a quiet joy.

Cookie had done an outstanding job planning the party. The venue was packed, and the crowd buzzed with anticipation. I'd leaked some details to the vultures intentionally, and like I'd envisioned, the press was eating it up. Funny, I couldn't really care less about fame for fame's sake: I needed the press to make my idea take hold. Public flogging was *so* Middle Ages, but I was bringing it back.

As the gallery continued to fill, I lingered by the entrance, eavesdropping at the critics' circle.

"It's quite a brilliant metaphor, the artist who shamelessly prostitutes herself."

"Oh, yes. Bold move, I'd say. And the structure…"

"A symbol of our earthly transience. We're mere visitors."

"Like Warhol said, we all have fifteen minutes."

It was the first cool night in a while, the type of late summer evening where you could smell autumn on its way.

Monika peeked out from the crowd and tapped my shoulder. "They're about to start the projector. You coming?"

"On my way," I said.

✳

Four months later, I was an anonymous traveler in Paris. I was loosely following an itinerary based off places mentioned in André Breton's surrealist diary, *Nadja*. Like Breton, my "point of departure" was the *Hôtel des Grands Hommes*, a fabulous hotel whose lobby boasted tiny potted succulent cacti and a parrot. This city was so organic and light compared to the rigid, carnivorous climate of New York. In Manhattan, the faceless masses traveled from point A to point B, mechanically, through oscillating glass doors and concrete pavement. But here, people and gardens and buildings had faces—they could see me and I could see them. I finally felt like I could breathe easy rather than gasping for my last breath of air.

It's funny, even though I was anonymous, my feet were firmly planted, and in this I knew that I was part of something larger than myself. I'd been a naïf, an artist, a whore, and now I was an artist once again. I'd been hurt and hurtful. Victim and perpetrator. But the whole time I was me. I'd always said divides were silly, useless constructions, as most interesting people are just that—split, but unified. It's a tricky philosophy, but as I watched a Parisian street performer dressed crudely in an altered suit examine a watch from the fob inside his vest, his three-legged dog by his side, I knew I was in the right company.

Reviews of *Beautiful Garbage* came out in all the important papers, and were overwhelmingly raves. Of course some feminists were outraged, and some stuffy critics appalled, but the show had pinched a nerve. I had interviews coming out in *Time*, *Vanity Fair*, *Life*, and *Rolling Stone*, way beyond the confines of downtown's precious little scene. I'd signed an iron-clad contract with Paula's dealer and had a press agent who plugged me as, finally, "A woman artist so in complete control of her sexuality that she dictates its structure." My balloon structure, or so mused the critics, signaled a maturity and self-assurance that belied solid form. It was, and I'm quoting Rene Ricard here, "A way to self-promote without drawing the exploitation card."

It wasn't just my buzz; something else had shifted in my process. I used to cast forms methodically, afraid of what would happen if the clay took over. Then a switch went off, and I realized, whatever came out would be all right. I thought of Basquiat's power to needle the public back when he was SAMO—the Same Old Shit.

I was just lucky enough that my show hit at the right time. The game was bullshit; there was no other way around it. It was a monster you couldn't take seriously. And for some reason, knowing this made me all the more appealing. Little did I know that by the early 1990s, scholars would take a renewed interest in the study and preservation of antiquity. The Met began excavating an off-site case housed in an anchorage on the Brooklyn side of the Brooklyn Bridge. It was full of plaster casts.

*

Paris was the first time I'd traveled so far from home. I wandered narrow streets for *masions* and *manoirs*, movie theatres, flea markets, and places of delicious abandon where bottles were uncorked and bread was broken then smeared with butter and chocolate. I accepted dinner invites when they turned up— learned the history of the Gallic peoples from travelers like me—and ate and drank alone in negative space.

This particular late afternoon, a woman had approached me and asked if she could buy my meal. She looked familiar, flaunting a taut body that more than anything looked lived in. Her poise and self-possession as she pulled a chair from my table gave her away. I'd recognize that body anywhere.

It was Lynda Benglis, the sculptor who'd posed nude for *Artforum* all oiled up with a vein-ribbed dildo at her crotch. We'd toasted to Lynda, Monika and I, the night we first met, and here she was, in the flesh.

"You're Jodi Plum, aren't you?" What she had was real swagger, taking a seat in the wiry, iron chair. "Let's eat *les moules* and get whimsically drunk."

"I used to have your picture from *Artforum* on my wall."

"Full bush and dildo?" She laughed. "That was for an ad for an upcoming show, you know."

A waitress came by and brought a carafe, some baguette, and an assortment of herb-infused oils. She and Lynda exchanged dialogue in a brusque yet sensual way that was so French, and so beyond my capabilities. The thing was, you didn't need to know how to *speak* well to *live* well here, as opposed to in New York where everyone spoke a language built up of exclusive grammar.

"It's almost been fifteen years since that photo, that show," she remarked. Just then a little Parisian boy ran up to our table, and, with a pudgy hand, smacked Lynda on the knee.

Lynda screamed and gestured wildly at the kid. "*Va t'en, garçon petit diable!*"

His mother called after him in a loud shriek, and the boy ran off in the opposite direction.

"I hate kids," began Lynda. "Devilish, narcissistic creatures."

I swallowed. I began to feel that familiar nausea in my gut, but something had shifted. Rather than feeling the uncomfortable pit in my stomach, I felt a warm gush of sympathy for children—the boy, Isla, even for myself. The French kid didn't bother me, because for the first time I felt separate from the child in me. I could understand this Parisian child, because I was no longer a child myself.

"Can't blame them," I said. "The world should belong to kids."

Lynda Benglis tore off a crusty piece of baguette and pointed it at me.

My heart stopped, and for a moment I could breathe. I mean *really* breathe and feel my body in this place, here with me. Lynda must've understood me—there was a reason Monika and I had toasted to her—because she said, "Don't confuse your personal bullshit with the art you make. Of course the two are inextricably linked, but if it was that easy, everyone would be Van Gogh."

I nodded. "Can I just say, your work… I mean, without you having the guts to go…"

"Stop," she interrupted. "We're eating *les moules*."

"But you *have* to tell me something," I said. "Something you've learned."

"And what was I just talking about? You want more?"

"Yes!" I insisted.

She laughed, swilled some wine, and said, "Female sexuality is way more powerful than male sexuality. But I suspect you've figured this out, as you've used the premise to ignite your career. If you haven't, then you've stumbled upon a happy accident, and you must've known it somewhere down there," she said, pointing to my gut, "so kudos either way. Don't ever waver. Don't give up your footing when people—men—and they will—try to take it out from under you. God, I remember when I was struggling so hard to make it," she said. "You know, bad apartments, bad food—or sometimes none at all, but there was that hope—and in a way, that's the best feeling in the world. Afterwards, you achieve success and then…"

I thought about the rotten kid I was. I never felt the world belonged to me. "Then," I said, "lives change."

"Not really." She sopped her bread in oil. "It's an illusion to think that lives change in any meaningful way. I mean, why would they change—when you achieve happiness? Happiness? We only become more comfortable with our inner sadness—I suppose that, in a way, is a form of happiness. But we're not going to discuss art and philosophy all night, are we?"

"What are you doing in Paris?"

She refilled her glass. "What does one do in Paris?"

When I got back to the hotel, I stumbled to the phone, and somehow my fingers found the correct numbers. "Monika," I squealed. "You'll never guess who bought me dinner tonight."

I told her, but she didn't seem to think it was a significant moment. In fact, I'm not even sure it registered with her. She started going off about some salesgirl who refused to sell her a Chanel scarf because she didn't like Monika's attitude. It hit me that people like Monika would never see outside the lines, the grid that was Manhattan. For so long I hoped she'd snap out of it—the narcissistic, material consumption that filled the void of her own misery. But I realized now that she only knew how to be *that* Monika. Wondering whether Monika was real or a fabrication didn't even matter any more, because I'd never really know. I couldn't spend my time trying to mine out the truth—there was no point; there was no truth. It was a sad moment, but one that had been brewing for a while, I suppose. Rather than let it eat away at me, I let it sit. I took the receiver and placed it away from my ear as she babbled on. You can't live in awe of someone forever, especially a girl caught in the excess of litany and violence that was downtown Manhattan, a city of whores.

Through the buzz of long distance, I said, "I wish you well, Monika. Goodbye."

There was a pause, and then, "Oh." She followed this with, "Of course, darling. Yes, of course."

We both knew it was the end, and whether we'd see each other again... I'd leave that up to fate.

*

The next morning, I was awakened by the woman who ran the hotel. She was knocking at my door with purpose, speaking so quickly that I only barely made out that a special package had come in the morning's post.

"*J'arrive!*" I called, searching for my morning fag.

The package was from my press agent in New York and was

nothing but a stack of reviews. The furnishings in my room were simple: bed, small dresser, footstool, and a wooden chair that I dragged to the window where I could sit and read through the clippings in a steady stream of sunlight. The recognition factor was good; yes, I couldn't lie, it felt wonderful to be praised, but I was more aroused by the passersby outside my window, on their way to the market to buy silk or whatever Parisians purchase on particularly bright Tuesday mornings.

Then an item in one of the gossip pages caught my eye. It was a picture of a familiar creep—the art dealer Vincent Frand. It seemed he had recently contracted a sexually transmitted disease that had left him disfigured, and he'd hightailed it out of New York, leaving behind a bevy of clients that no one would touch. The feeling I had for Vincent Frand was not contempt but true sadness, until I realized that my sadness was about Walter. I'd never treated him well. His disease had made me uncomfortable. Disgusted me. Frightened me. Enraged me. I couldn't stand to think of the body being such a canvas for pain—or perhaps I understood it too well. Either way, I couldn't face it when your body acted against you. How many times had I gotten wet from the repulsive johns who'd touched me the right way? Many. The body has desires; it gets excited when you don't want it to—even the boy understood. The body breaks down when you don't want it to.

It hit me then that a triangle had been reconfigured, only this time, the boy—Walter—was taken, lost to a plague that no one wanted to see.

I kept the item about Vincent Frand with my press clippings and then walked the length of the hallway, hoping the bathroom would be vacant so I could bathe and then explore the city.

✷

Hours ago I was in a bookstore called *The Humanité*, where I smoked hashish and bought eighty francs worth of antique books. Later that evening, I'd met a man and woman who'd told me about a new type of mechanical sculpture debuting at a new museum. I'd studied their faces as they spoke, the shape of their lips as words exited their mouths, the creases in their brows as they shared with me what they knew. Out of kindness, they'd taken ten minutes to explain walking directions from the park, the place of our encounter. When the sun had set, and the street was lit dimly by streetlamps, I'd tested my sense of direction and gone about finding this new place.

In the morning, I found myself in a sculpture garden of such macabre splendor it had to be an ancient cemetery. Scattered throughout, jagged tombstones pierced the foliage and reached skyward. It had started to drizzle, but the sun managed shafts of light through the cloudscape, casting an impermanent haze upon me. Silence sluiced my body, and I collapsed onto the damp grass, devoid of doubt or strangeness.

Acknowledgments

Thank you to my parents, Anna Marie and John Di Donato, my sister, and multiple-draft-reader, Sara Listas, my other mom, Judith Kuppersmith, PhD, early readers Christopher Daish, Susan Gould, Caroline Hagood, Monique Raphel High, Doretta Lau, Claudia B. Manley, Jessica Mingus, editor, Joanna Yas, art historian, Theodore Ward Barrow, PhD, powerhouse Lauren Rayner, my assistant, Nicole Bagnarol, and all my writing teachers and peers.

About the Author

A Brooklyn native, Jill Di Donato writes a sex column for *The Huffington Post*. This is her debut novel.